FOUR EYES

VOLUME ONE

FORGED IN FLAMES

WRITER
JOE KELLY

ILLUSTRATOR
MAX FIUMARA

LETTERING, LOGO & DESIGN
DREW GILL

2ND ED. EDITING & DESIGN
THOMAS MAUER

CREATED BY
JOE KELLY & MAX FIUMARA

MAN OF action ENTERTAINMENT
www.manofaction.tv

FOUR EYES, VOL. 1: FORGED IN FLAMES

ISBN: 978-1-63215-424-8
Second Edition. July 2015. Published by Image Comics, Inc.
Office of publication: 2001 Center Street, Sixth Floor, Berkeley, CA 94704.

For information regarding the CPSIA on this printed material call: 203-595-3636 and provide reference #RICH-624837.

For international rights, contact:
foreignlicensing@imagecomics.com

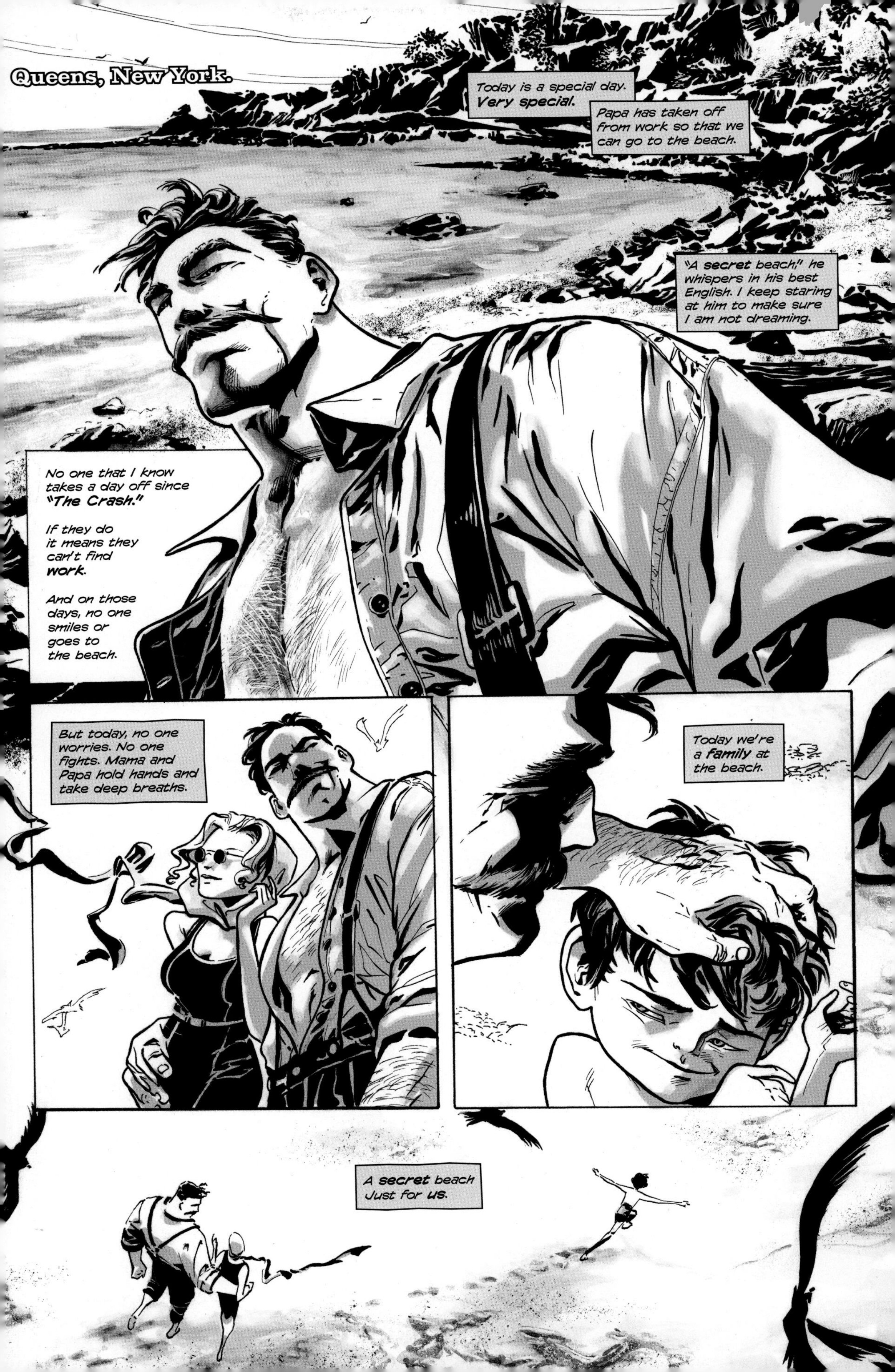
Queens, New York.
Today is a special day. **Very special.**
Papa has taken off from work so that we can go to the beach.
"A **secret** beach," he whispers in his best English. I keep staring at him to make sure I am not dreaming.
No one that I know takes a day off since **"The Crash."**
If they do it means they can't find **work**.
And on those days, no one smiles or goes to the beach.
But today, no one worries. No one fights. Mama and Papa hold hands and take deep breaths.
Today we're a **family** at the beach.
A **secret** beach Just for **us**.

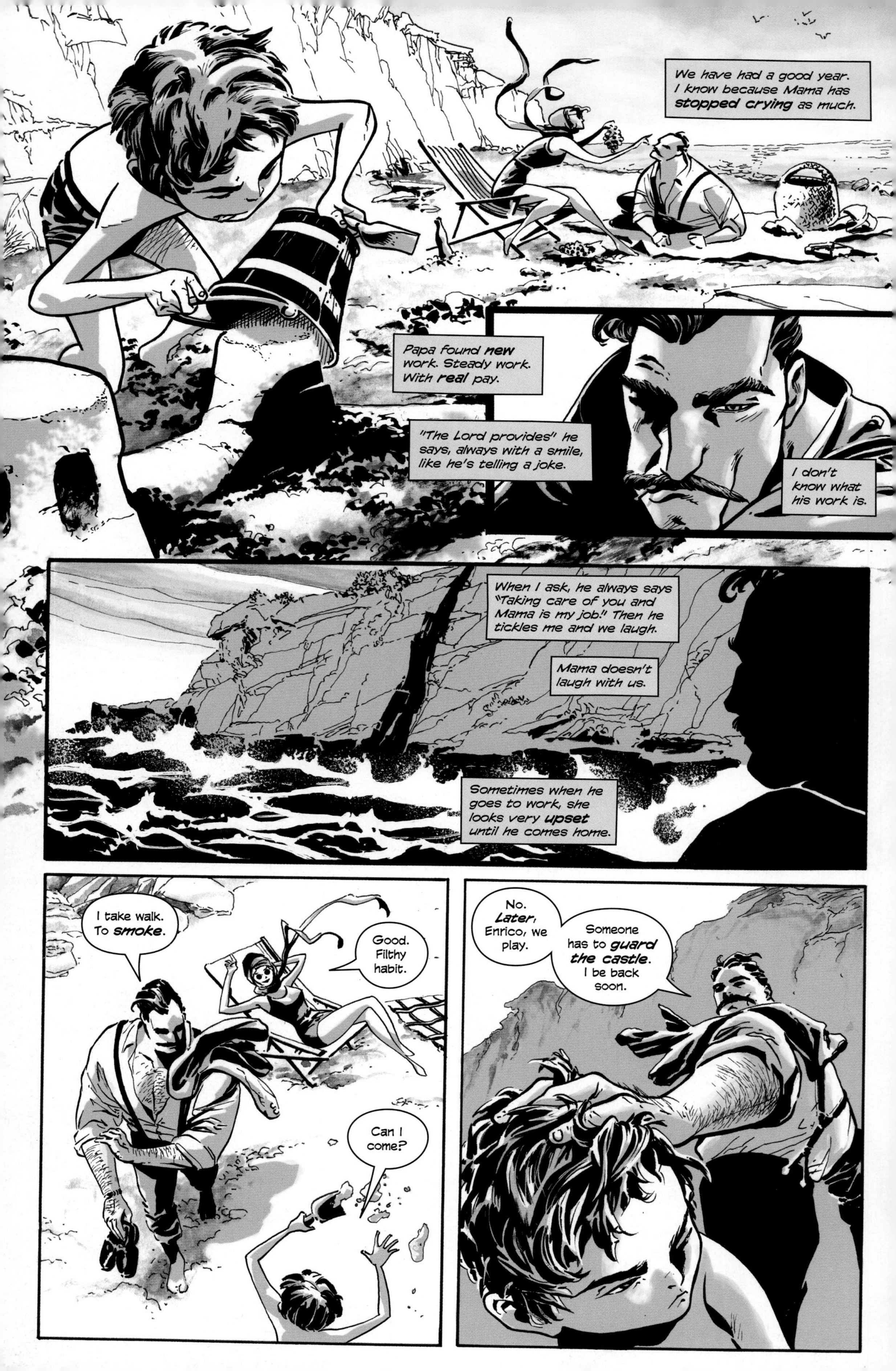
We have had a good year.
I know because Mama has **stopped crying** as much.
Papa found **new** work. Steady work. With **real** pay.
"The Lord provides" he says, always with a smile, like he's telling a joke.
I don't know what his work is.
When I ask, he always says "Taking care of you and Mama is my job." Then he tickles me and we laugh.
Mama doesn't laugh with us.
Sometimes when he goes to work, she looks very **upset** until he comes home.
I take walk. To **smoke**.
Good. Filthy habit.
Can I come?
No. **Later**, Enrico, we play.
Someone has to **guard the castle**. I be back soon.

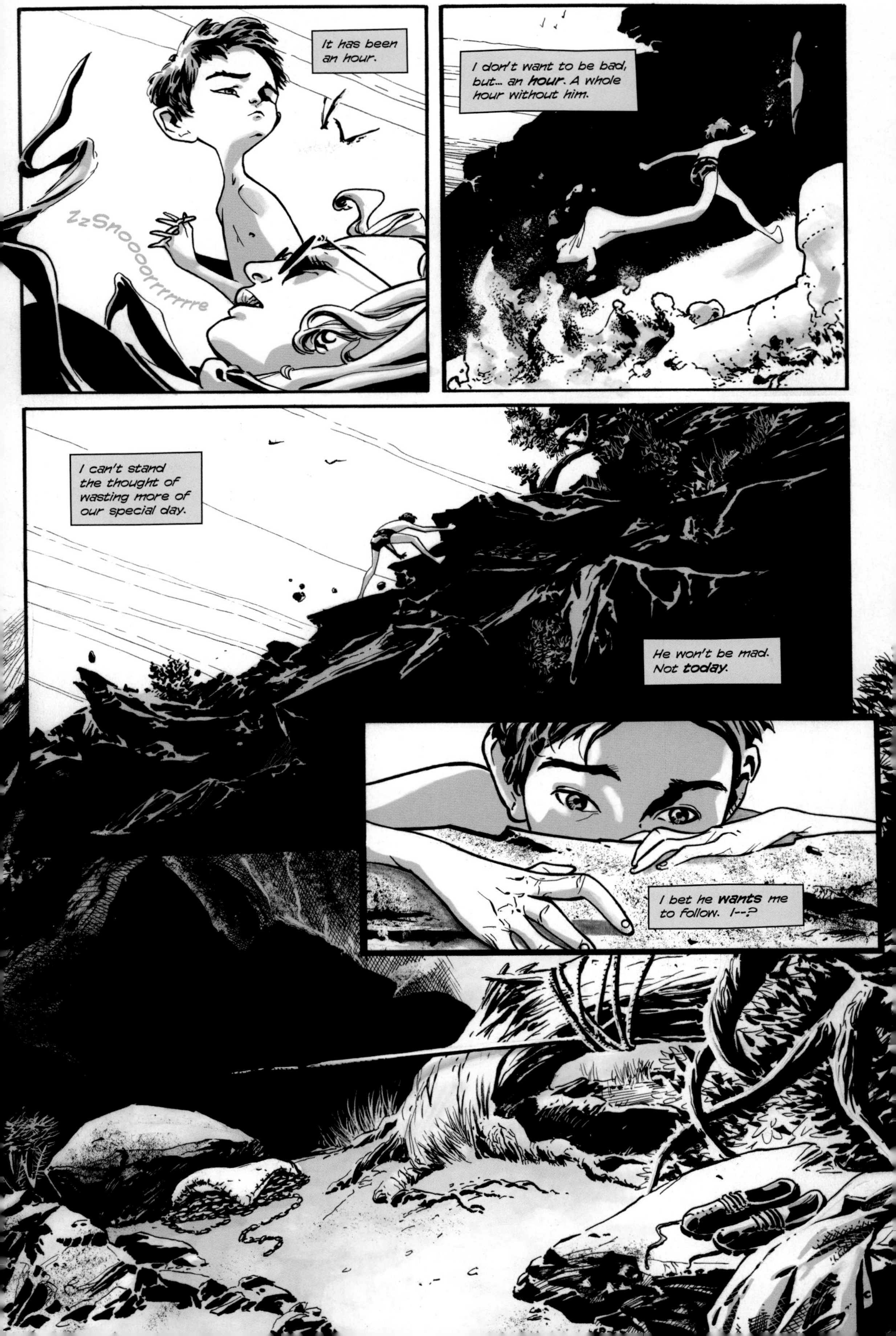
It has been an hour.
ZzSnooooorrrrrrre
I don't want to be bad, but... an hour. A whole hour without him.
I can't stand the thought of wasting more of our special day.
He won't be mad. Not today.
I bet he wants me to follow. I--?

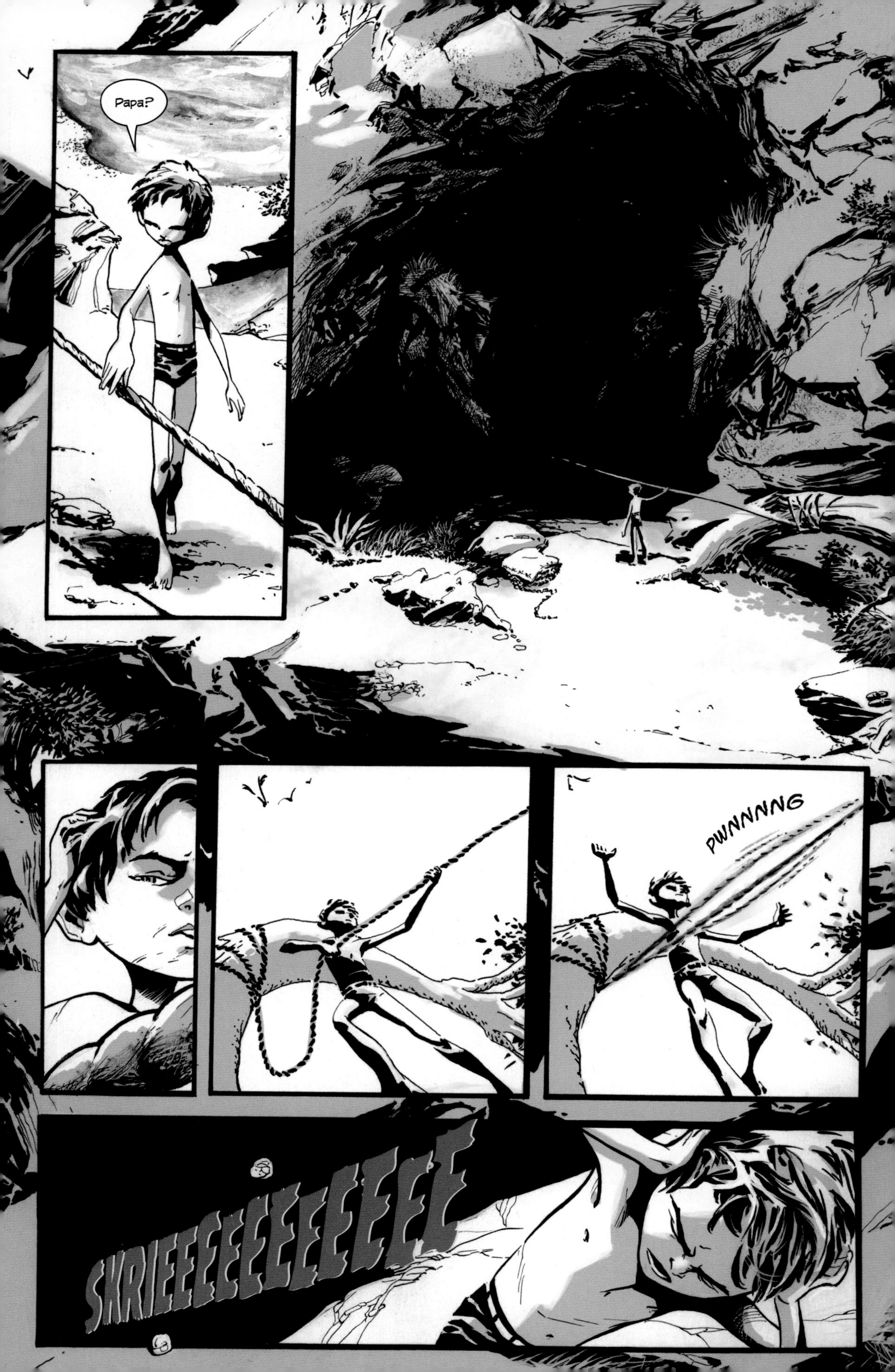
Papa?
PWNNNNG
SKRIEEEEEEEEEEEEEE

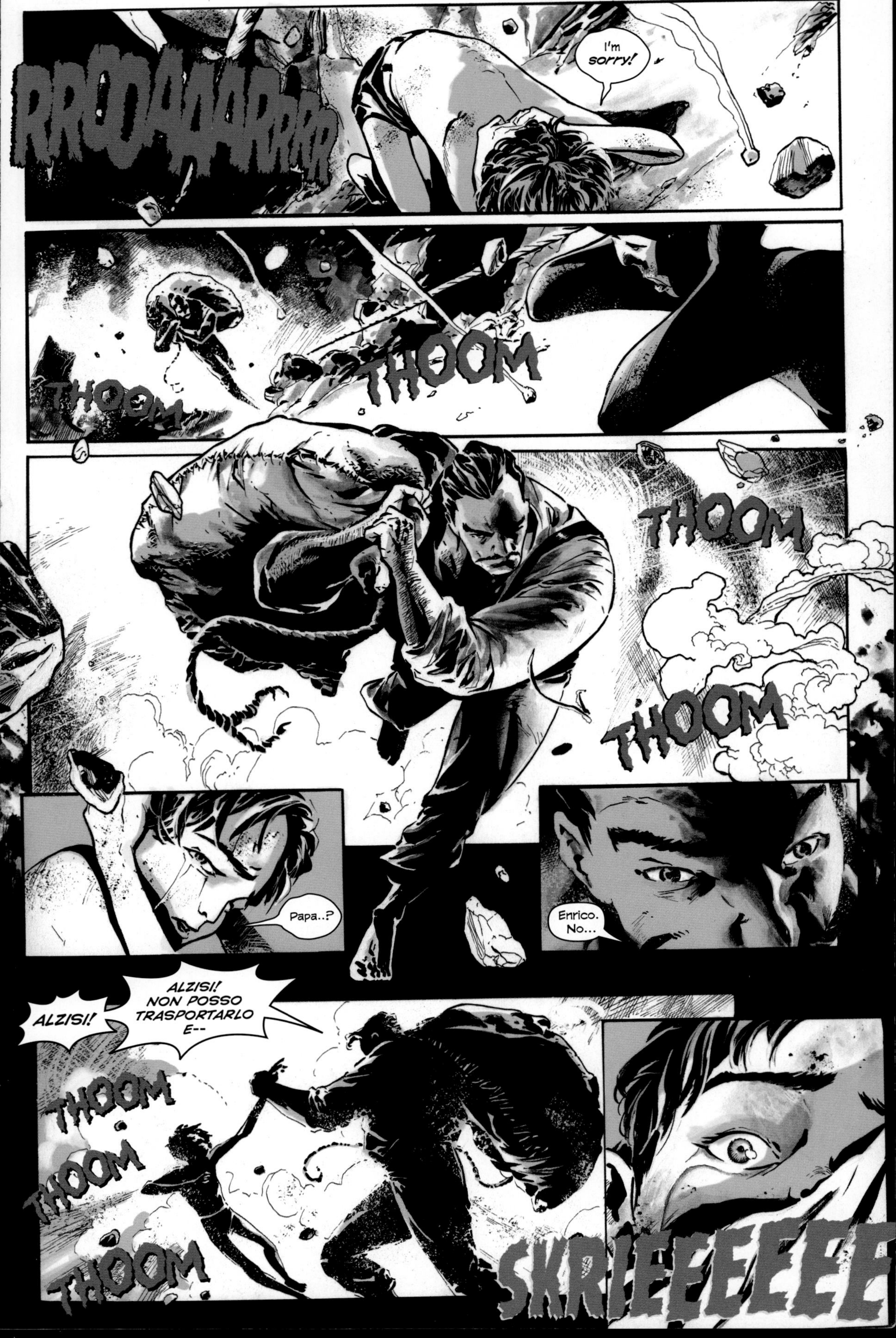
RROOAAARRRR
I'm sorry!
THOOM
THOOM
THOOM
THOOM
Papa..?
Enrico. No...
ALZISI!
ALZISI! NON POSSO TRASPORTARLO E--
THOOM
THOOM
THOOM
SKRIEEEEEE

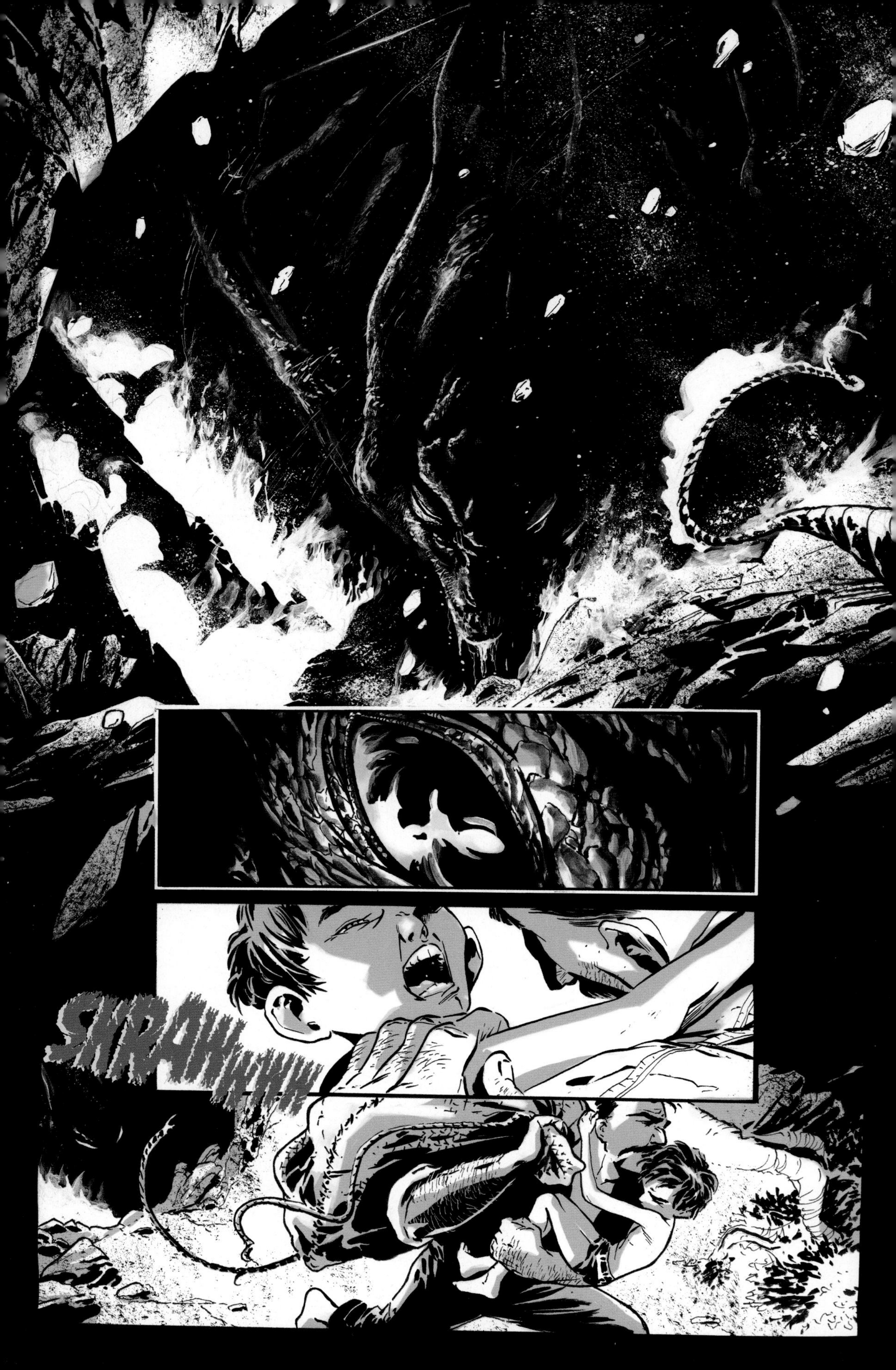
SKRAHHHHHH

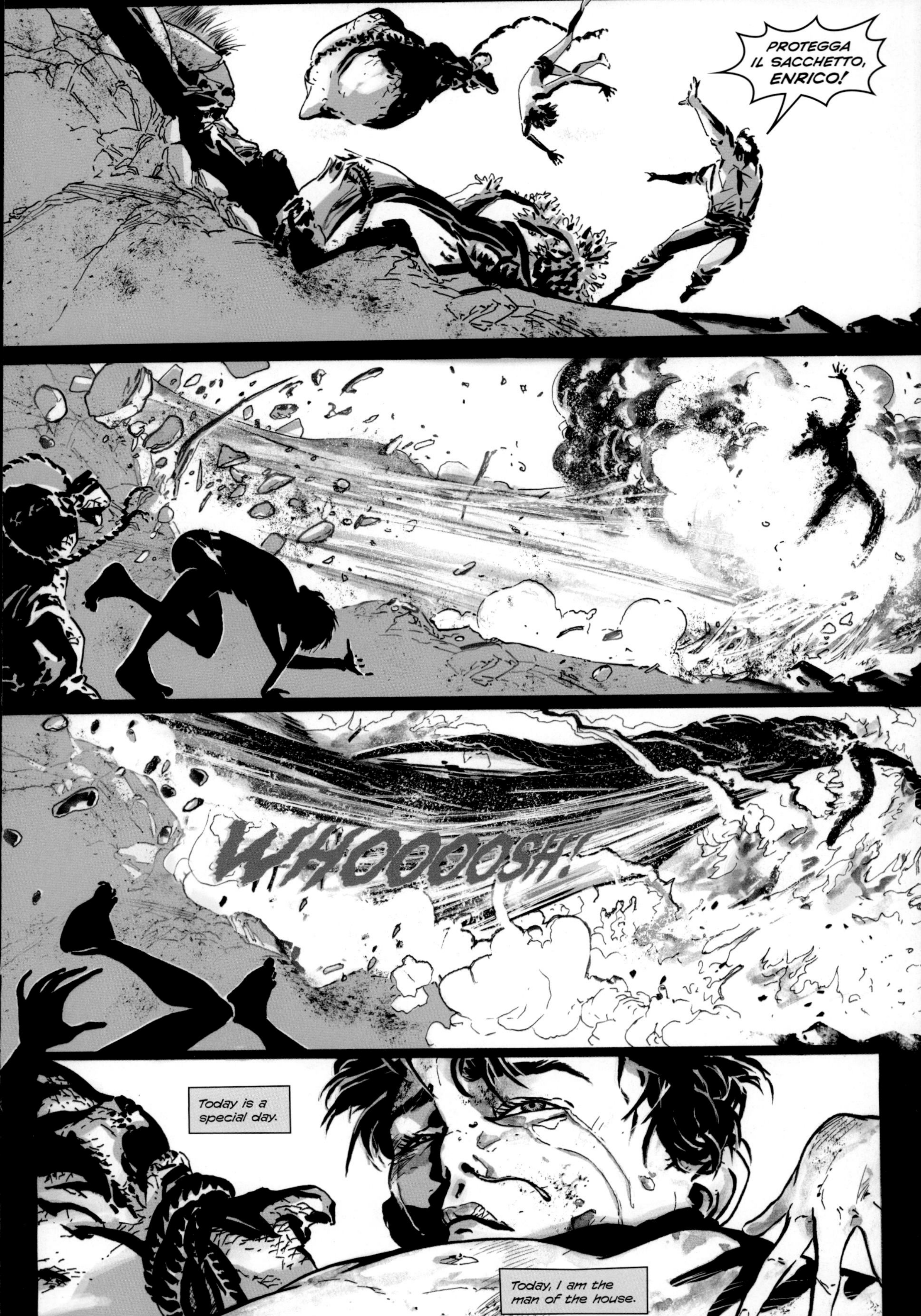
PROTEGGA IL SACCHETTO, ENRICO!
WHOOOOOSH!
Today is a special day.
Today, I am the man of the house.

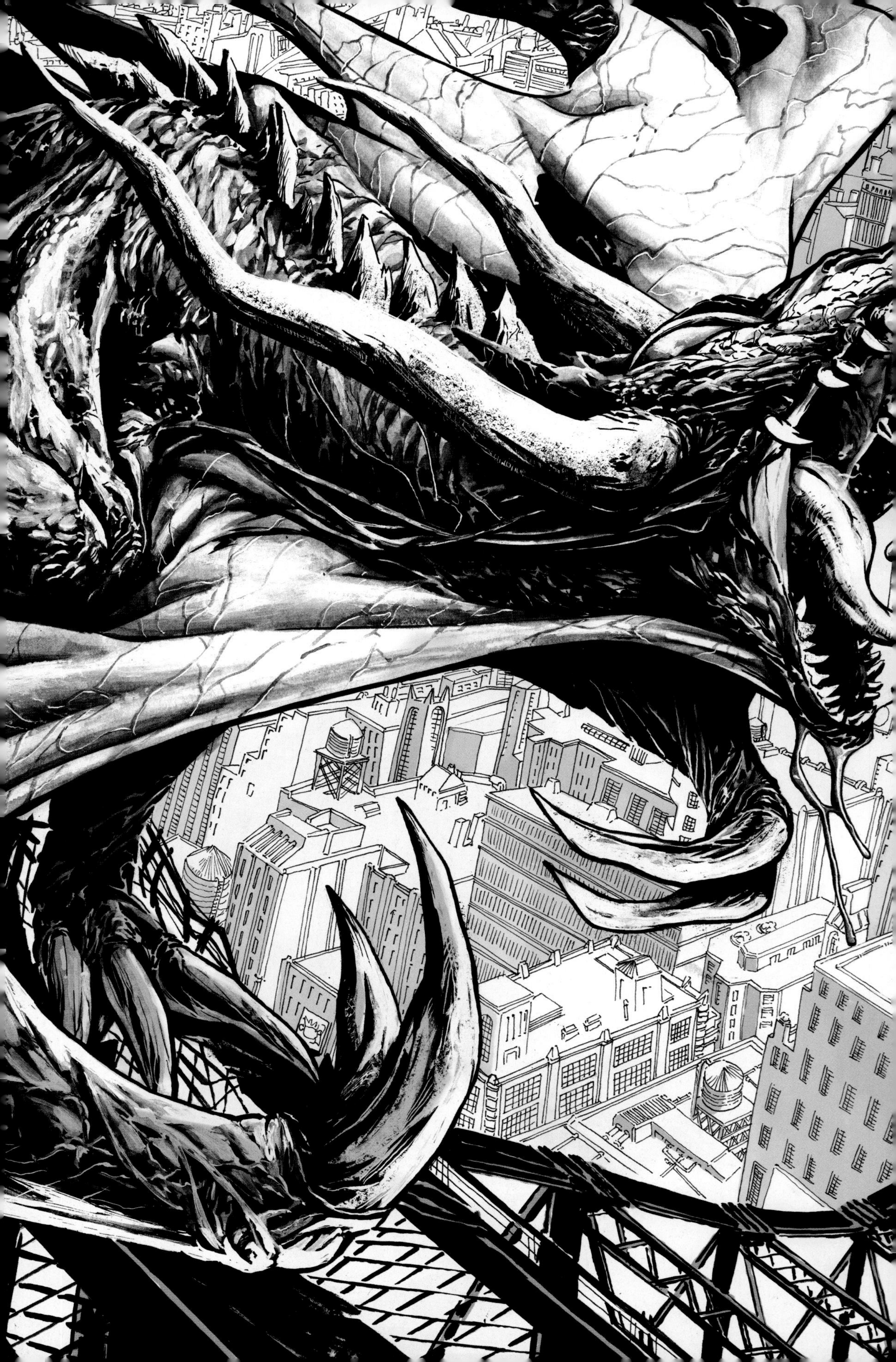

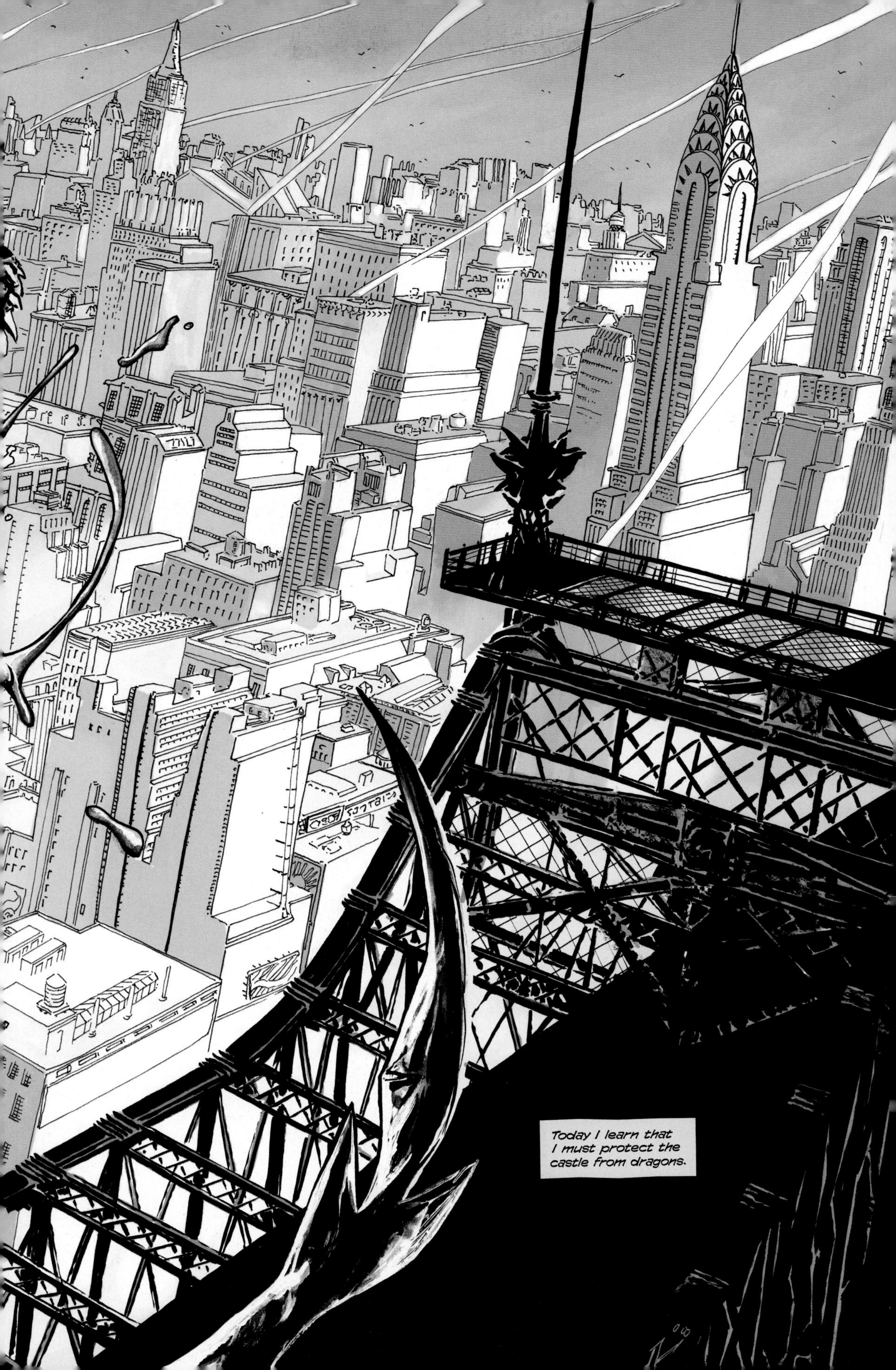
Today I learn that I must protect the castle from dragons.

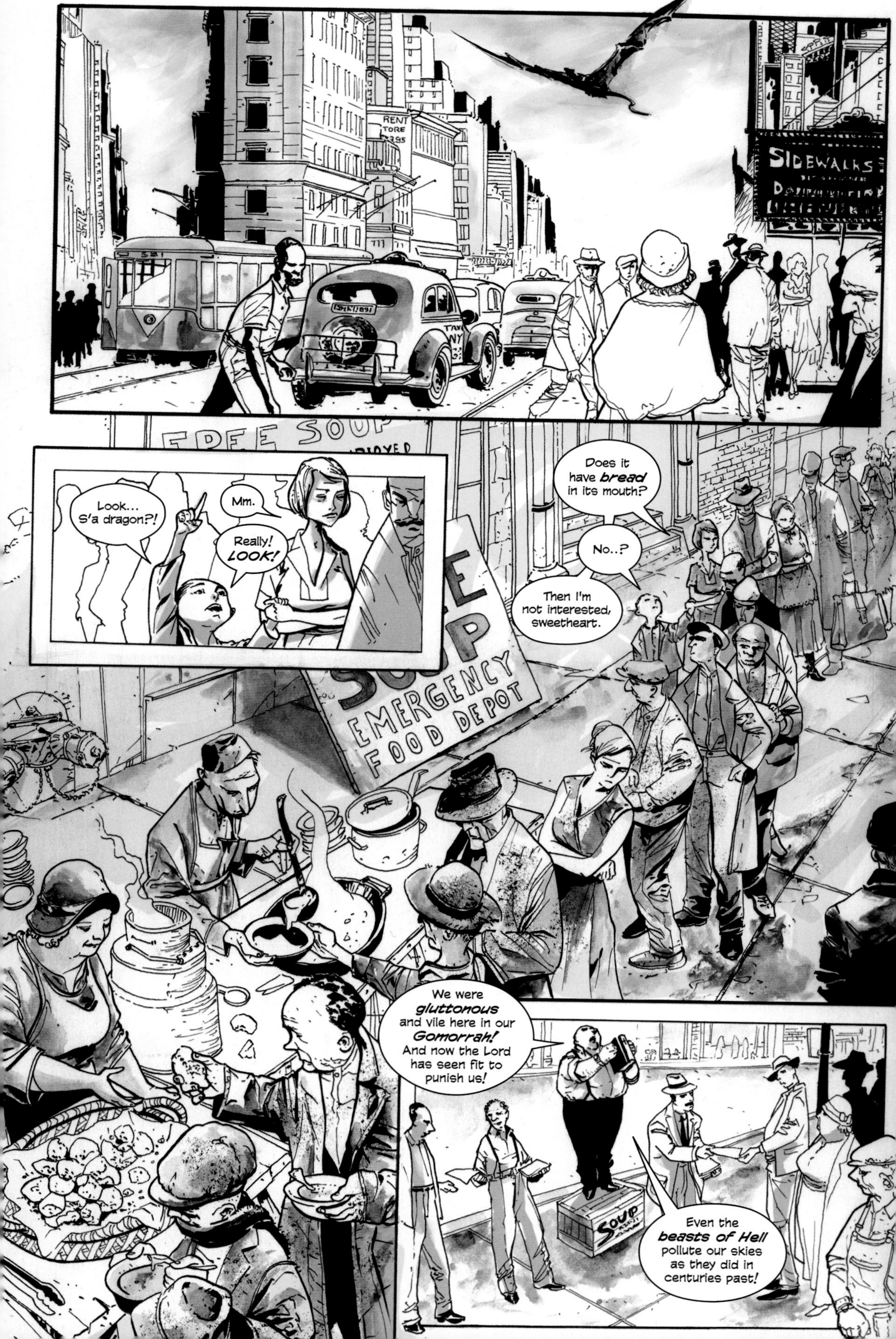
SIDEWALKS
FREE SOUP
Look... S'a dragon?!
Mm.
Really! LOOK!
Does it have bread in its mouth?
No..?
Then I'm not interested, sweetheart.
SOUP
EMERGENCY FOOD DEPOT
We were gluttonous and vile here in our Gomorrah! And now the Lord has seen fit to punish us!
SOUP
Even the beasts of Hell pollute our skies as they did in centuries past!

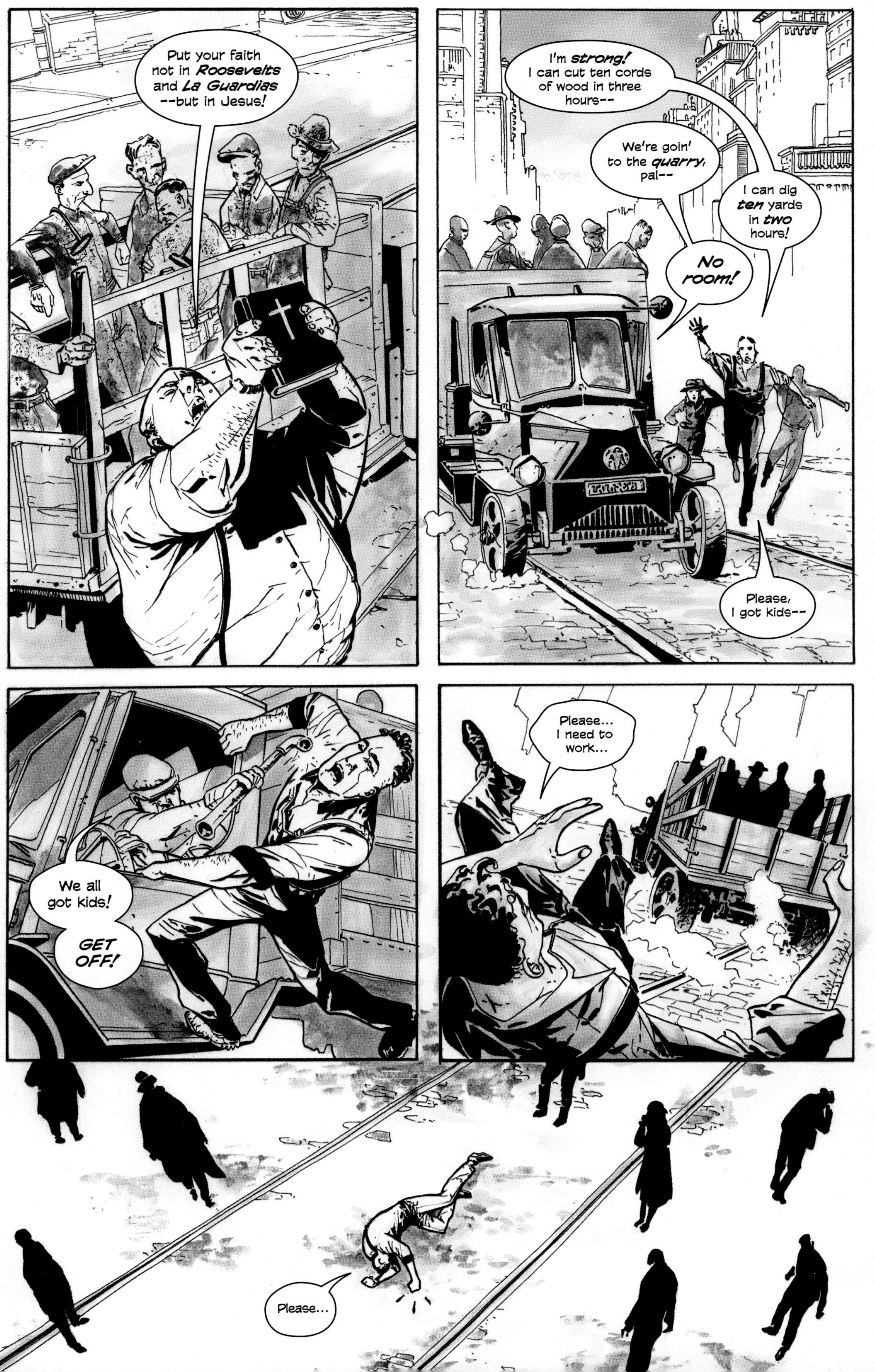

Put your faith not in *Roosevelts* and *La Guardias* --but in Jesus!
I'm ***strong!*** I can cut ten cords of wood in three hours--
We're goin' to the ***quarry,*** pal--
I can dig ***ten*** yards in ***two*** hours!
No room!
Please, I got kids--
We all got kids*!*
GET OFF!
Please... I need to work...
Please...

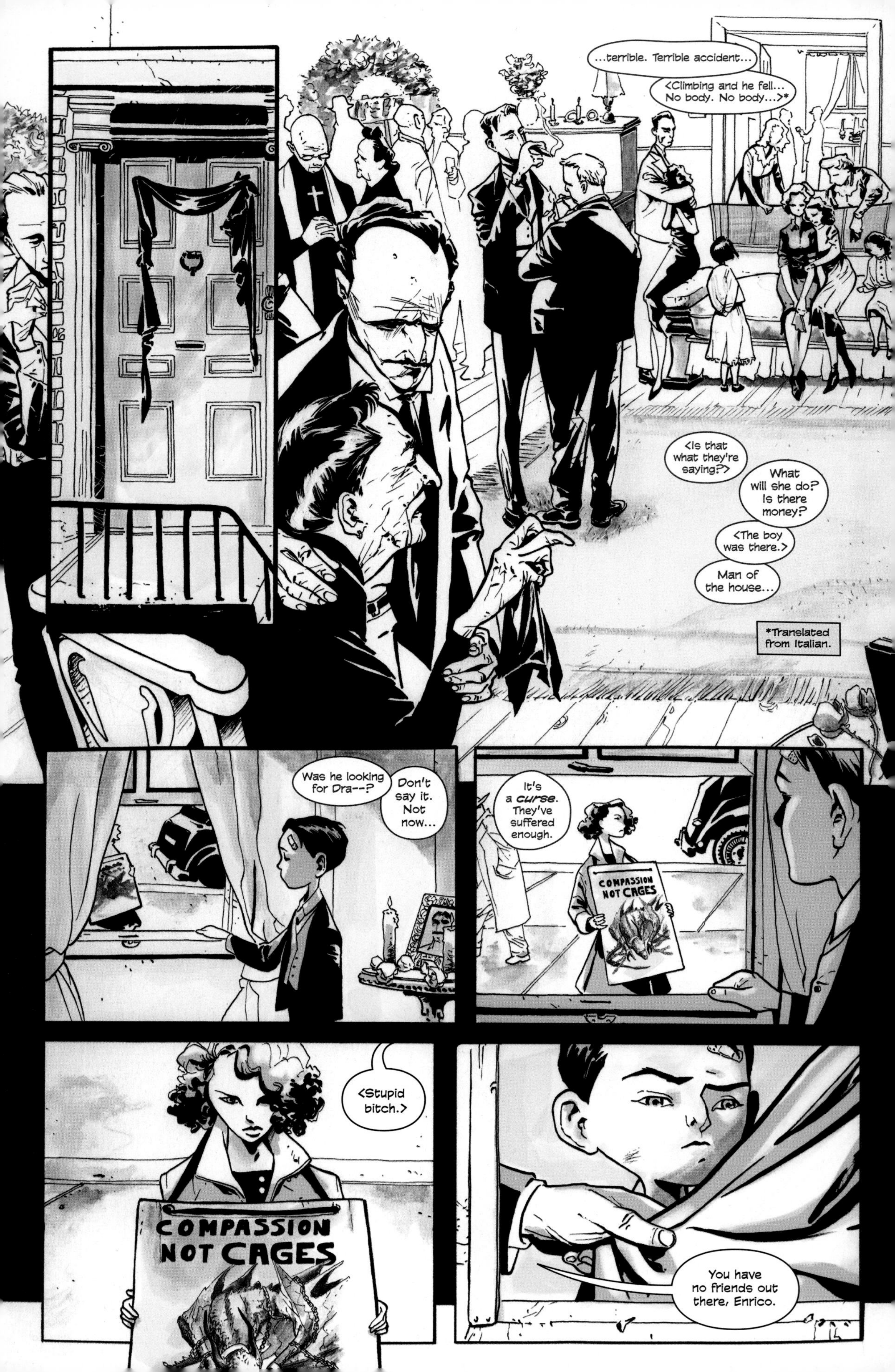
...terrible. Terrible accident...
<Climbing and he fell... No body. No body...>*
<Is that what they're saying?>
What will she do? Is there money?
<The boy was there.>
Man of the house...
*Translated from Italian.
Was he looking for Dra--?
Don't say it. Not now...
It's a *curse*. They've suffered enough.
COMPASSION NOT CAGES
<Stupid bitch.>
COMPASSION NOT CAGES
You have no friends out there, Enrico.

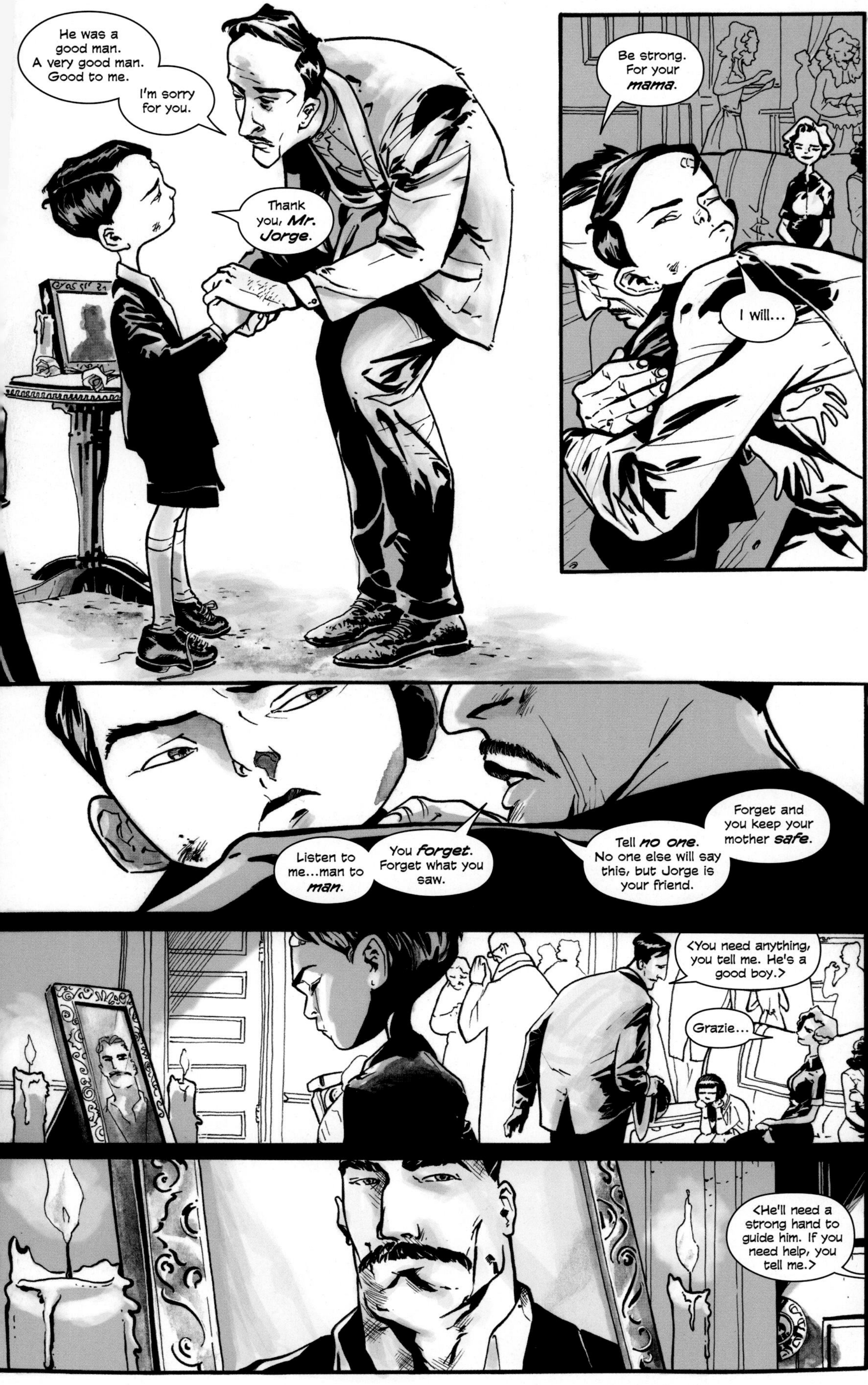
He was a good man. A very good man. Good to me.
I'm sorry for you.
Thank you, Mr. Jorge.
Be strong. For your mama.
I will...
Listen to me...man to man.
You forget. Forget what you saw.
Tell no one. No one else will say this, but Jorge is your friend.
Forget and you keep your mother safe.
<You need anything, you tell me. He's a good boy.>
Grazie...
<He'll need a strong hand to guide him. If you need help, you tell me.>

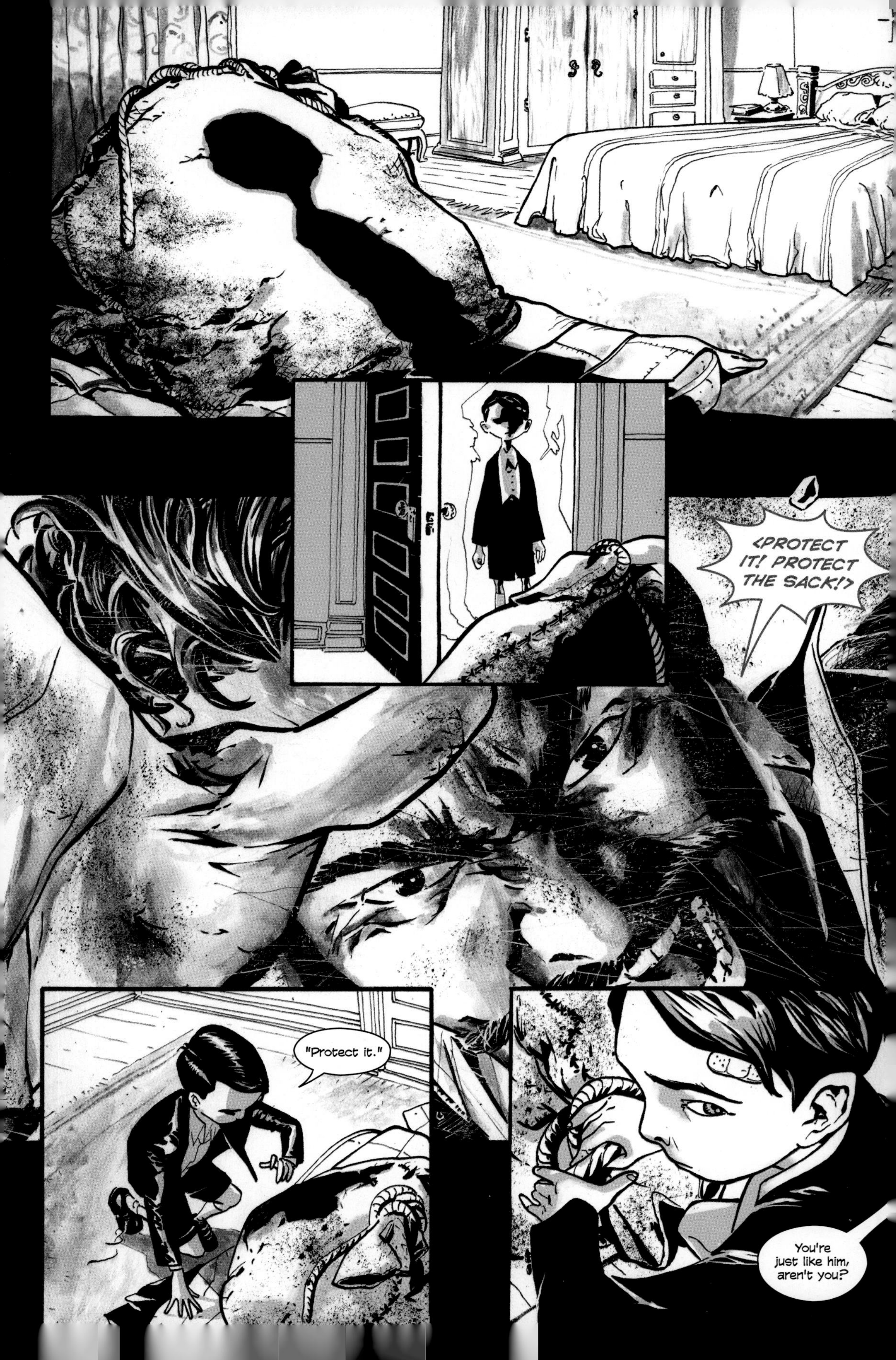
<PROTECT IT! PROTECT THE SACK!>
"Protect it."
You're just like him, aren't you?

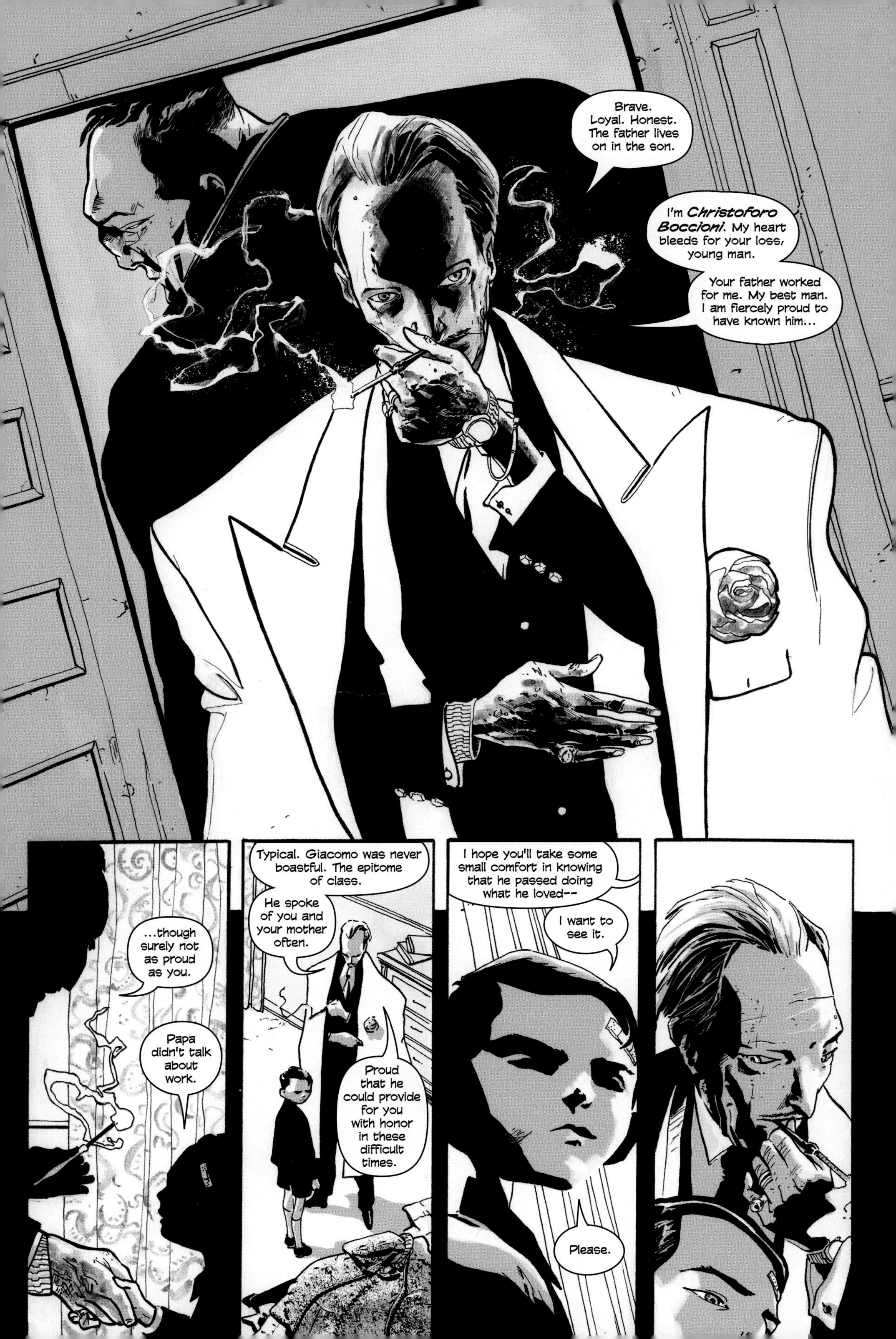
Brave. Loyal. Honest. The father lives on in the son.
I'm *Christoforo Boccioni*. My heart bleeds for your loss, young man.
Your father worked for me. My best man. I am fiercely proud to have known him...
...though surely not as proud as you.
Papa didn't talk about work.
Typical. Giacomo was never boastful. The epitome of class.
He spoke of you and your mother often.
Proud that he could provide for you with honor in these difficult times.
I hope you'll take some small comfort in knowing that he passed doing what he loved--
I want to see it.
Please.

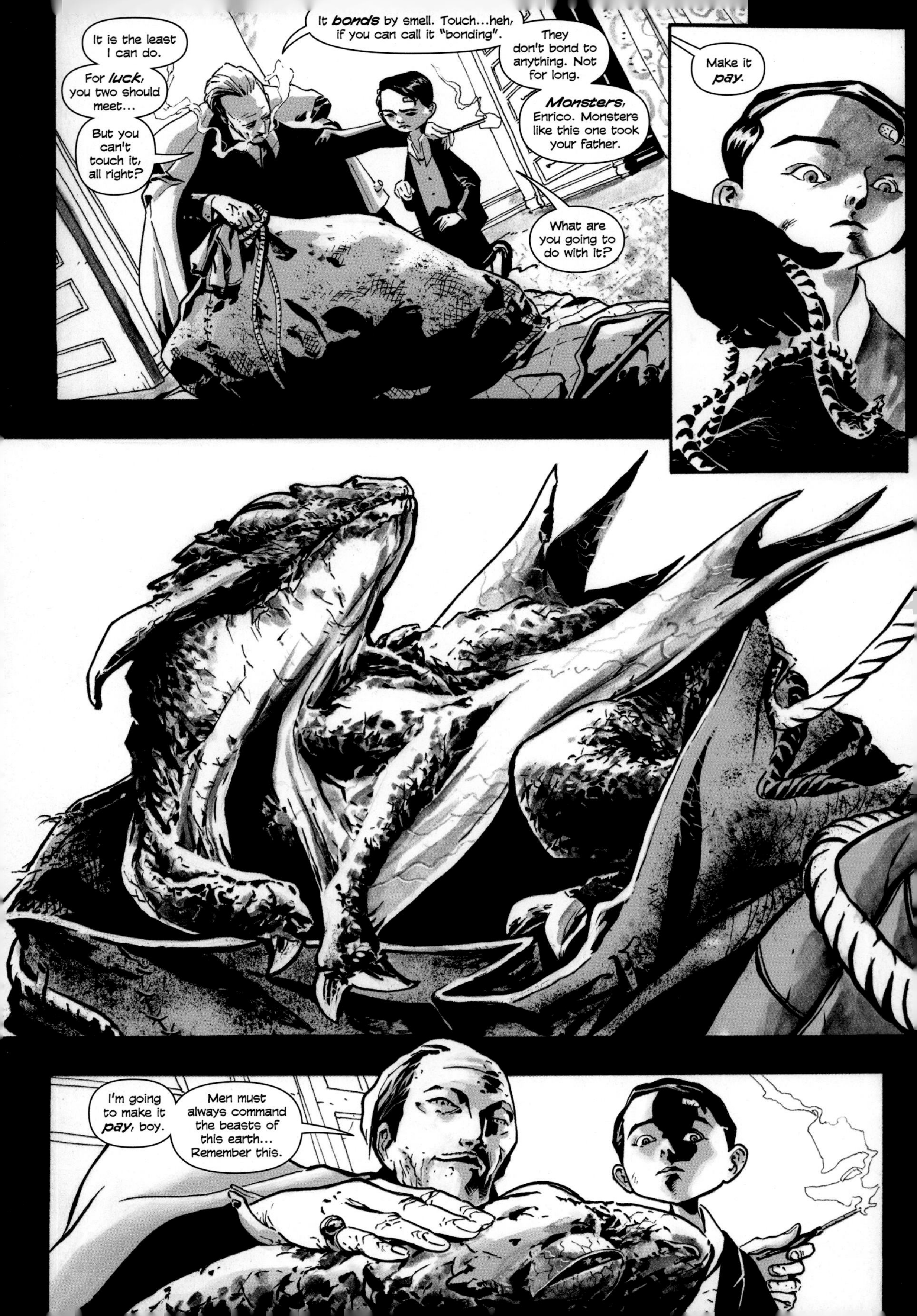

It is the least I can do.
For *luck*, you two should meet...
But you can't touch it, all right?
It *bonds* by smell. Touch...heh, if you can call it "bonding".
They don't bond to anything. Not for long.
Monsters, Enrico. Monsters like this one took your father.
What are you going to do with it?
Make it *pay*.
I'm going to make it *pay*, boy.
Men must always command the beasts of this earth... Remember this.

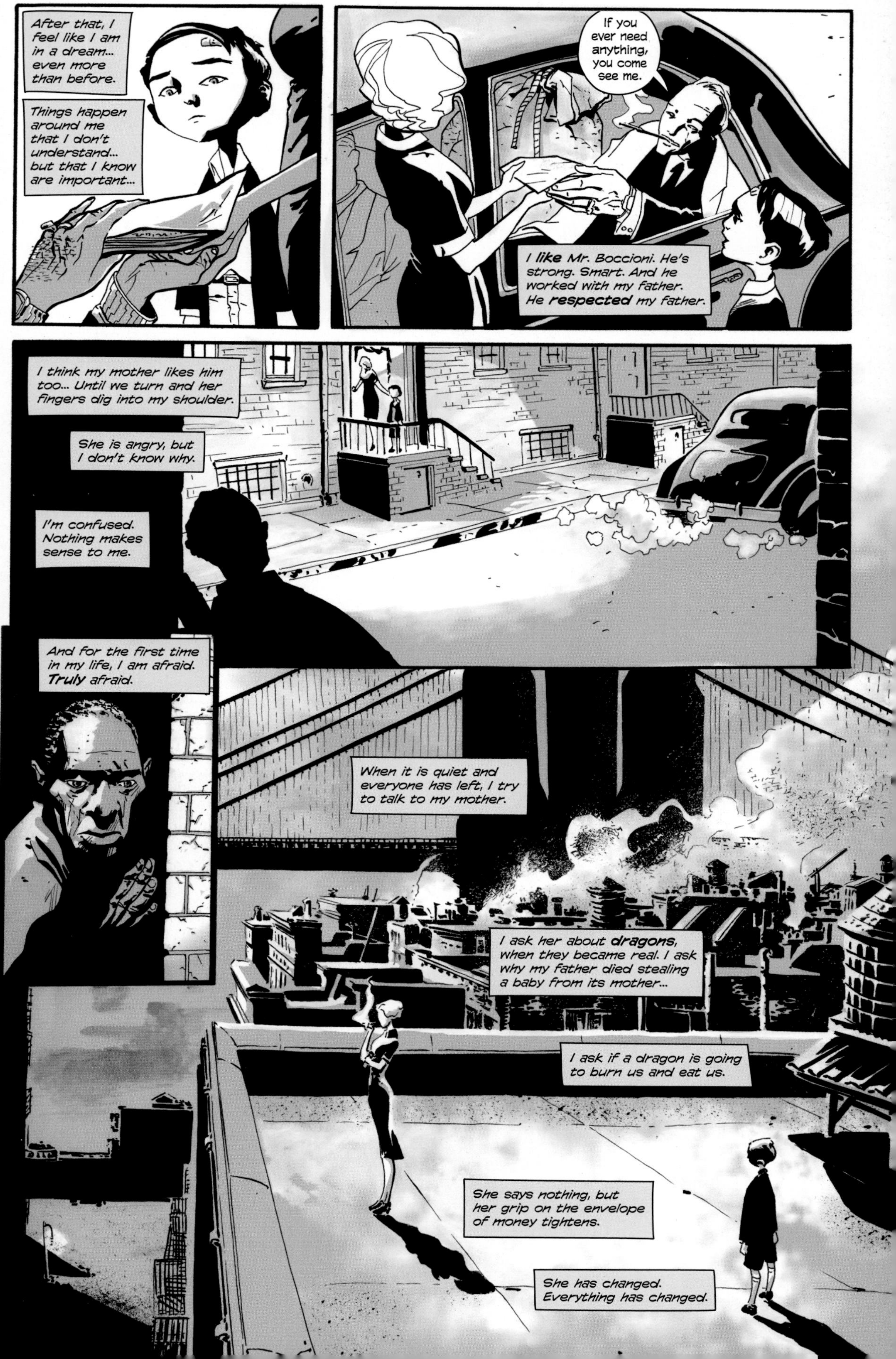
After that, I feel like I am in a dream... even more than before.
Things happen around me that I don't understand... but that I know are important...
If you ever need anything, you come see me.
I **like** Mr. Boccioni. He's strong. Smart. And he worked with my father. He **respected** my father.
I think my mother likes him too... Until we turn and her fingers dig into my shoulder.
She is angry, but I don't know why.
I'm confused. Nothing makes sense to me.
And for the first time in my life, I am afraid. **Truly** afraid.
When it is quiet and everyone has left, I try to talk to my mother.
I ask her about **dragons**, when they became real. I ask why my father died stealing a baby from its mother...
I ask if a dragon is going to burn us and eat us.
She says nothing, but her grip on the envelope of money tightens.
She has changed. Everything has changed.

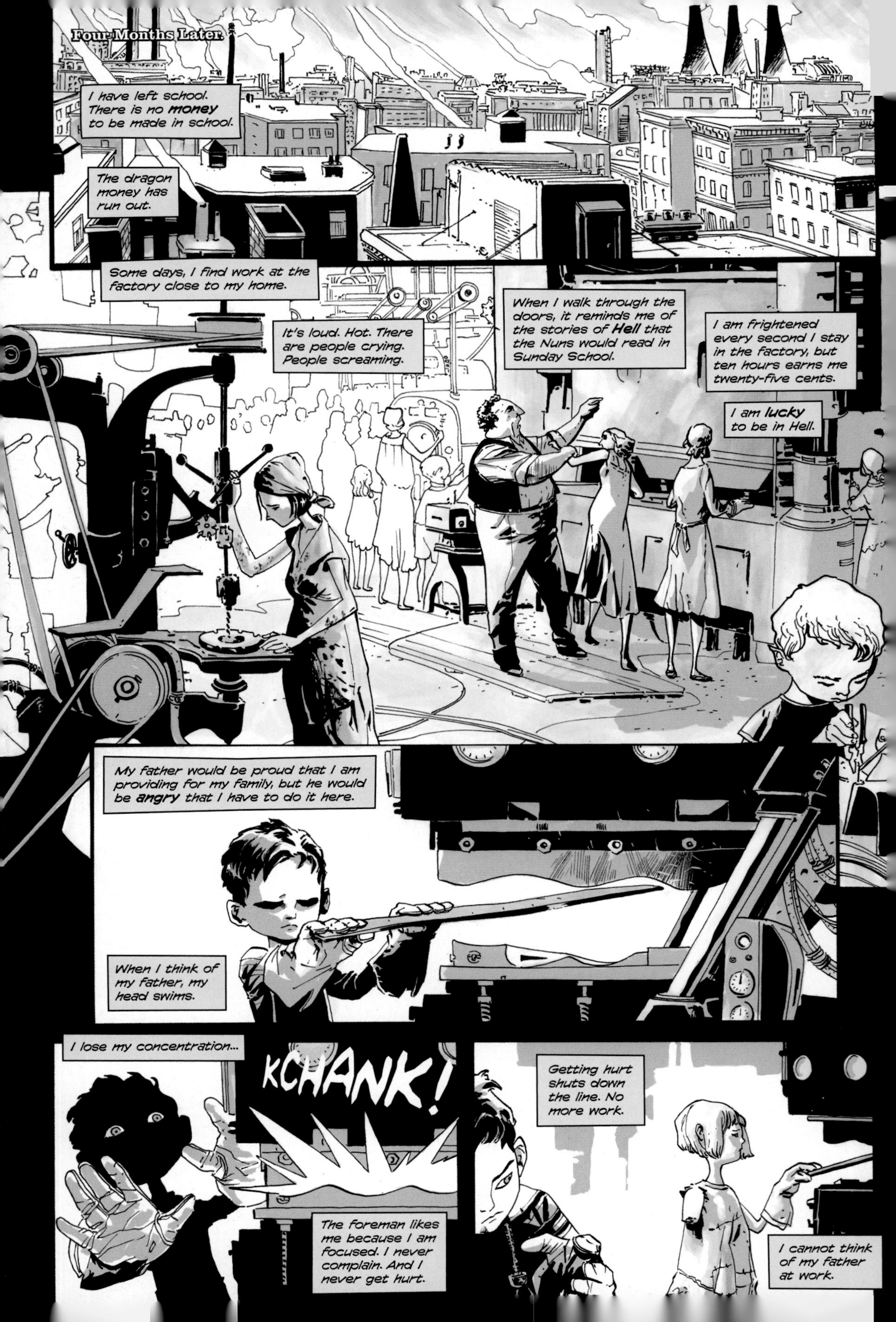
Four Months Later.
I have left school. There is no money to be made in school.
The dragon money has run out.
Some days, I find work at the factory close to my home.
It's loud. Hot. There are people crying. People screaming.
When I walk through the doors, it reminds me of the stories of Hell that the Nuns would read in Sunday School.
I am frightened every second I stay in the factory, but ten hours earns me twenty-five cents.
I am lucky to be in Hell.
My father would be proud that I am providing for my family, but he would be angry that I have to do it here.
When I think of my father, my head swims.
I lose my concentration...
kCHANK!
The foreman likes me because I am focused. I never complain. And I never get hurt.
Getting hurt shuts down the line. No more work.
I cannot think of my father at work.

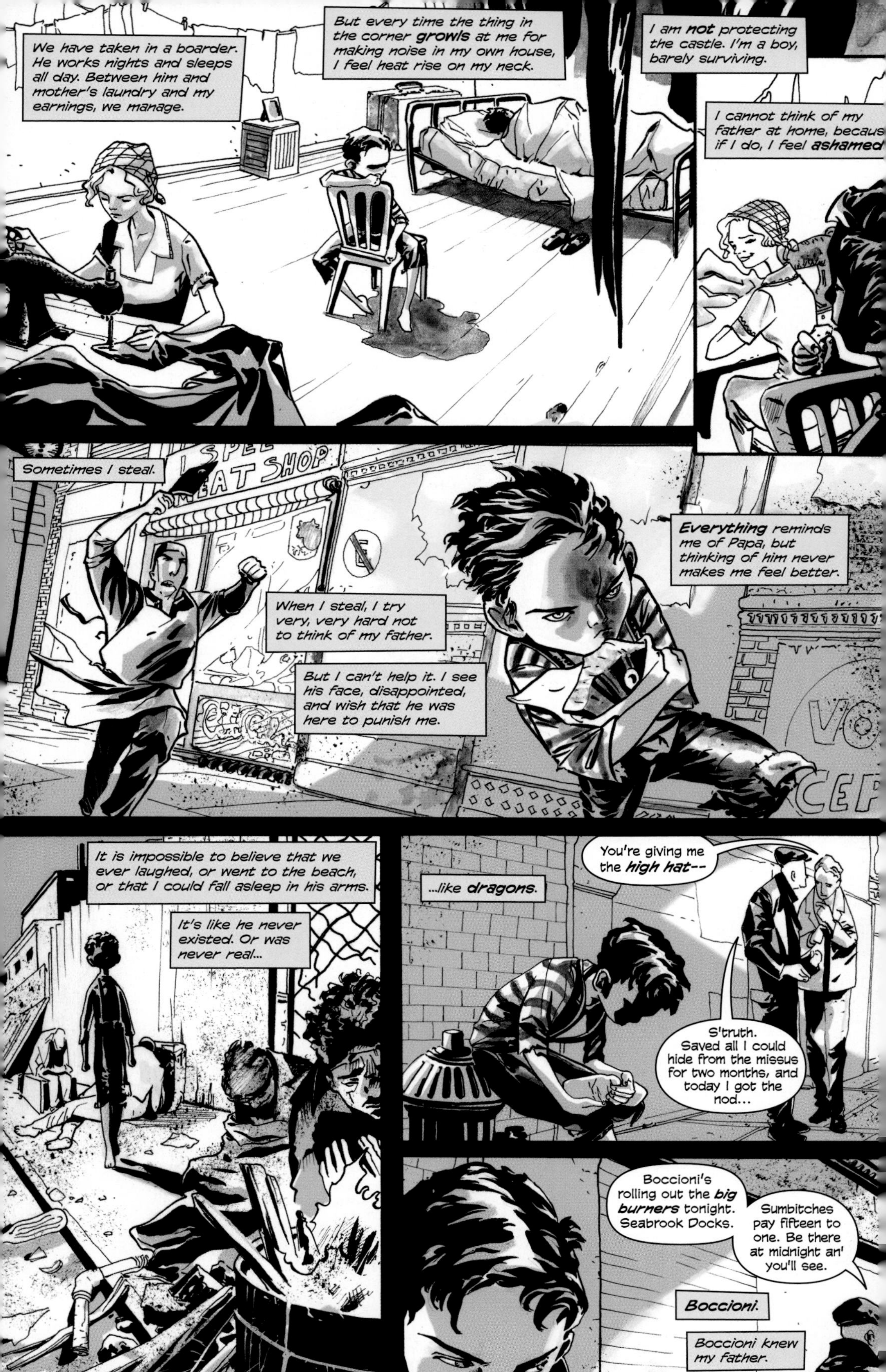
We have taken in a boarder. He works nights and sleeps all day. Between him and mother's laundry and my earnings, we manage.
But every time the thing in the corner growls at me for making noise in my own house, I feel heat rise on my neck.
I am not protecting the castle. I'm a boy, barely surviving.
I cannot think of my father at home, becaus if I do, I feel ashamed
Sometimes I steal.
MEAT SHOP
Everything reminds me of Papa, but thinking of him never makes me feel better.
When I steal, I try very, very hard not to think of my father.
But I can't help it. I see his face, disappointed, and wish that he was here to punish me.
It is impossible to believe that we ever laughed, or went to the beach, or that I could fall asleep in his arms.
It's like he never existed. Or was never real...
...like dragons.
You're giving me the high hat--
S'truth. Saved all I could hide from the missus for two months, and today I got the nod...
Boccioni's rolling out the big burners tonight. Seabrook Docks.
Sumbitches pay fifteen to one. Be there at midnight an' you'll see.
Boccioni.
Boccioni knew my father.

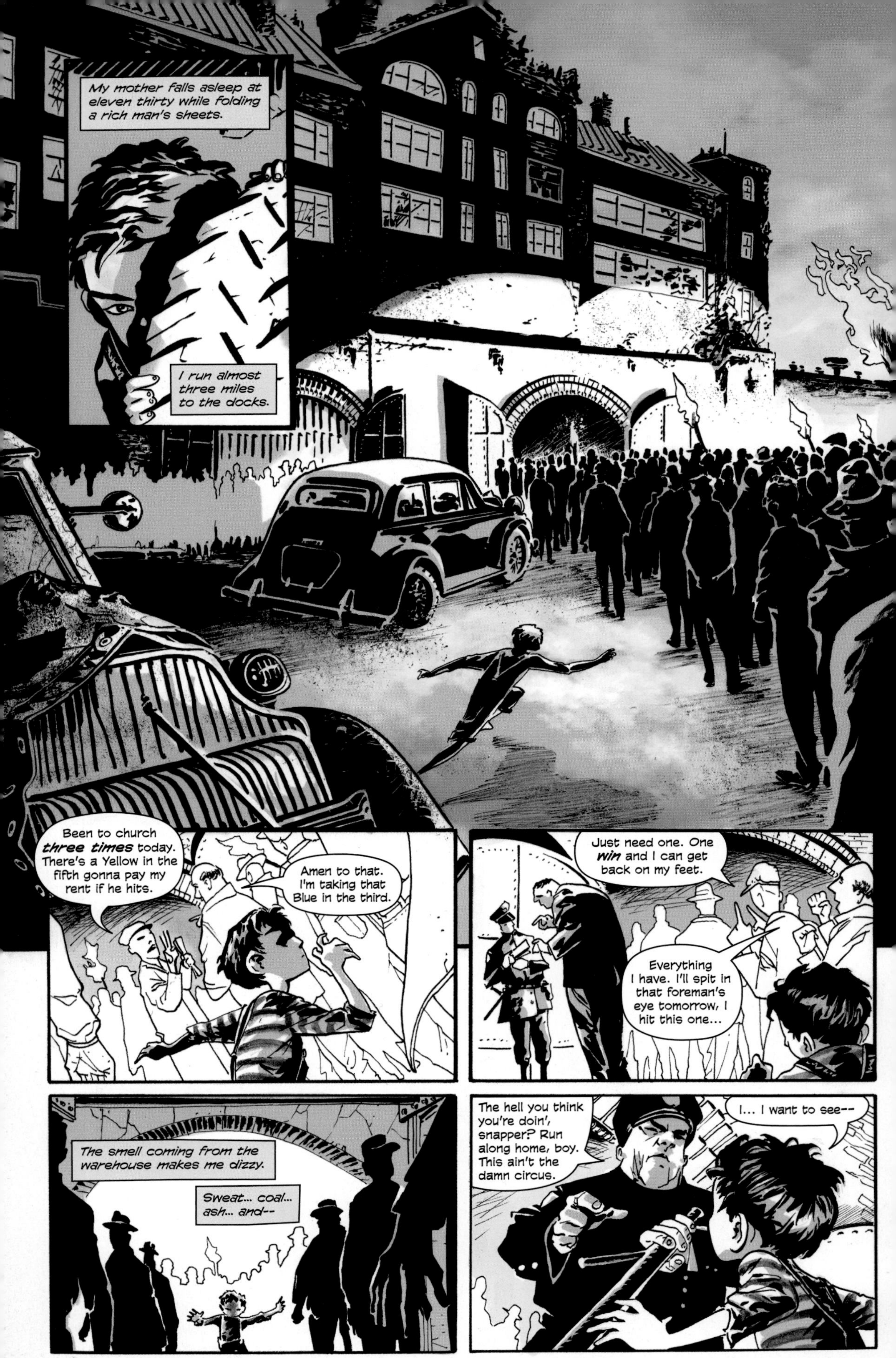

My mother falls asleep at eleven thirty while folding a rich man's sheets.
I run almost three miles to the docks.
Been to church *three times* today. There's a Yellow in the fifth gonna pay my rent if he hits.
Amen to that. I'm taking that Blue in the third.
Just need one. One *win* and I can get back on my feet.
Everything I have. I'll spit in that foreman's eye tomorrow, I hit this one...
The smell coming from the warehouse makes me dizzy.
Sweat... coal... ash... and--
The hell you think you're doin', snapper? Run along home, boy. This ain't the damn circus.
I... I want to see--

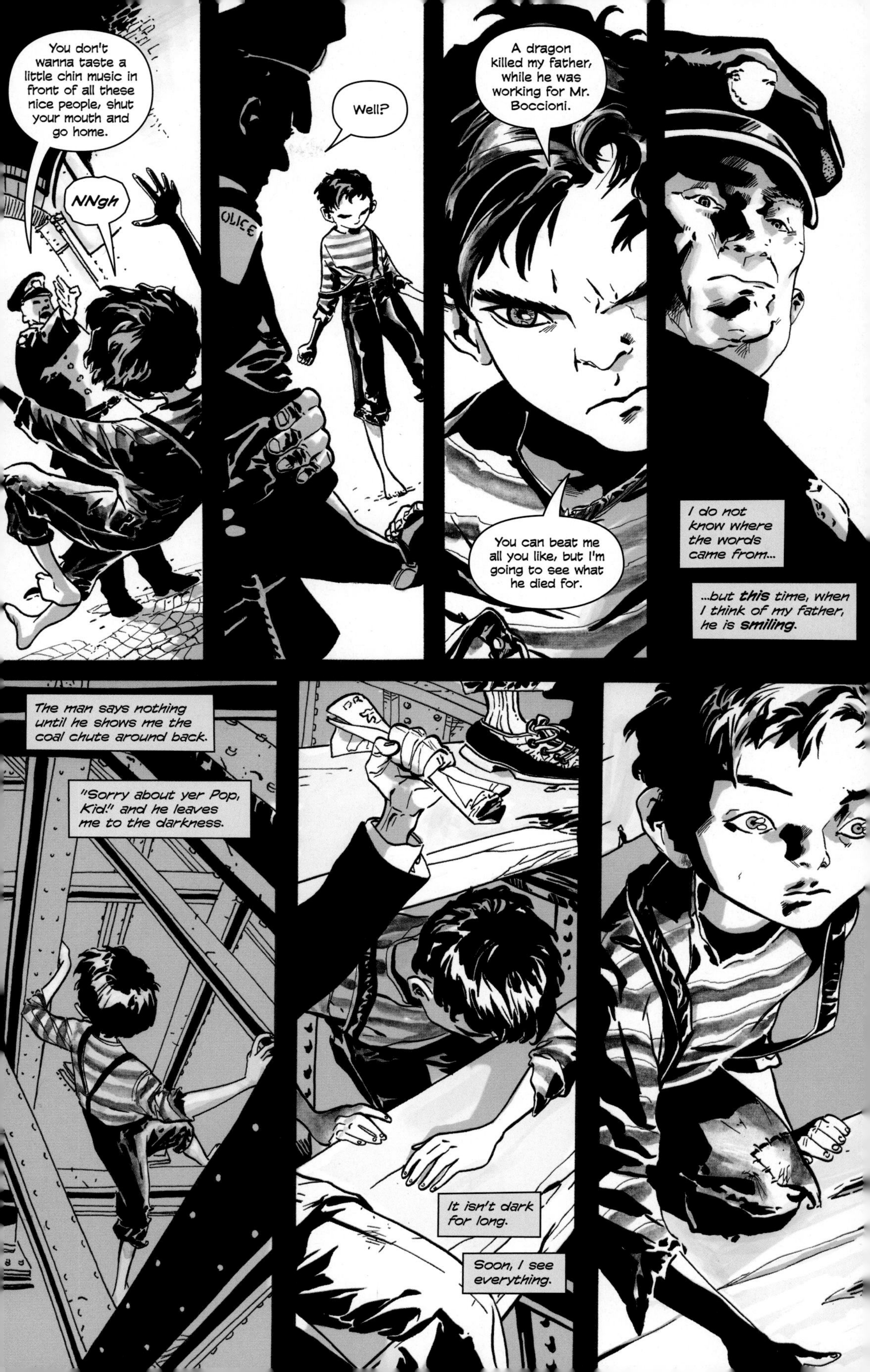
You don't wanna taste a little chin music in front of all these nice people, shut your mouth and go home.
NNgh
Well?
A dragon killed my father, while he was working for Mr. Boccioni.
You can beat me all you like, but I'm going to see what he died for.
I do not know where the words came from...
...but **this** time, when I think of my father, he is **smiling**.
The man says nothing until he shows me the coal chute around back.
"Sorry about yer Pop, Kid!" and he leaves me to the darkness.
It isn't dark for long.
Soon, I see everything.

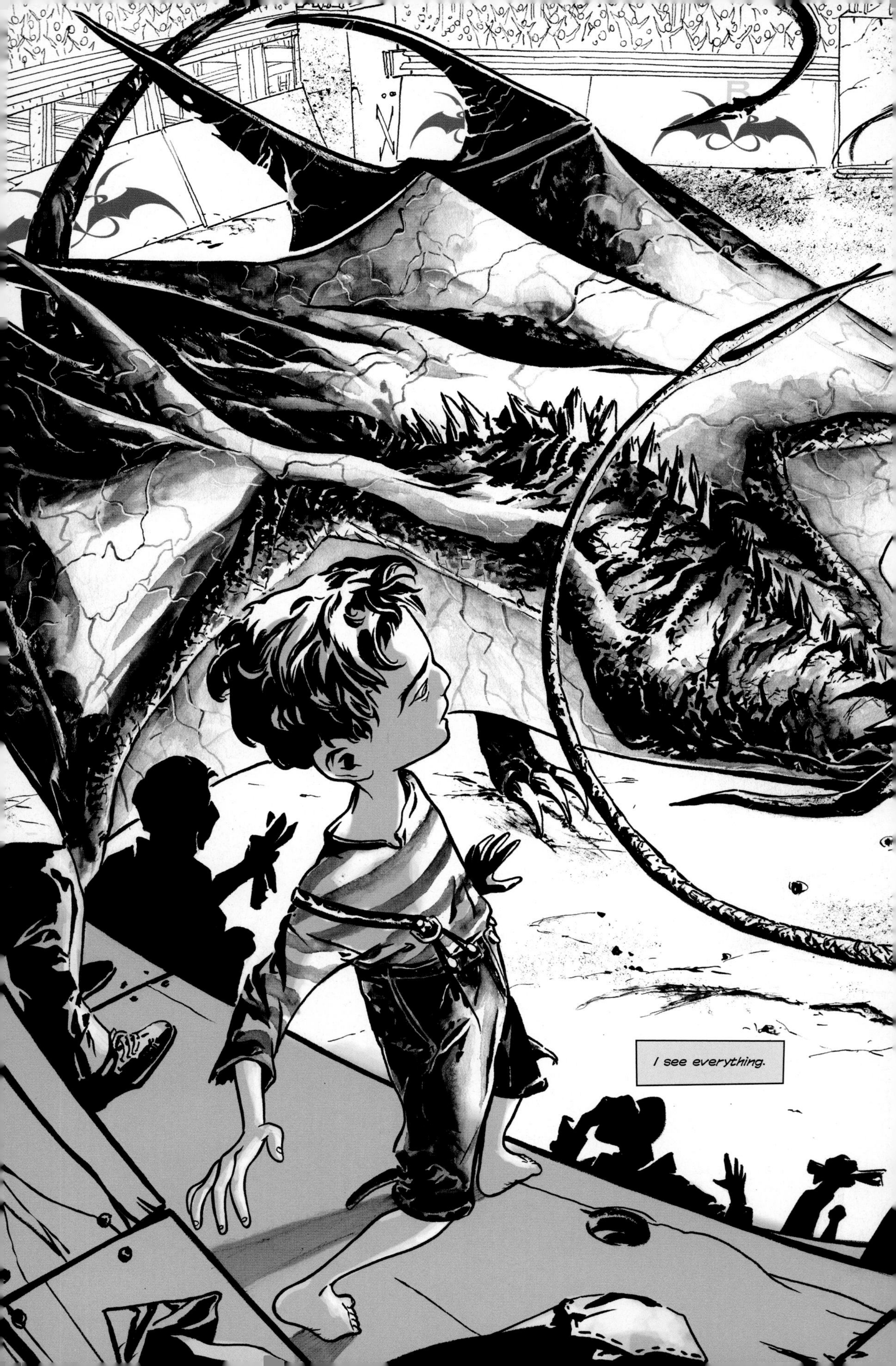
I see everything.

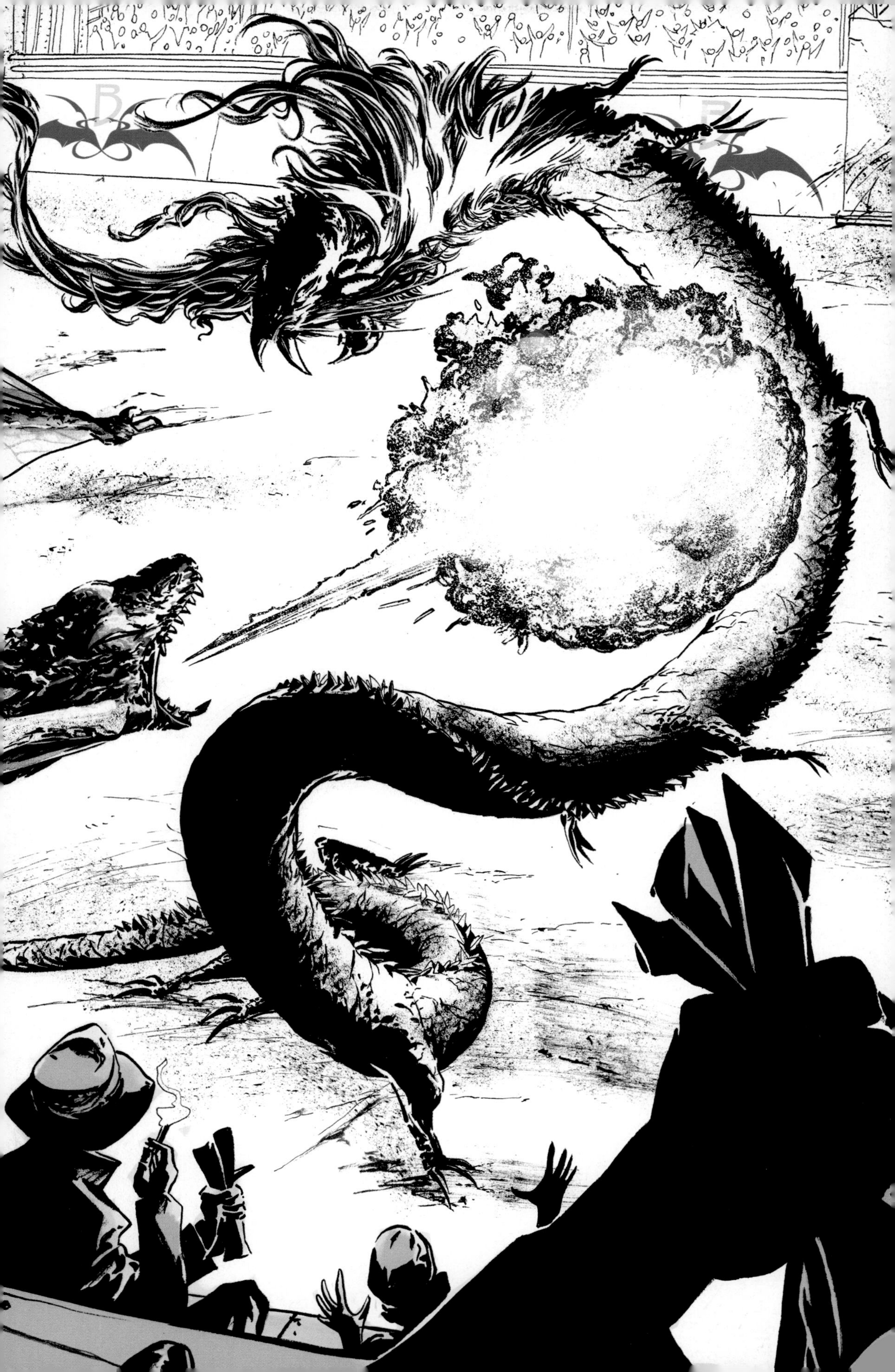

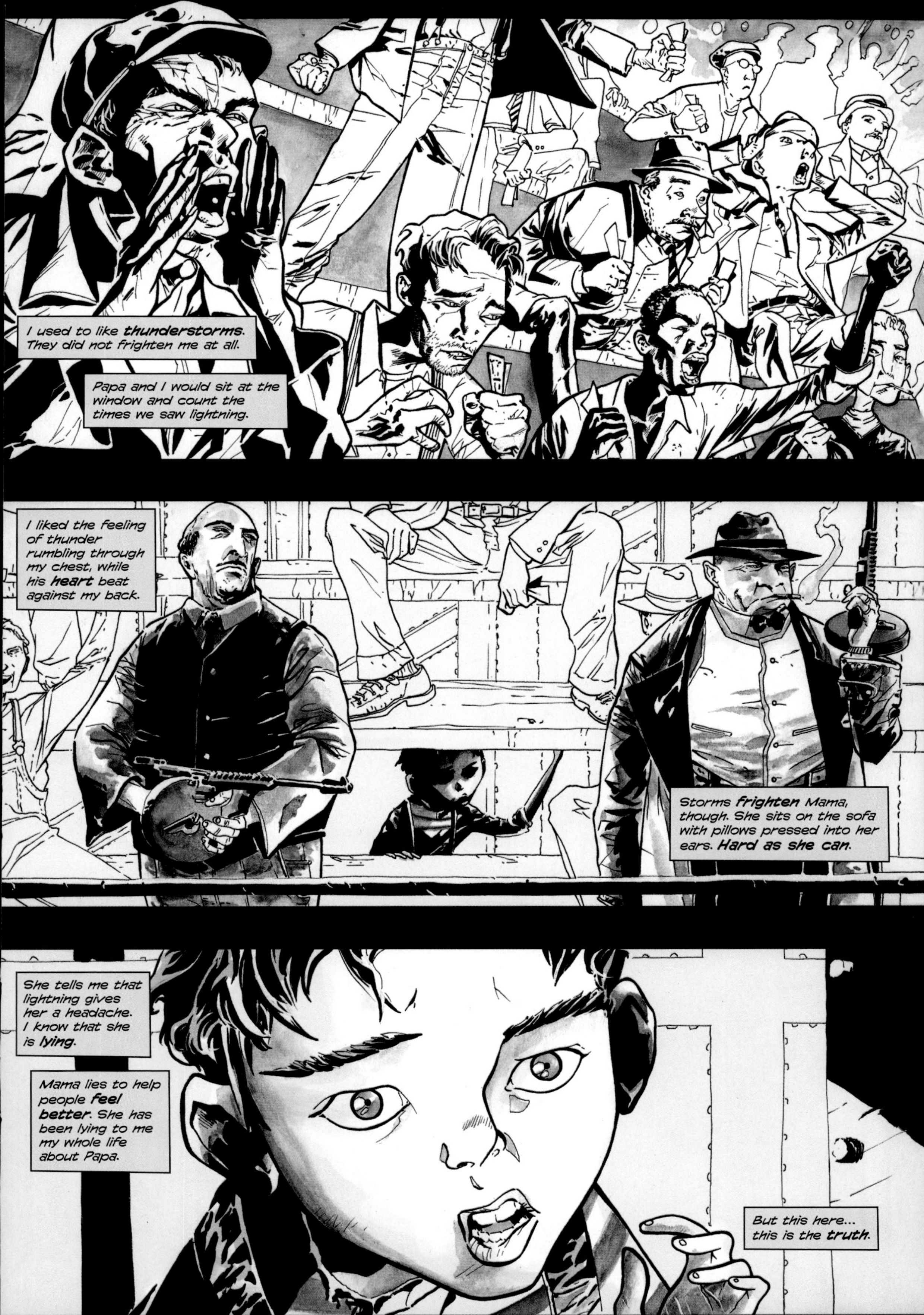
I used to like **thunderstorms**. They did not frighten me at all.
Papa and I would sit at the window and count the times we saw lightning.
I liked the feeling of thunder rumbling through my chest, while his **heart** beat against my back.
Storms **frighten** Mama, though. She sits on the sofa with pillows pressed into her ears. **Hard as she can**.
She tells me that lightning gives her a headache. I know that she is **lying**.
Mama lies to help people **feel better**. She has been lying to me my whole life about Papa.
But this here... this is the **truth**.

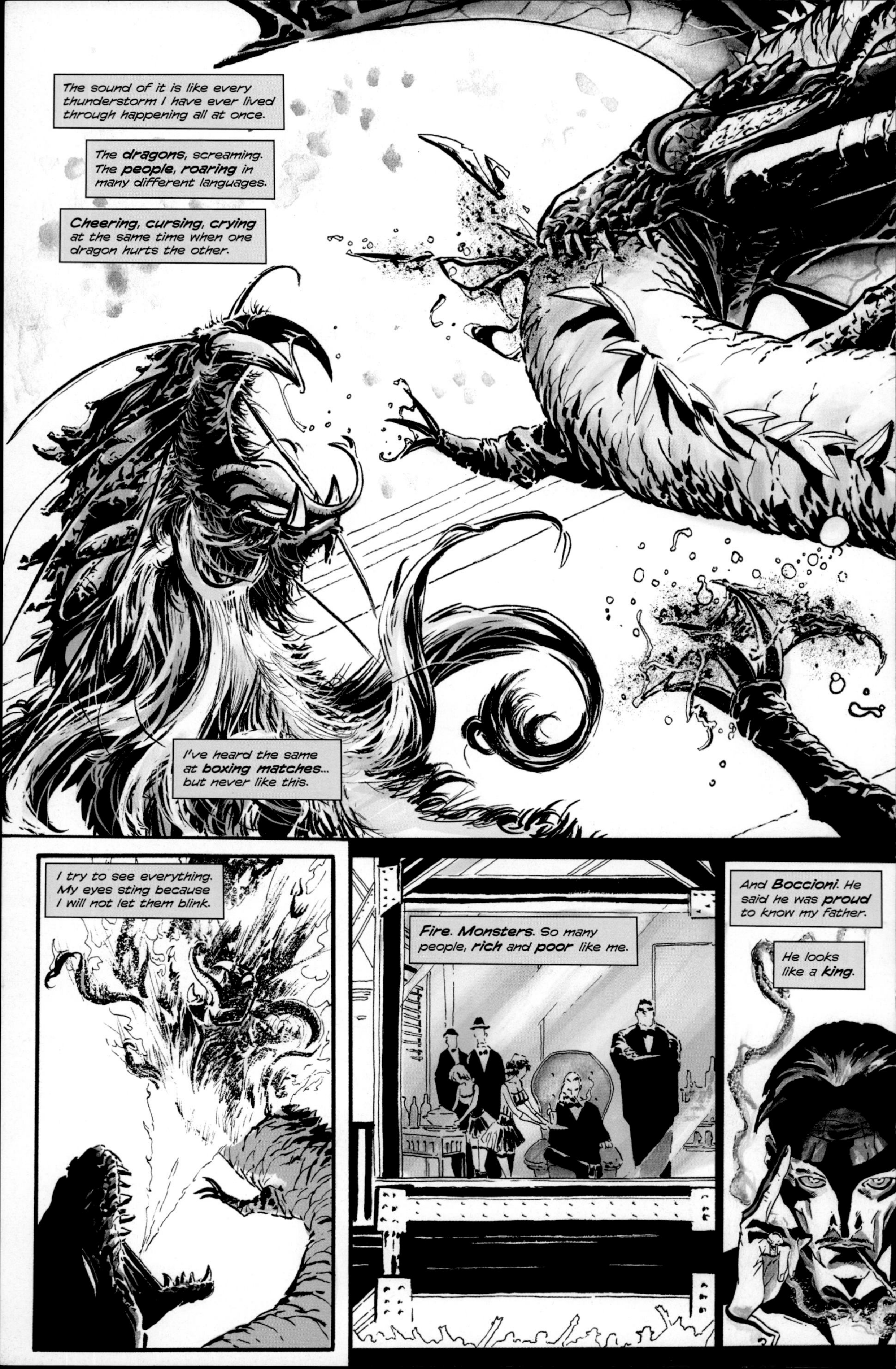
The sound of it is like every thunderstorm I have ever lived through happening all at once.
The **dragons**, screaming. The **people**, **roaring** in many different languages.
Cheering, **cursing**, **crying** at the same time when one dragon hurts the other.
I've heard the same at **boxing matches**... but never like this.
I try to see everything. My eyes sting because I will not let them blink.
Fire. **Monsters**. So many people, **rich** and **poor** like me.
And **Boccioni**. He said he was **proud** to know my father.
He looks like a **king**.

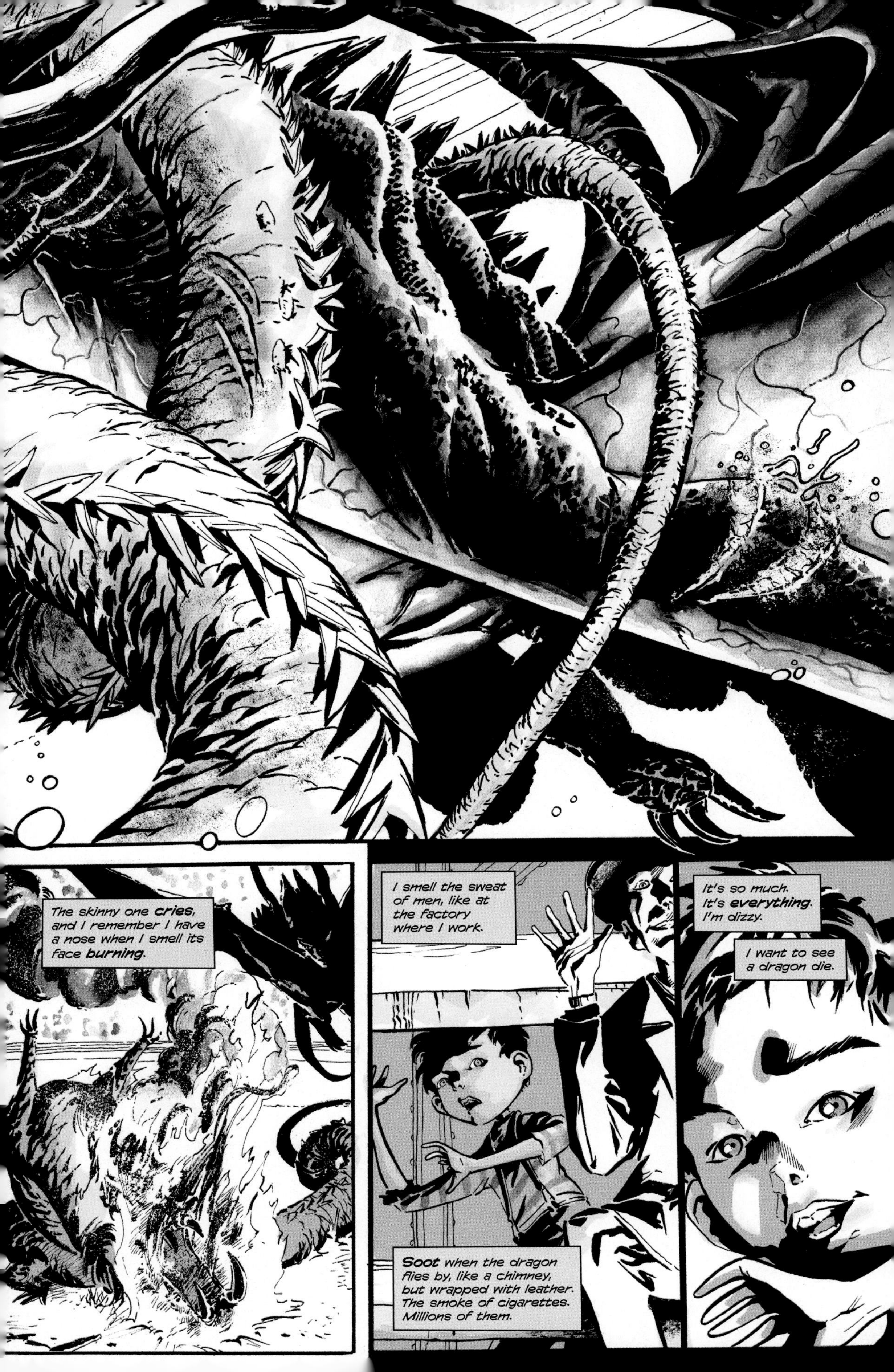
The skinny one **cries**, and I remember I have a nose when I smell its face **burning**.
I smell the sweat of men, like at the factory where I work.
Soot when the dragon flies by, like a chimney, but wrapped with leather. The smoke of cigarettes. Millions of them.
It's so much. It's **everything**. I'm dizzy.
I want to see a dragon die.

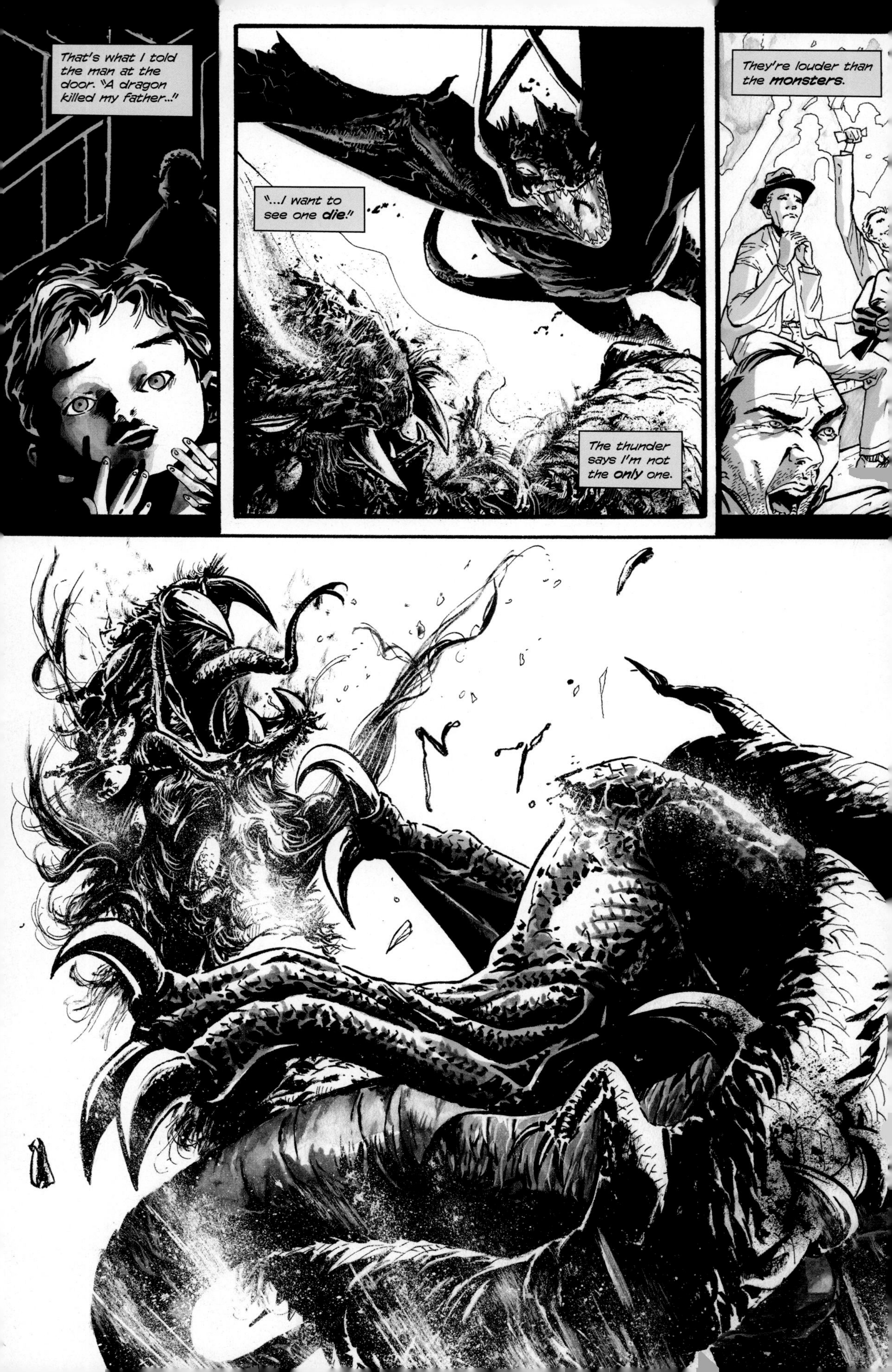

That's what I told the man at the door. "A dragon killed my father..."
"...I want to see one **die**."
The thunder says I'm not the **only** one.
They're louder than the **monsters**.

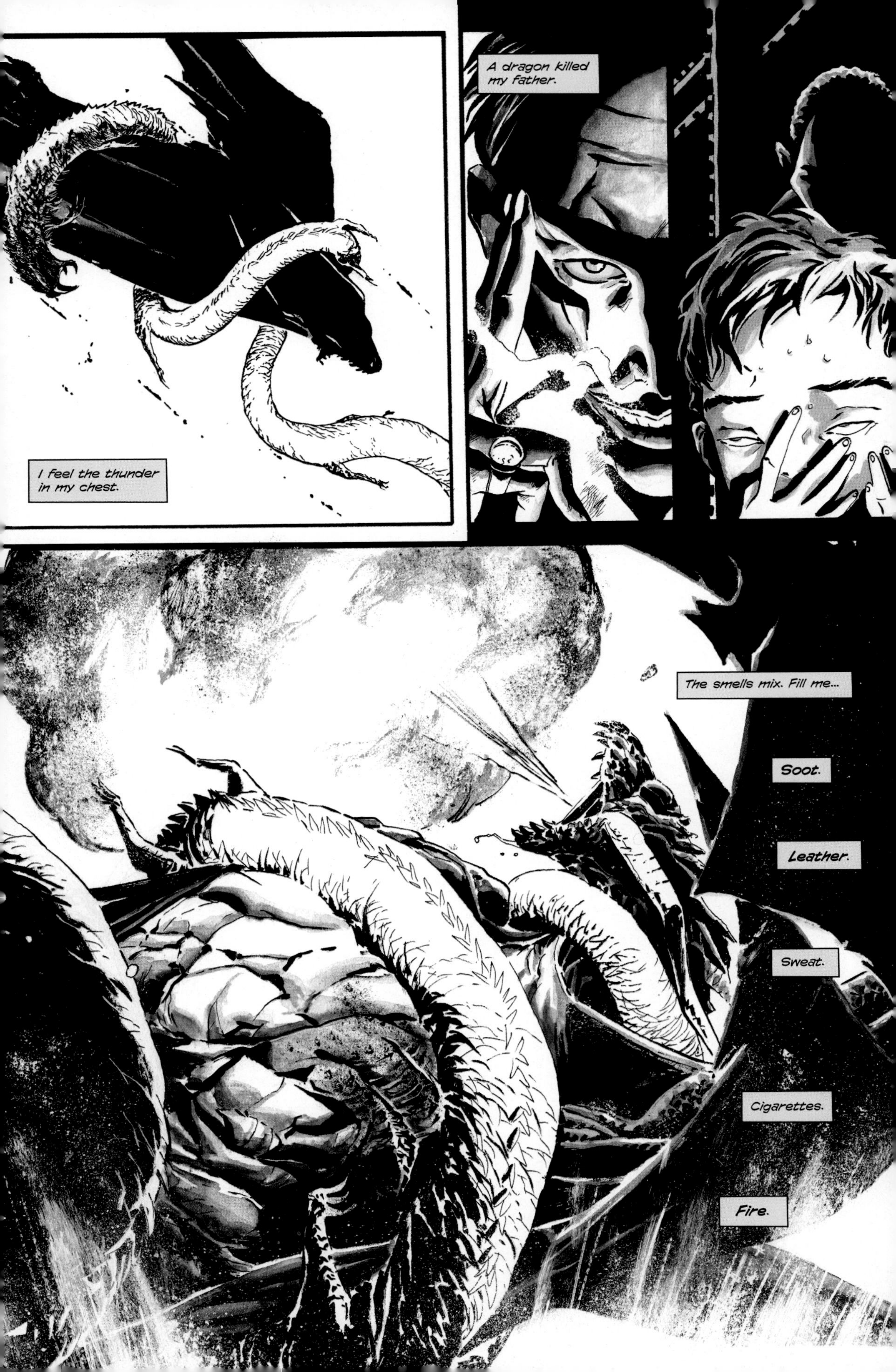
I feel the thunder in my chest.
A dragon killed my father.
The smells mix. Fill me...
Soot.
Leather.
Sweat.
Cigarettes.
Fire.

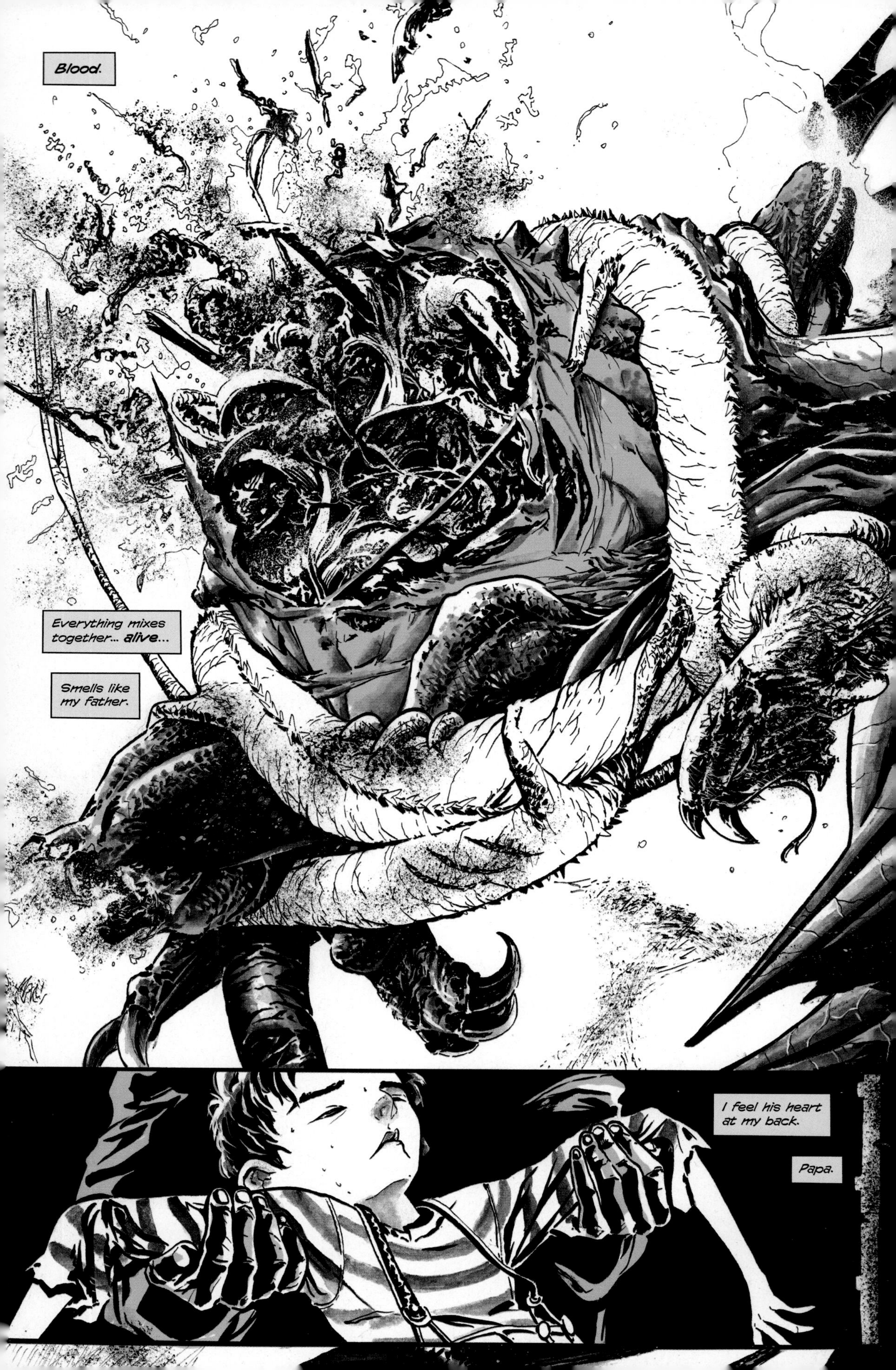
Blood.
Everything mixes together... alive...
Smells like my father.
I feel his heart at my back.
Papa.

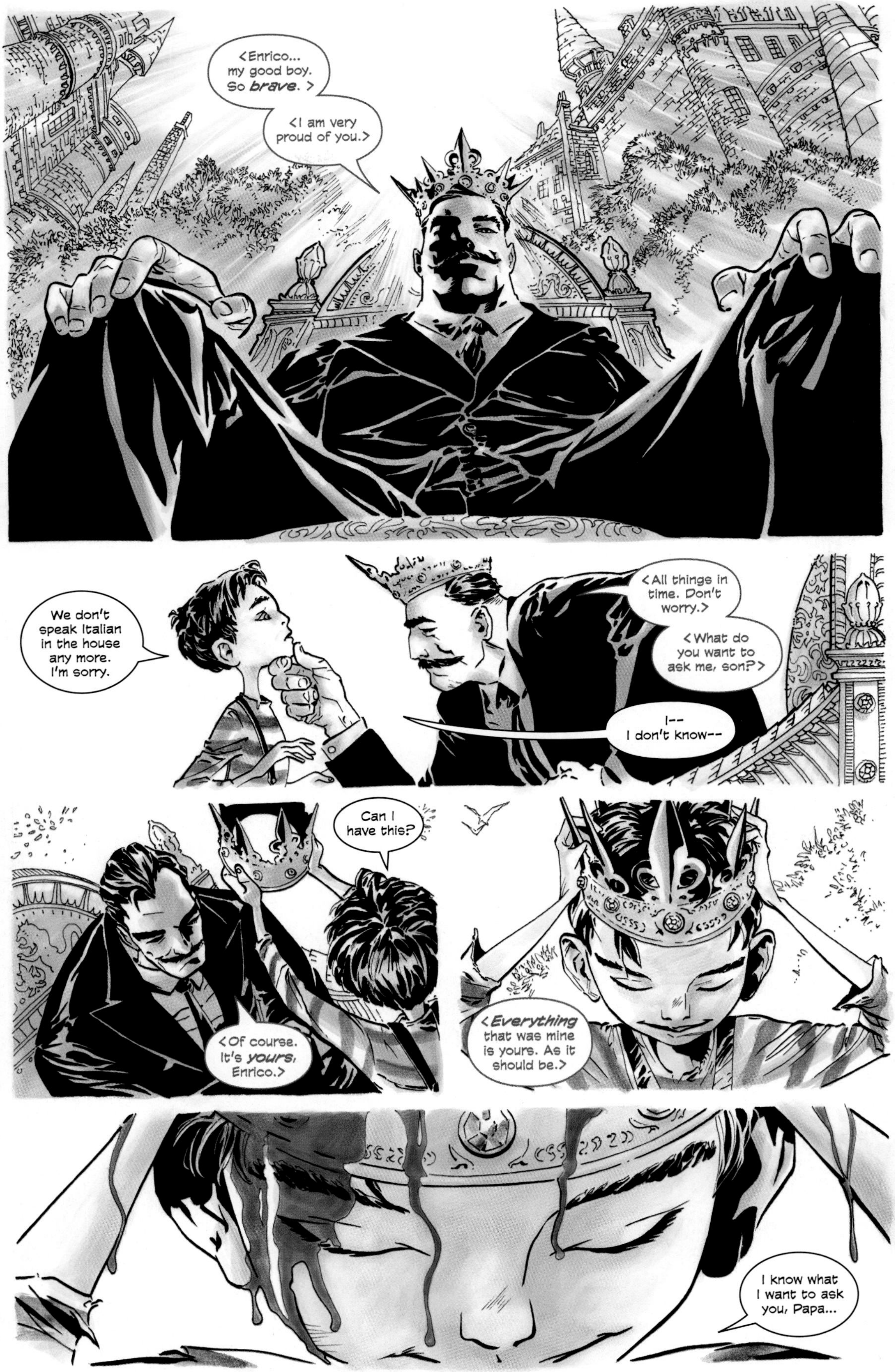
<Enrico... my good boy. So *brave*.>
<I am very proud of you.>
We don't speak Italian in the house any more. I'm sorry.
<All things in time. Don't worry.>
<What do you want to ask me, son?>
I-- I don't know--
Can I have this?
<Of course. It's *yours*, Enrico.>
<*Everything* that was mine is yours. As it should be.>
I know what I want to ask you, Papa...

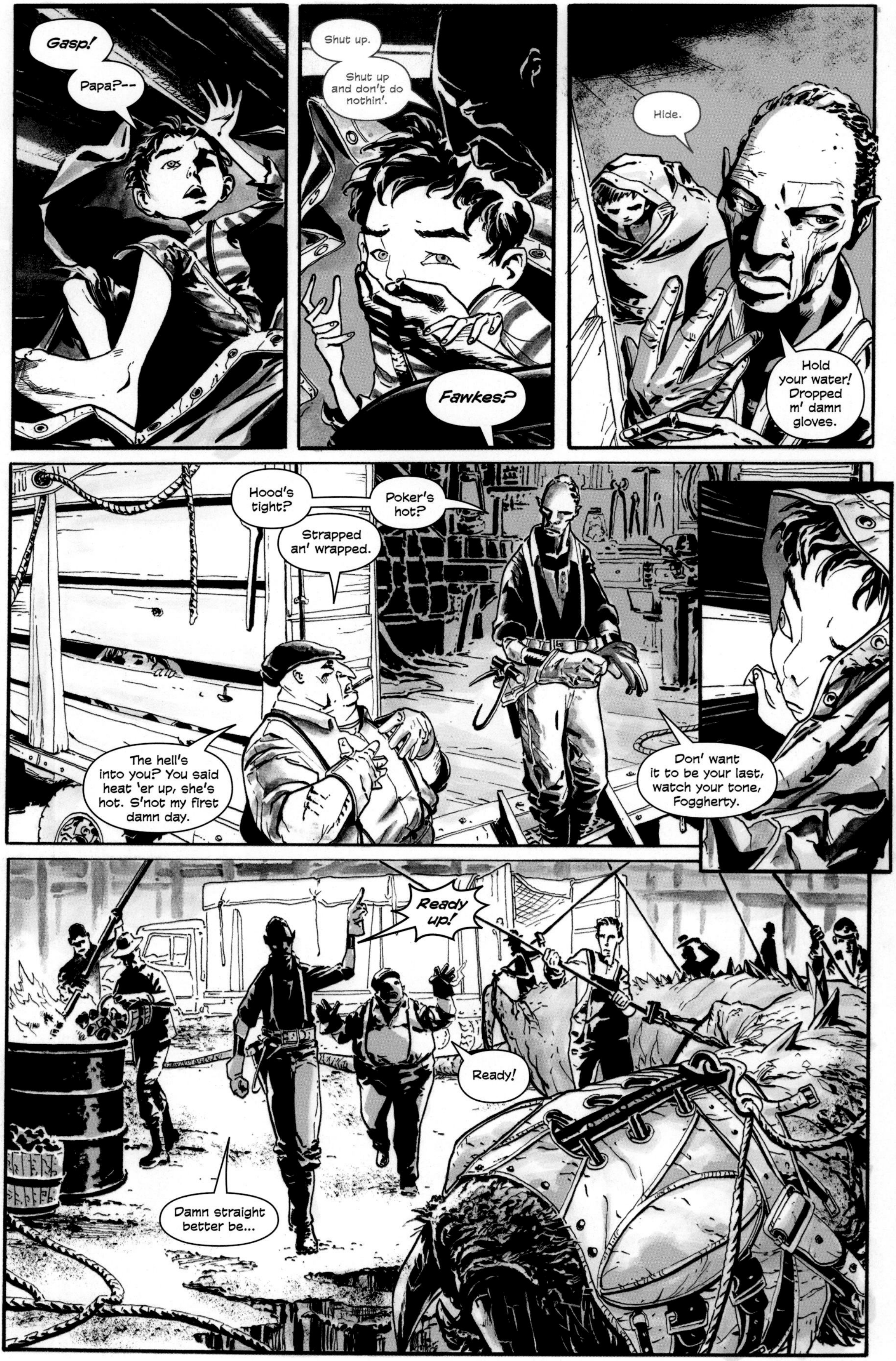
Gasp!
Papa?--
Shut up.
Shut up and don't do nothin'.
Fawkes?
Hide.
Hold your water! Dropped m' damn gloves.
Hood's tight?
Poker's hot?
Strapped an' wrapped.
The hell's into you? You said heat 'er up, she's hot. S'not my first damn day.
Don' want it to be your last, watch your tone, Foggherty.
Ready up!
Ready!
Damn straight better be...

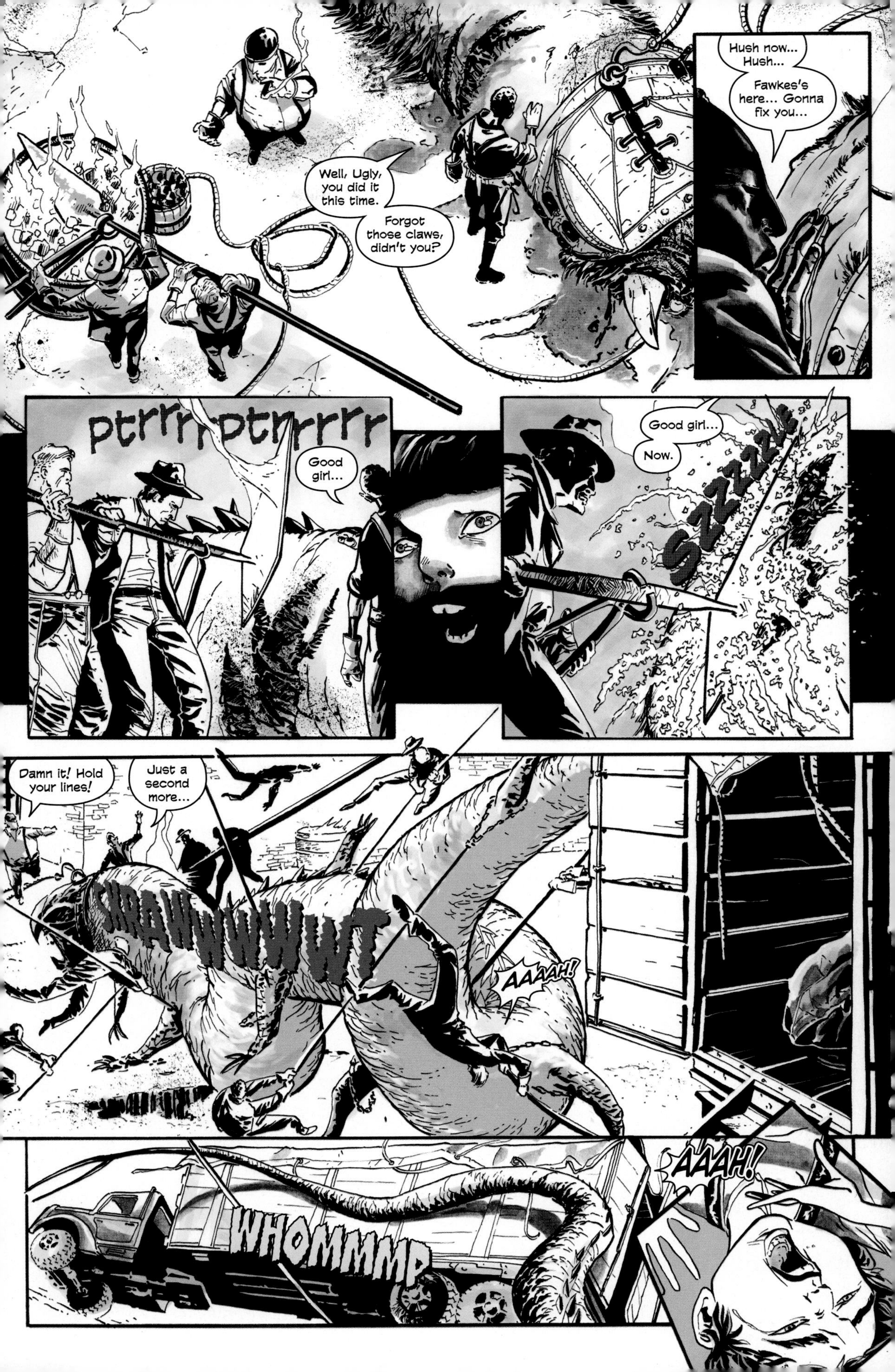
Well, Ugly, you did it this time.
Forgot those claws, didn't you?
Hush now... Hush...
Fawkes's here... Gonna fix you...
ptrrrrptrrrrr
Good girl...
Good girl...
Now.
SZZZZ
Damn it! Hold your lines!
Just a second more...
SKRAWWWWWWT
AAAAH!
WHOMMMMP
AAAH!

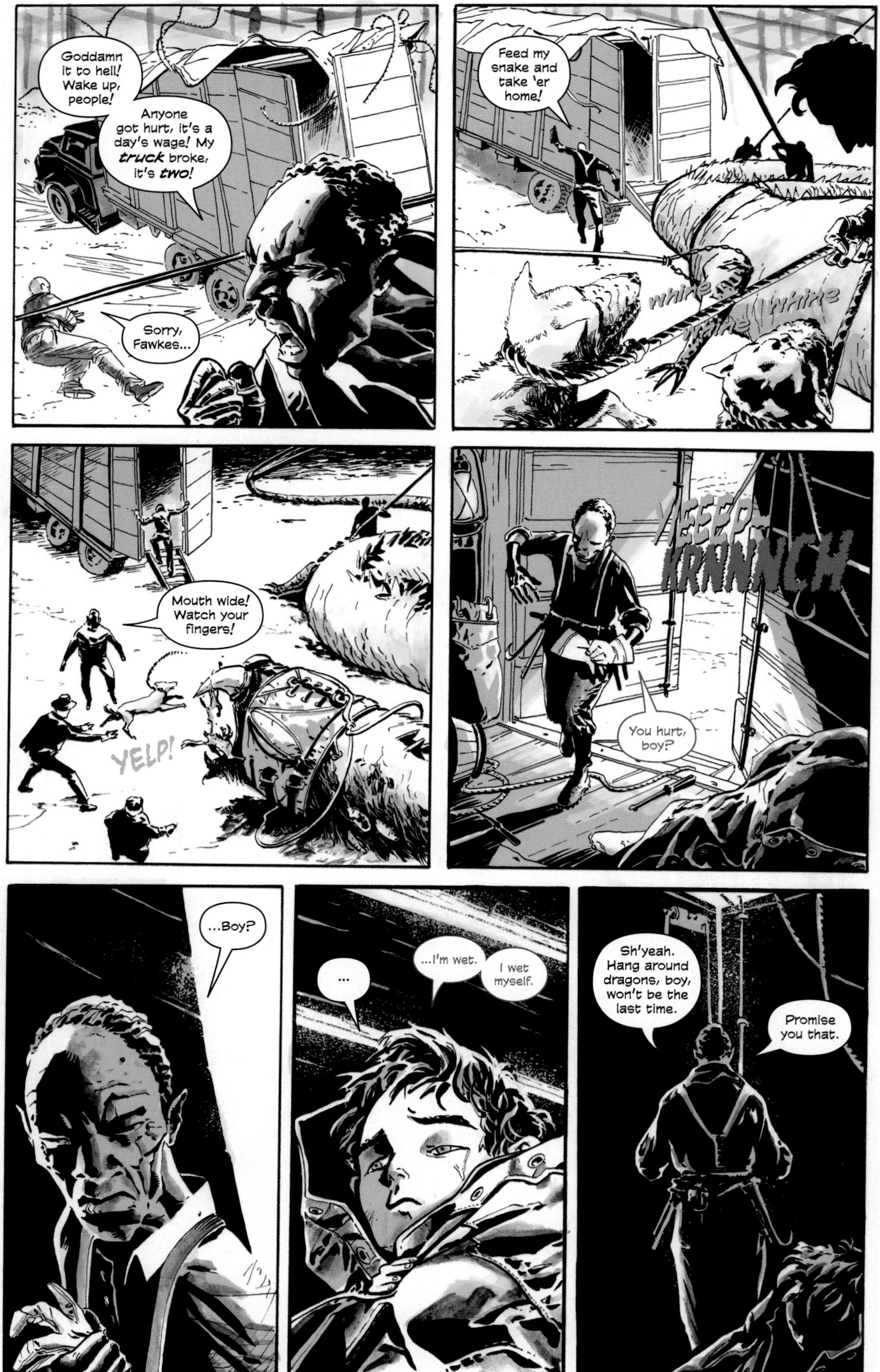
Goddamn it to hell! Wake up, people!
Anyone got hurt, it's a day's wage! My *truck* broke, it's *two*!
Sorry, Fawkes...
Feed my snake and take 'er home!
whine
whine
whine
Mouth wide! Watch your fingers!
YELP!
KRNNNCH
You hurt, boy?
...Boy?
...
...I'm wet.
I wet myself.
Sh'yeah. Hang around dragons, boy, won't be the last time.
Promise you that.

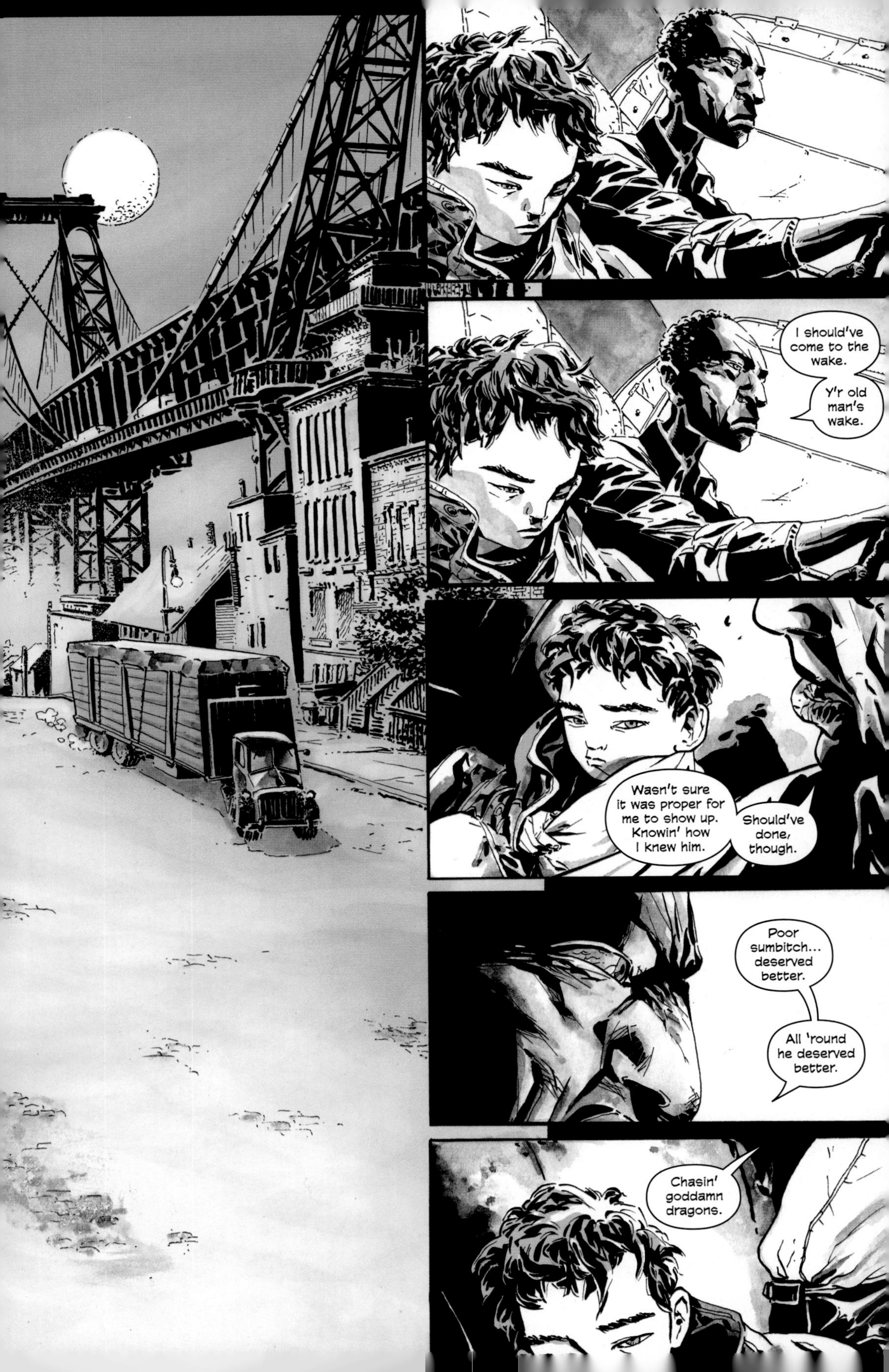

I should've come to the wake.
Y'r old man's wake.
Wasn't sure it was proper for me to show up. Knowin' how I knew him.
Should've done, though.
Poor sumbitch... deserved better.
All 'round he deserved better.
Chasin' goddamn dragons.

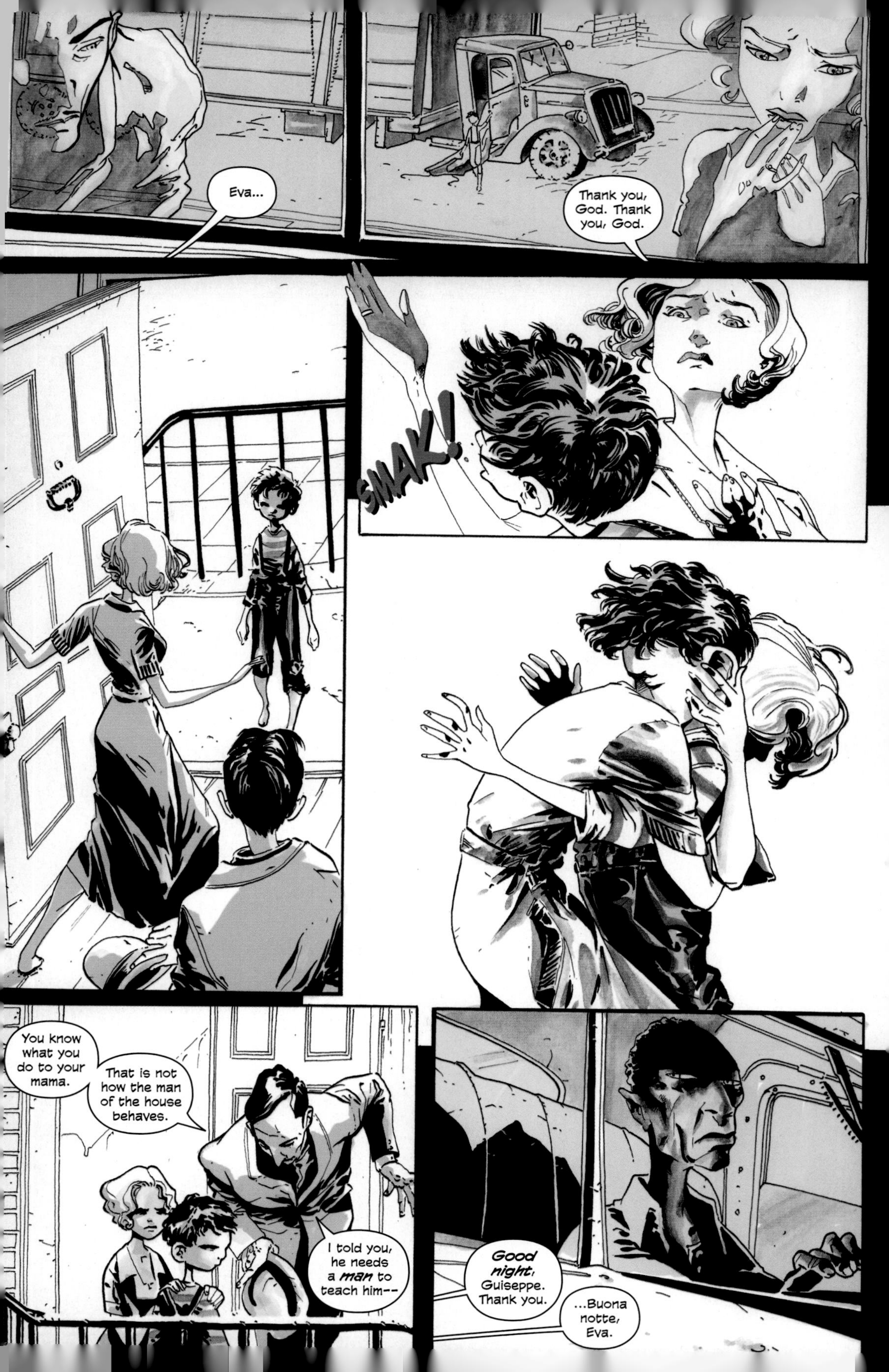
Eva...
Thank you, God. Thank you, God.
SMAK!
You know what you do to your mama.
That is not how the man of the house behaves.
I told you, he needs a *man* to teach him--
Good night, Guiseppe. Thank you.
...Buona notte, Eva.

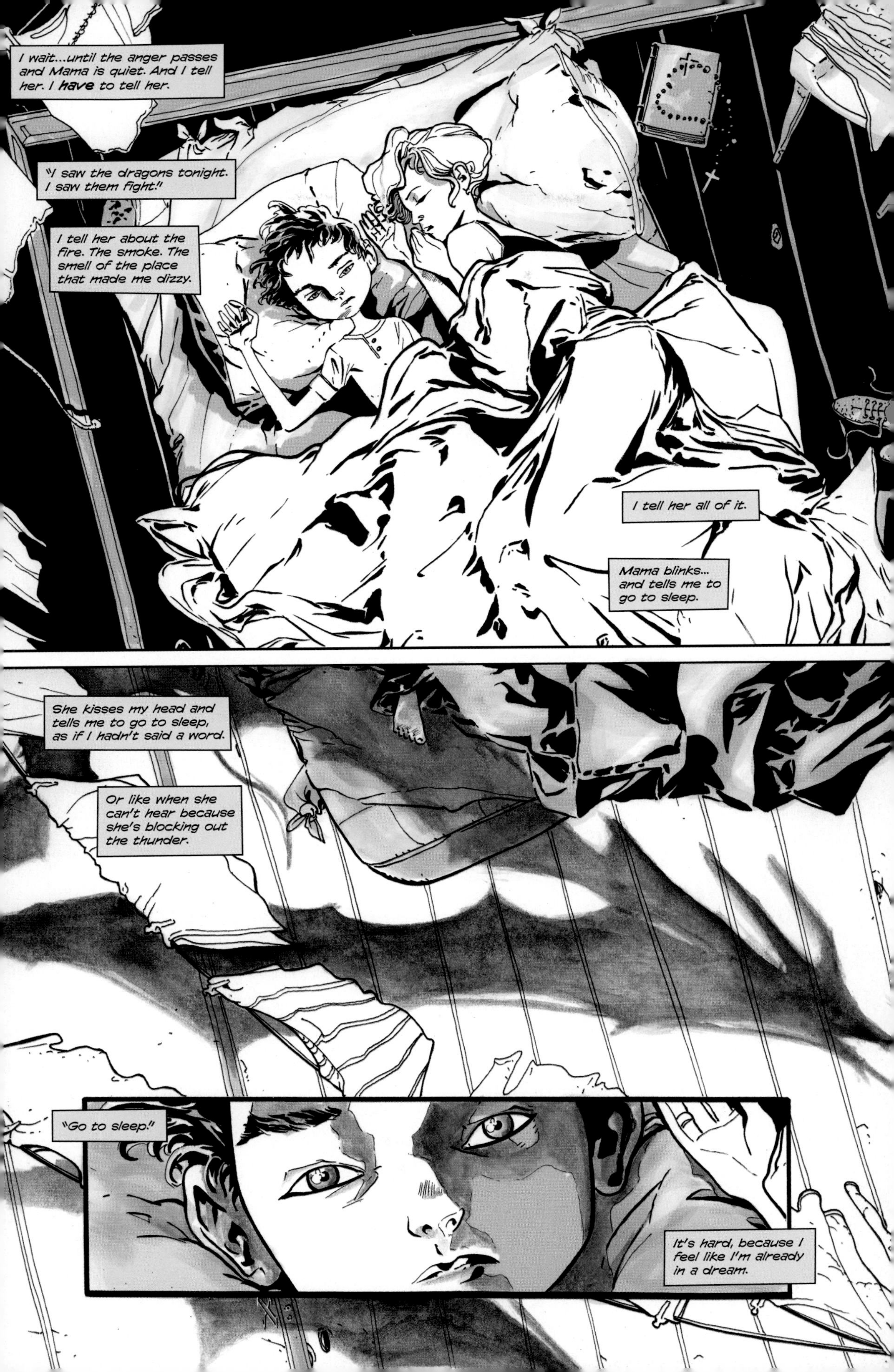
I wait...until the anger passes and Mama is quiet. And I tell her. I **have** to tell her.
"I saw the dragons tonight. I saw them fight!"
I tell her about the fire. The smoke. The smell of the place that made me dizzy.
I tell her all of it.
Mama blinks... and tells me to go to sleep.
She kisses my head and tells me to go to sleep, as if I hadn't said a word.
Or like when she can't hear because she's blocking out the thunder.
"Go to sleep!"
It's hard, because I feel like I'm already in a dream.

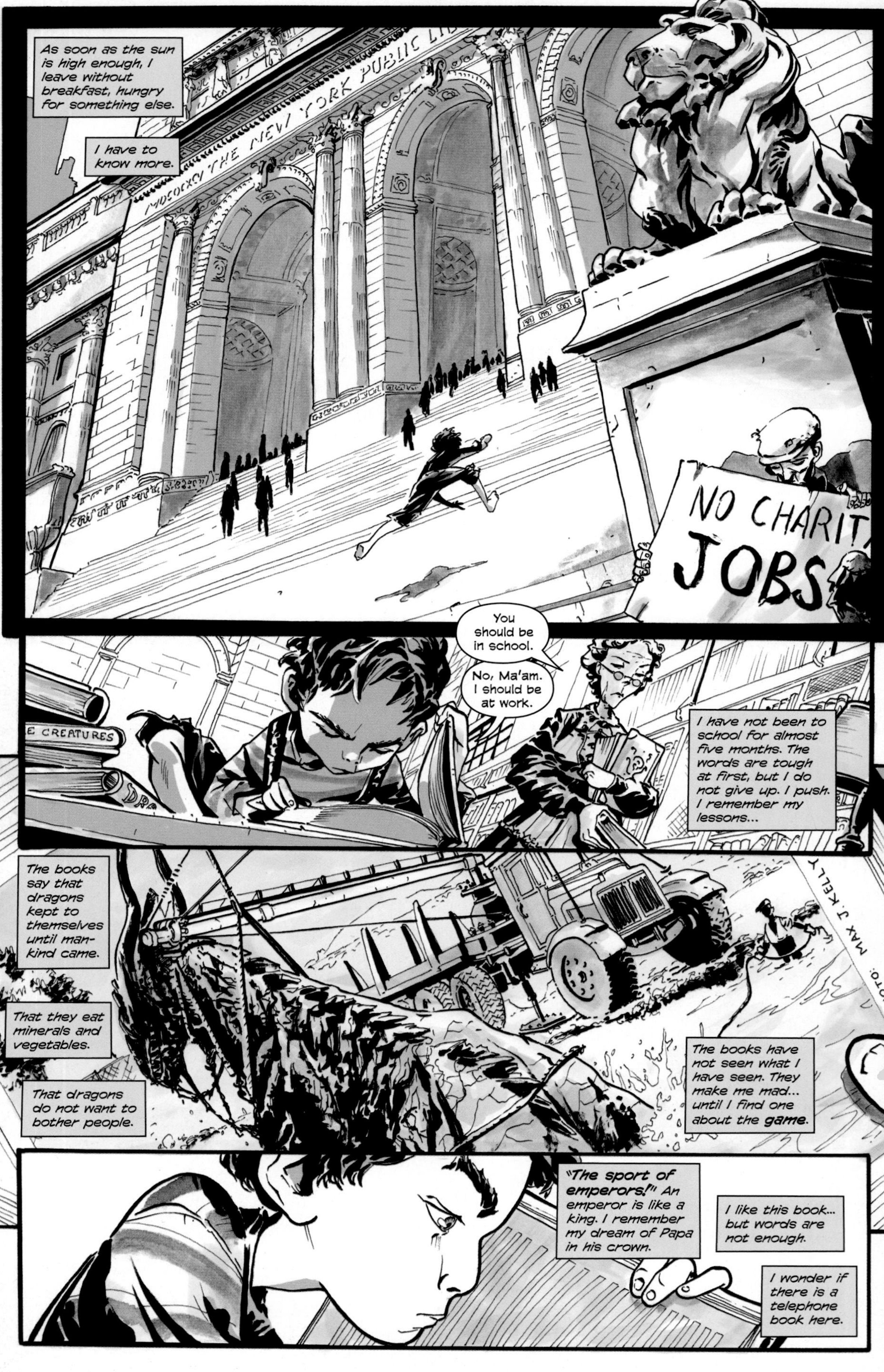
As soon as the sun is high enough, I leave without breakfast, hungry for something else.
THE NEW YORK PUBLIC LI
I have to know more.
NO CHARIT
JOBS
You should be in school.
No, Ma'am. I should be at work.
E CREATURES
DRA
I have not been to school for almost five months. The words are tough at first, but I do not give up. I push. I remember my lessons...
The books say that dragons kept to themselves until man-kind came.
That they eat minerals and vegetables.
That dragons do not want to bother people.
MAX J. KELLY
The books have not seen what I have seen. They make me mad... until I find one about the **game**.
"The sport of emperors!" An emperor is like a king. I remember my dream of Papa in his crown.
I like this book... but words are not enough.
I wonder if there is a telephone book here.

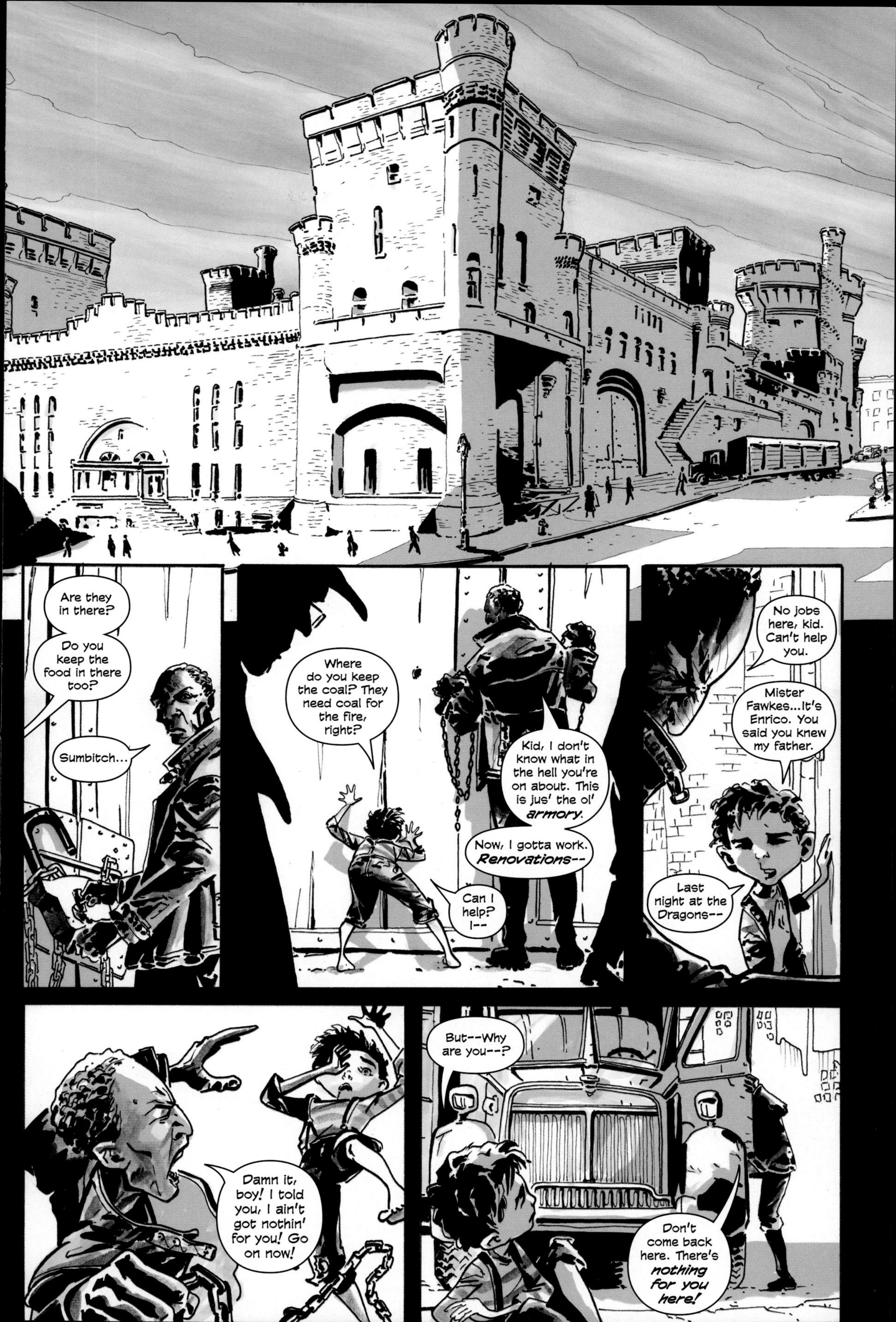

Are they in there?
Do you keep the food in there too?
Sumbitch...
Where do you keep the coal? They need coal for the fire, right?
Kid, I don't know what in the hell you're on about. This is jus' the ol' *armory*.
Now, I gotta work. *Renovations--*
Can I help? I--
No jobs here, kid. Can't help you.
Mister Fawkes...It's Enrico. You said you knew my father.
Last night at the Dragons--
Damn it, boy! I told you, I ain't got nothin' for you! Go on now!
But--Why are you--?
Don't come back here. There's *nothing for you here!*

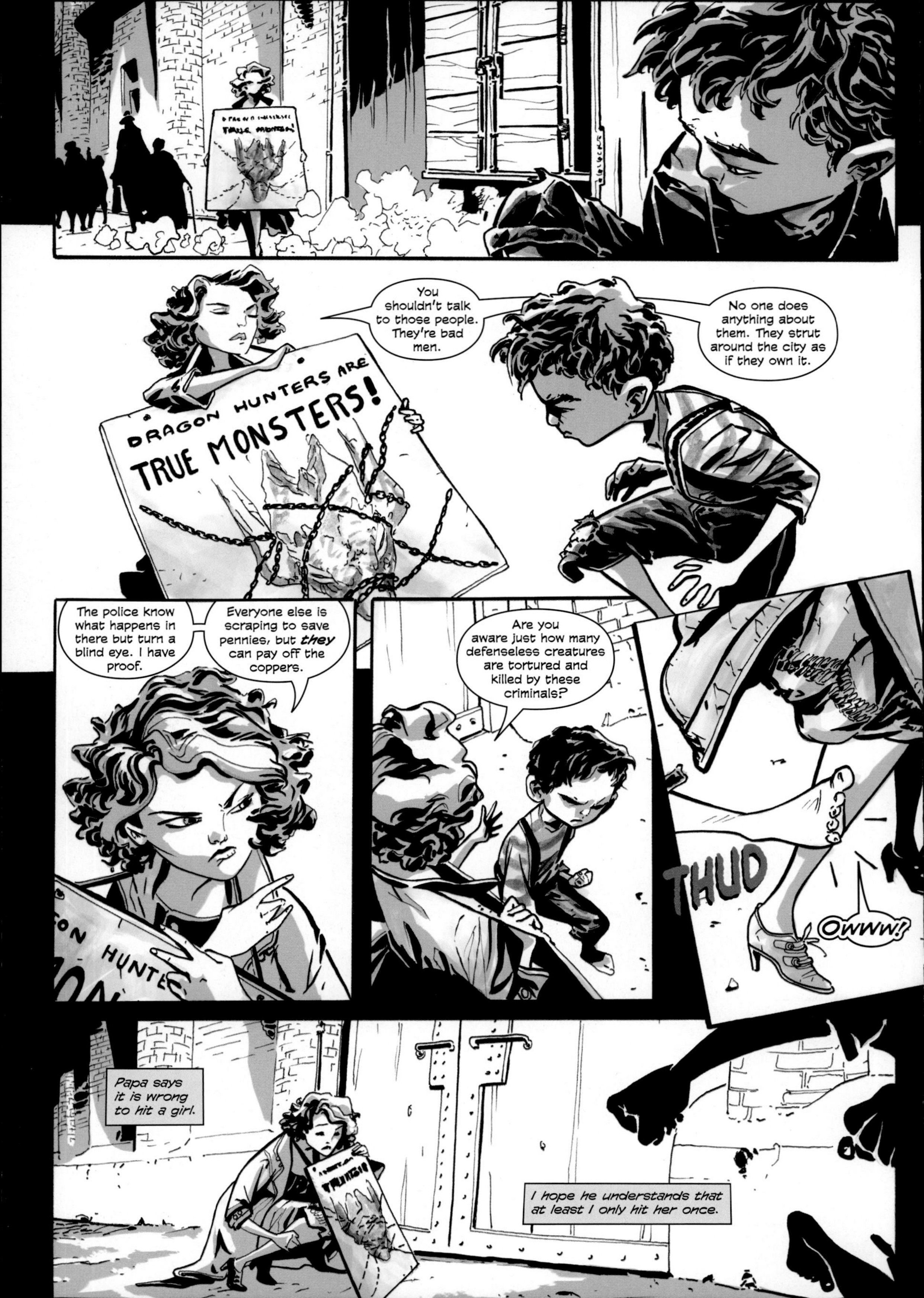

DRAGON HUNTERS ARE TRUE MONSTERS!
You shouldn't talk to those people. They're bad men.
No one does anything about them. They strut around the city as if they own it.
The police know what happens in there but turn a blind eye. I have proof.
Everyone else is scraping to save pennies, but *they* can pay off the coppers.
Are you aware just how many defenseless creatures are tortured and killed by these criminals?
THUD
OWWW!
Papa says it is wrong to hit a girl.
I hope he understands that at least I only hit her once.

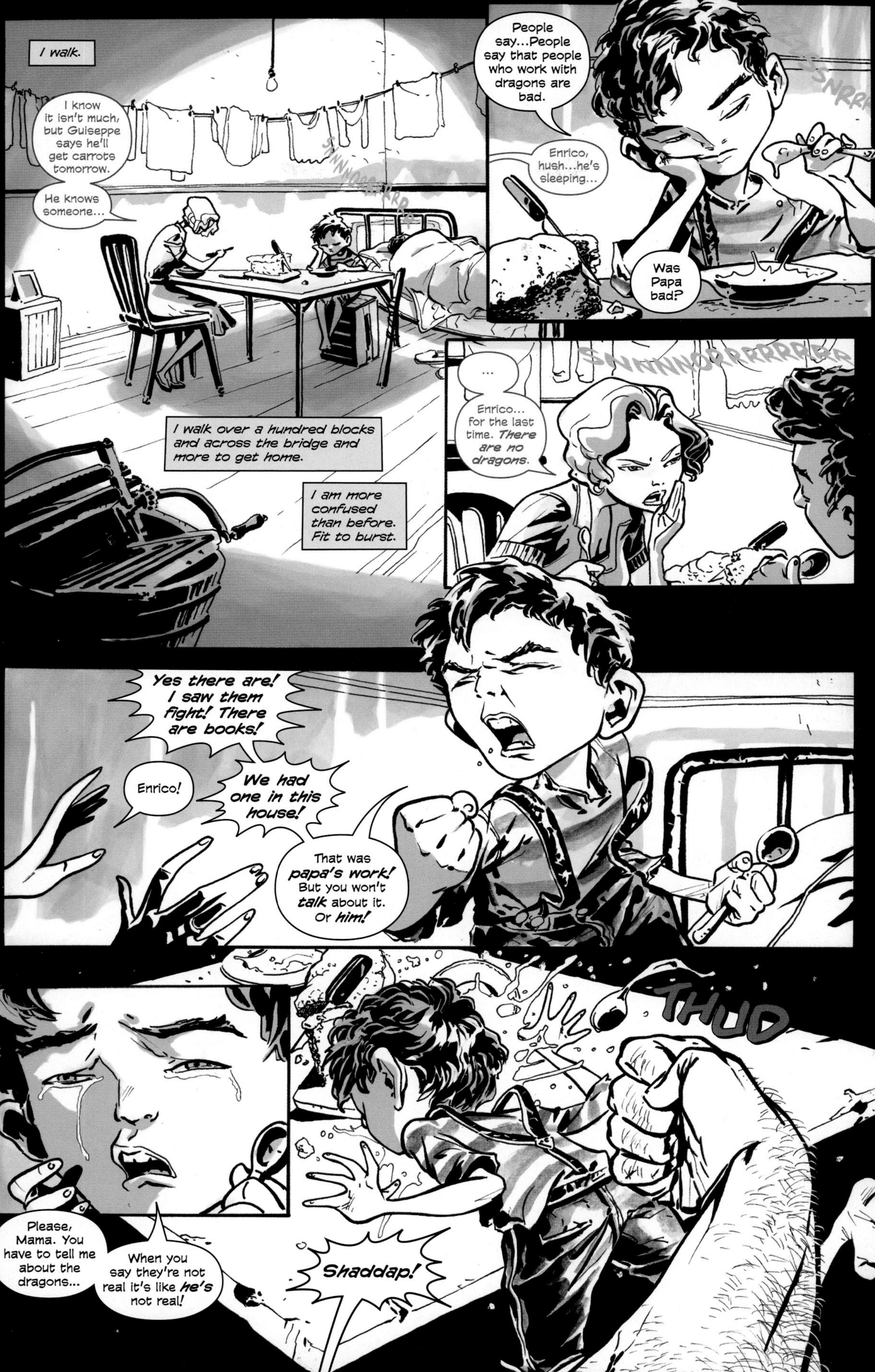
I walk.
I know it isn't much, but Guiseppe says he'll get carrots tomorrow.
He knows someone...
SNNNORRRRRR
People say...People say that people who work with dragons are bad.
SNRR
Enrico, hush...he's sleeping...
Was Papa bad?
I walk over a hundred blocks and across the bridge and more to get home.
I am more confused than before. Fit to burst.
SNNNNORRRRRRRRR
...
Enrico... for the last time. There are no dragons.
Yes there are! I saw them fight! There are books!
Enrico!
We had one in this house!
That was papa's work! But you won't talk about it. Or him!
THUD
Please, Mama. You have to tell me about the dragons...
When you say they're not real it's like he's not real!
Shaddap!

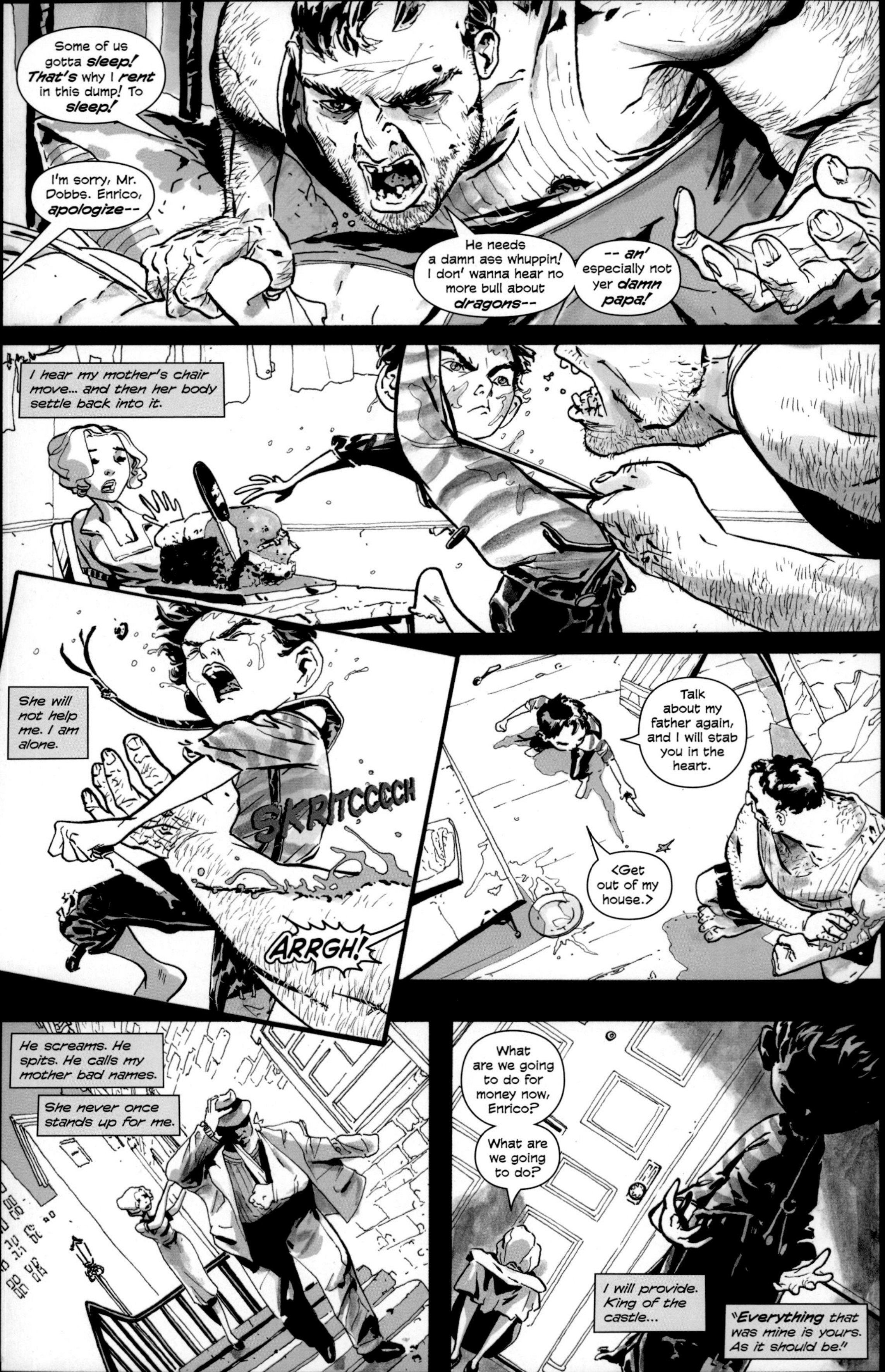
Some of us gotta sleep! That's why I rent in this dump! To sleep!
I'm sorry, Mr. Dobbs. Enrico, apologize--
He needs a damn ass whuppin! I don' wanna hear no more bull about dragons--
-- an' especially not yer damn papa!
I hear my mother's chair move... and then her body settle back into it.
She will not help me. I am alone.
SKRITCCCCH
ARRGH!
Talk about my father again, and I will stab you in the heart.
<Get out of my house.>
He screams. He spits. He calls my mother bad names.
She never once stands up for me.
What are we going to do for money now, Enrico?
What are we going to do?
I will provide. King of the castle...
"Everything that was mine is yours. As it should be."

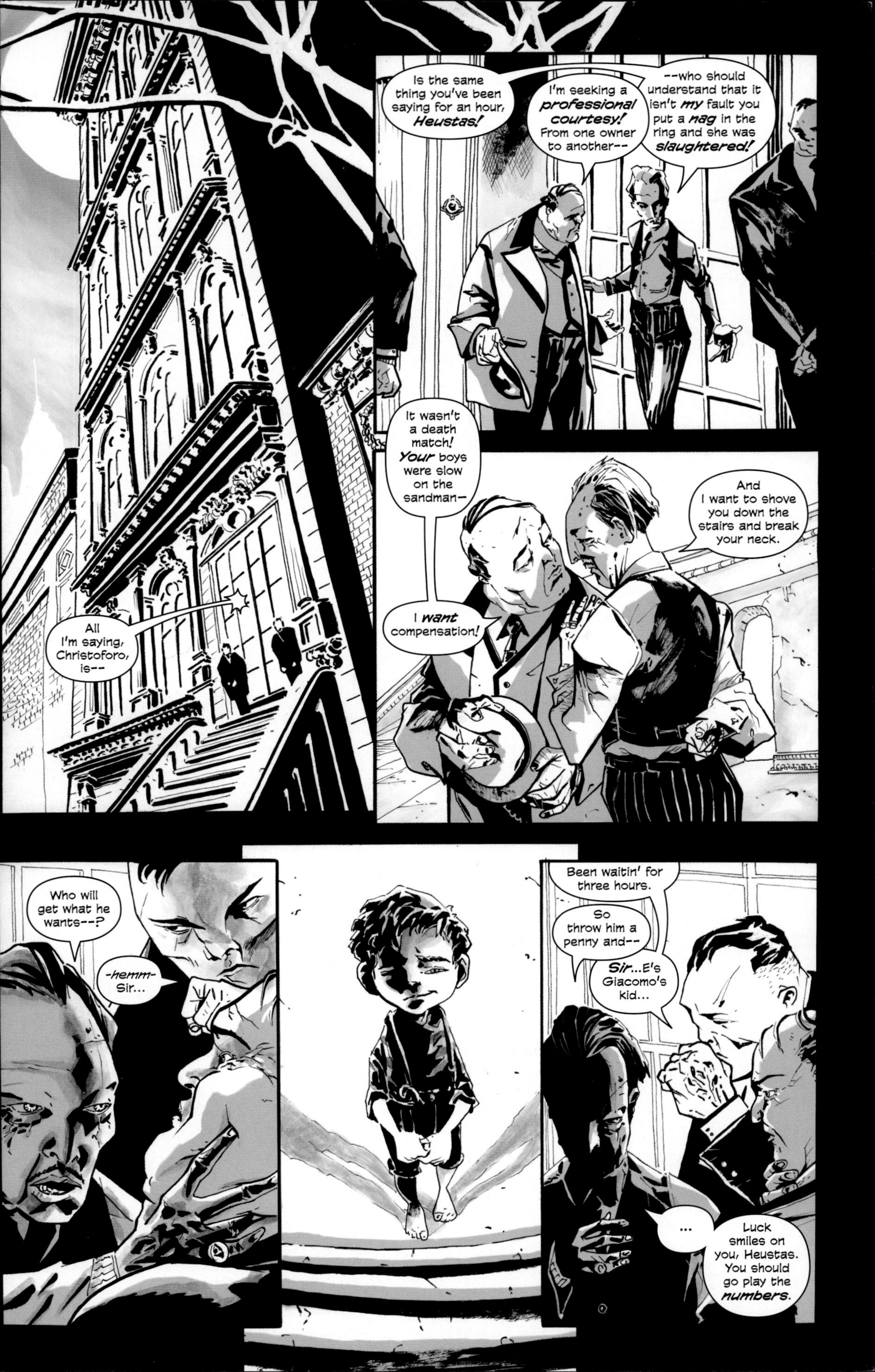
All I'm saying, Christoforo, is--
Is the same thing you've been saying for an hour, Heustas!
I'm seeking a professional courtesy! From one owner to another--
--who should understand that it isn't my fault you put a nag in the ring and she was slaughtered!
It wasn't a death match! Your boys were slow on the sandman—
I want compensation!
And I want to shove you down the stairs and break your neck.
Who will get what he wants--?
-hemm- Sir...
Been waitin' for three hours.
So throw him a penny and--
Sir...E's Giacomo's kid...
...
Luck smiles on you, Heustas. You should go play the numbers.

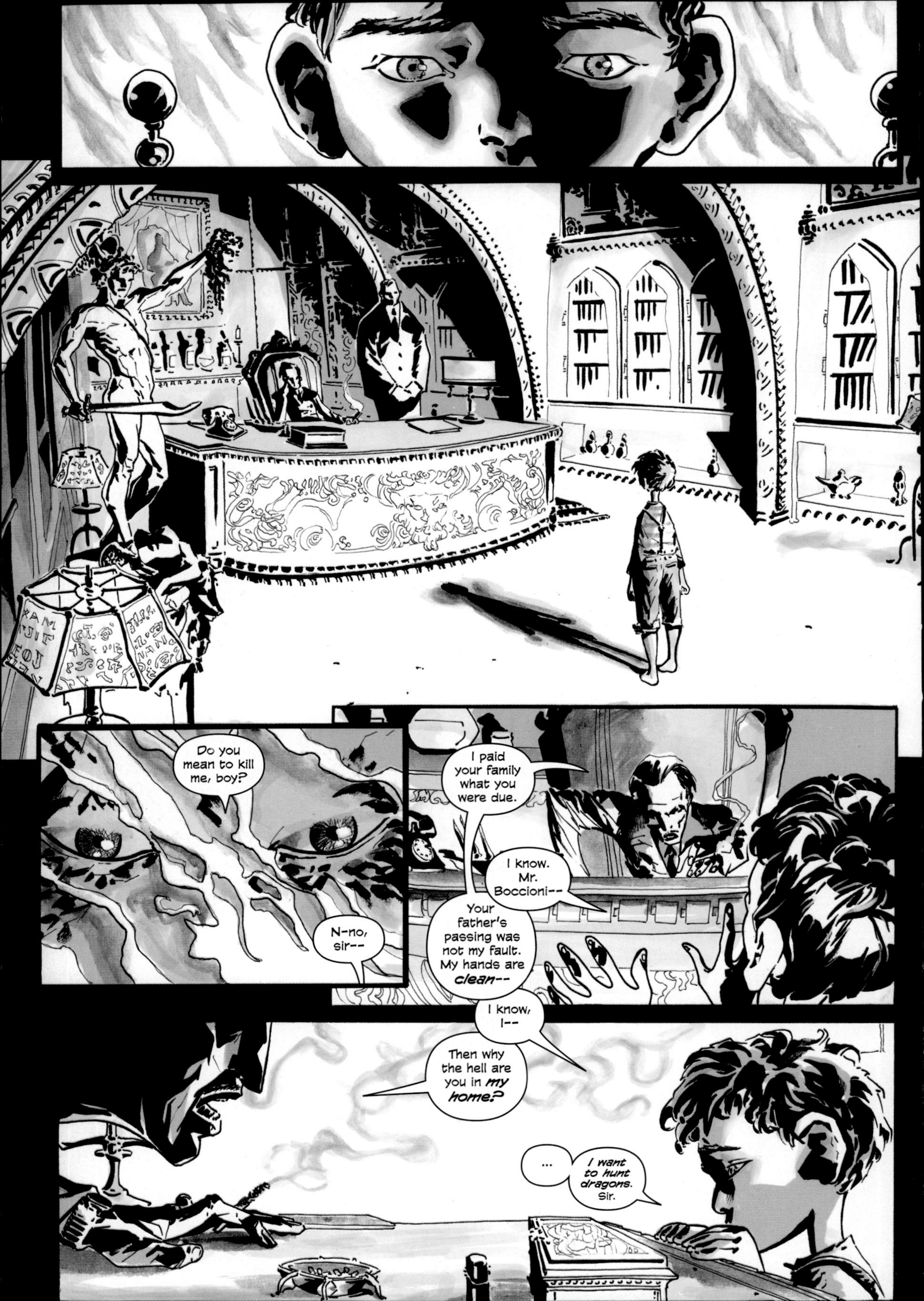
Do you mean to kill me, boy?
N-no, sir--
I paid your family what you were due.
I know. Mr. Boccioni--
Your father's passing was not my fault. My hands are *clean--*
I know, I--
Then why the hell are you in *my home?*
...
I want to hunt dragons. Sir.

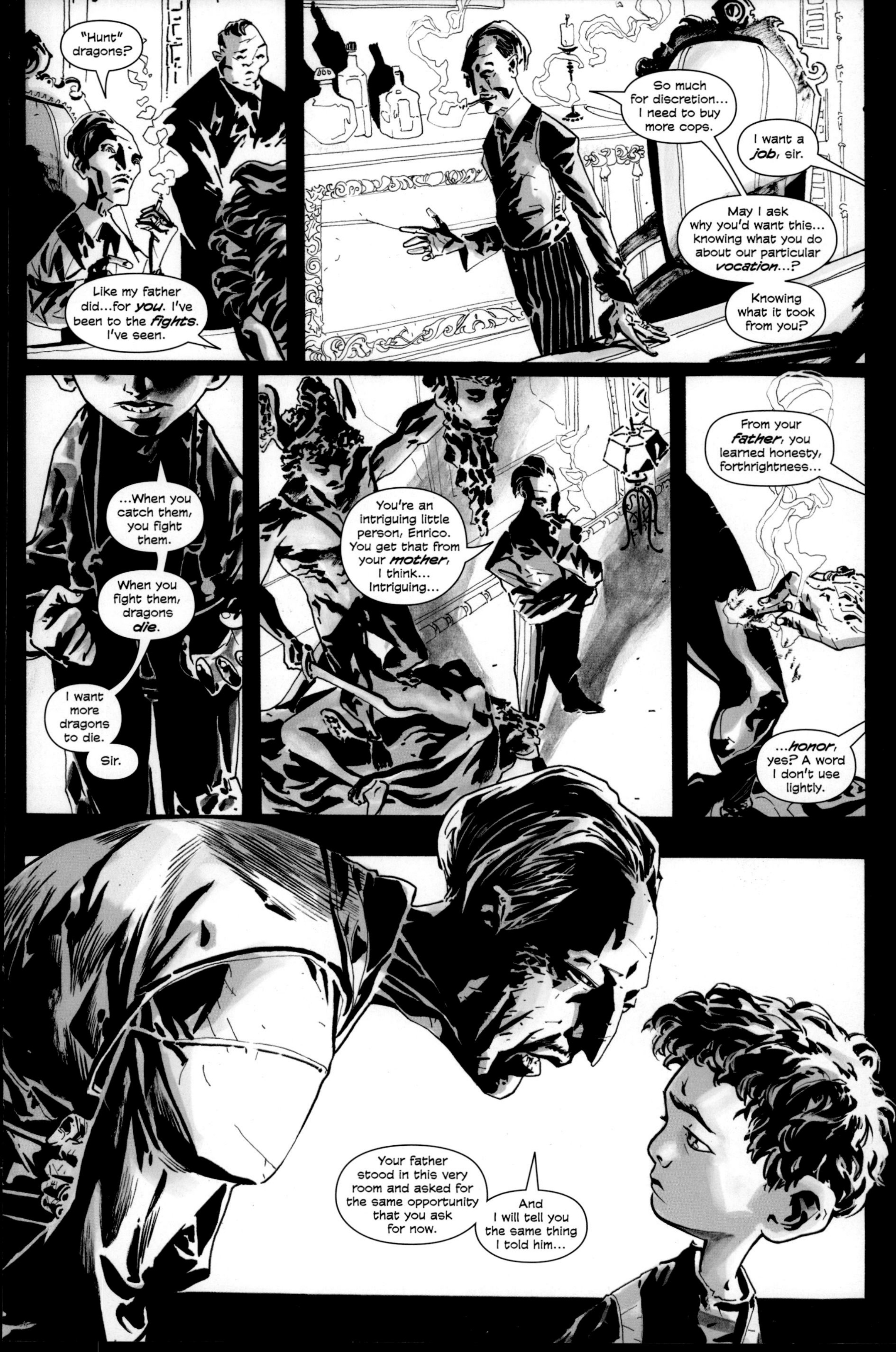
"Hunt" dragons?
Like my father did...for *you*. I've been to the *fights*. I've seen.
So much for discretion... I need to buy more cops.
I want a *job*, sir.
May I ask why you'd want this... knowing what you do about our particular *vocation*...?
Knowing what it took from you?
...When you catch them, you fight them.
When you fight them, dragons *die*.
I want more dragons to die.
Sir.
You're an intriguing little person, Enrico. You get that from your *mother*, I think... Intriguing...
From your *father*, you learned honesty, forthrightness...
...*honor*, yes? A word I don't use lightly.
Your father stood in this very room and asked for the same opportunity that you ask for now.
And I will tell you the same thing I told him...

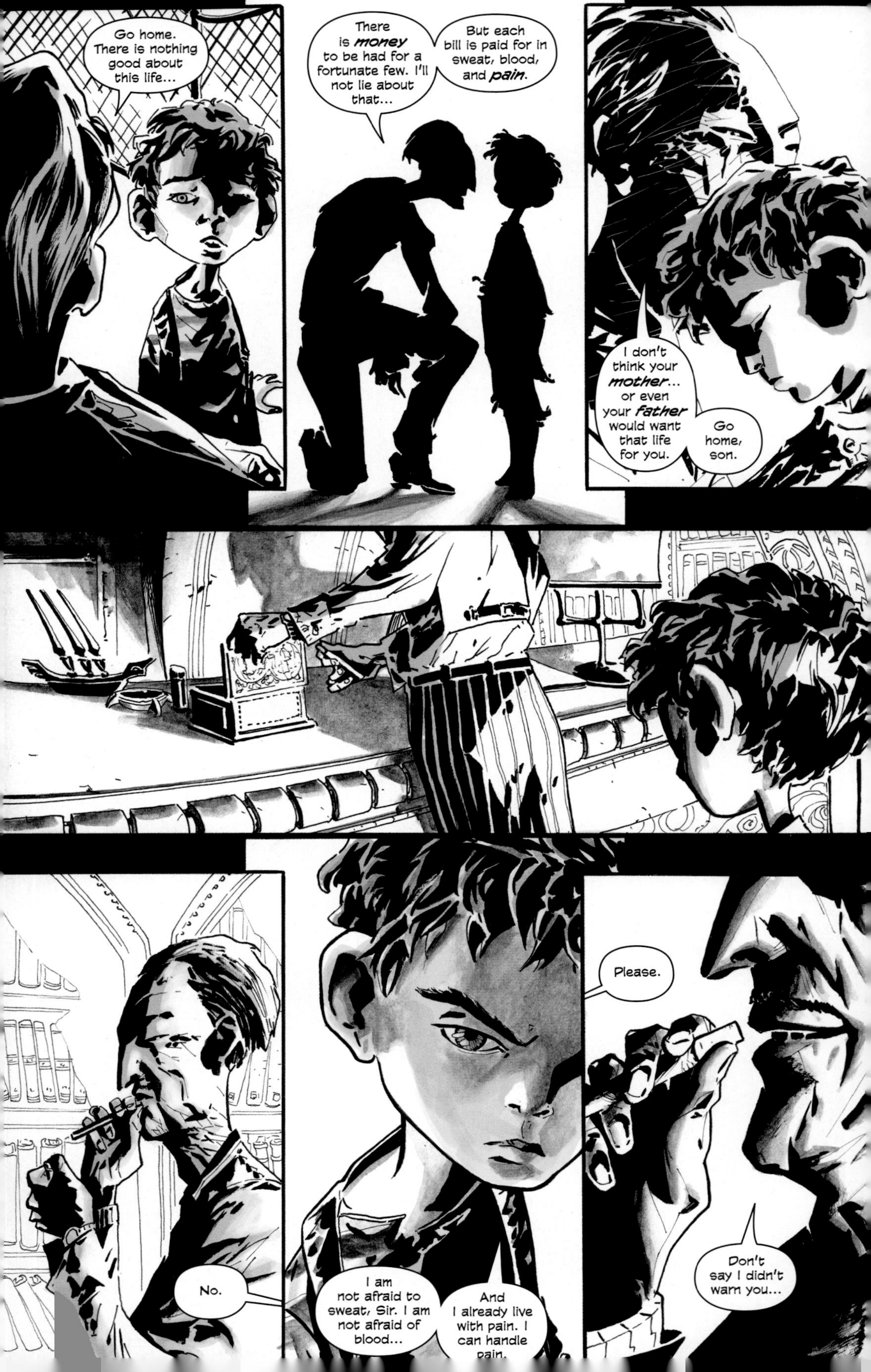

Go home. There is nothing good about this life...
There is *money* to be had for a fortunate few. I'll not lie about that...
But each bill is paid for in sweat, blood, and *pain*.
I don't think your *mother*... or even your *father* would want that life for you.
Go home, son.
No.
I am not afraid to sweat, Sir. I am not afraid of blood...
And I already live with pain. I can handle pain.
Please.
Don't say I didn't warn you...

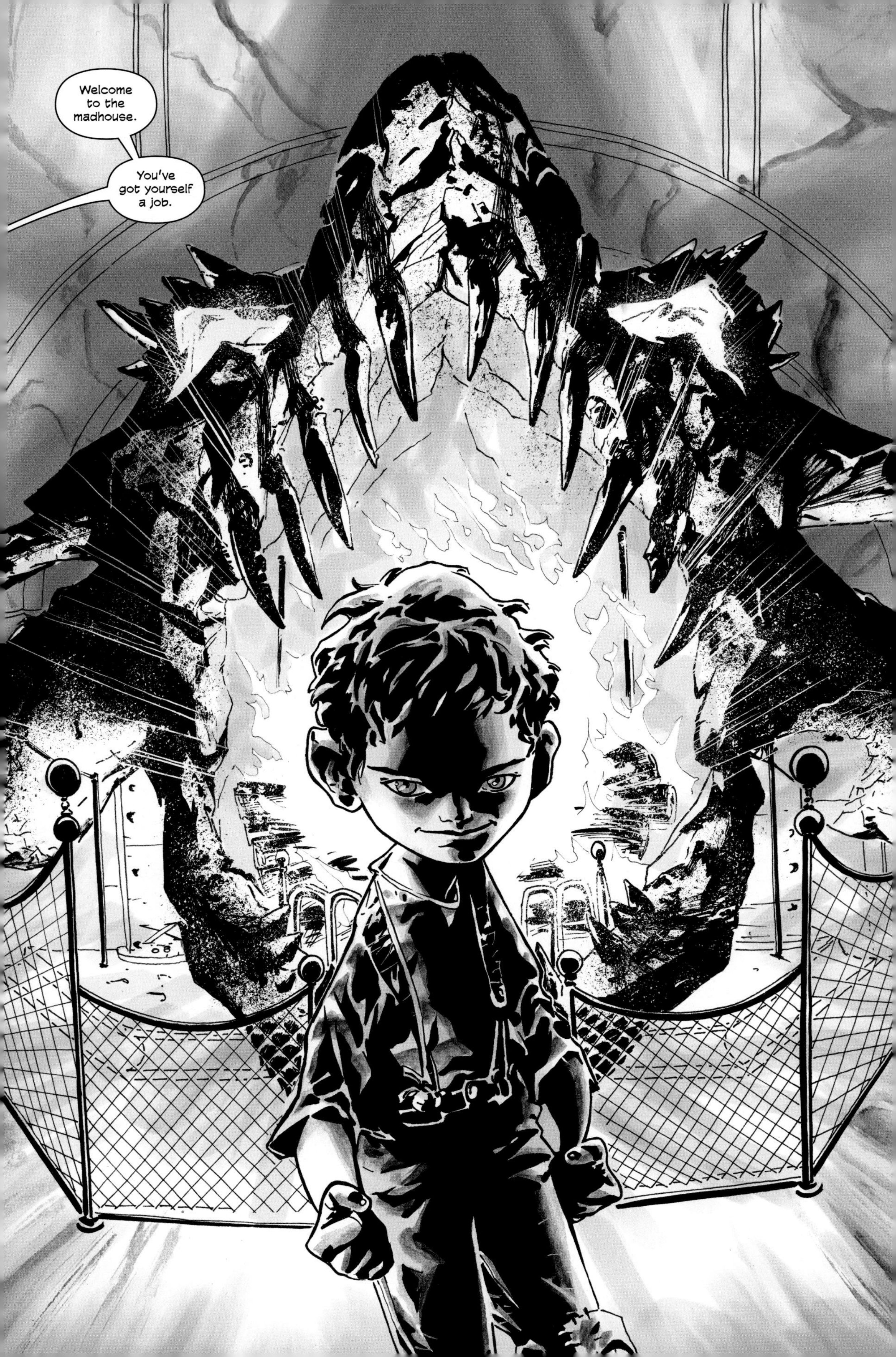
Welcome to the madhouse.
You've got yourself a job.

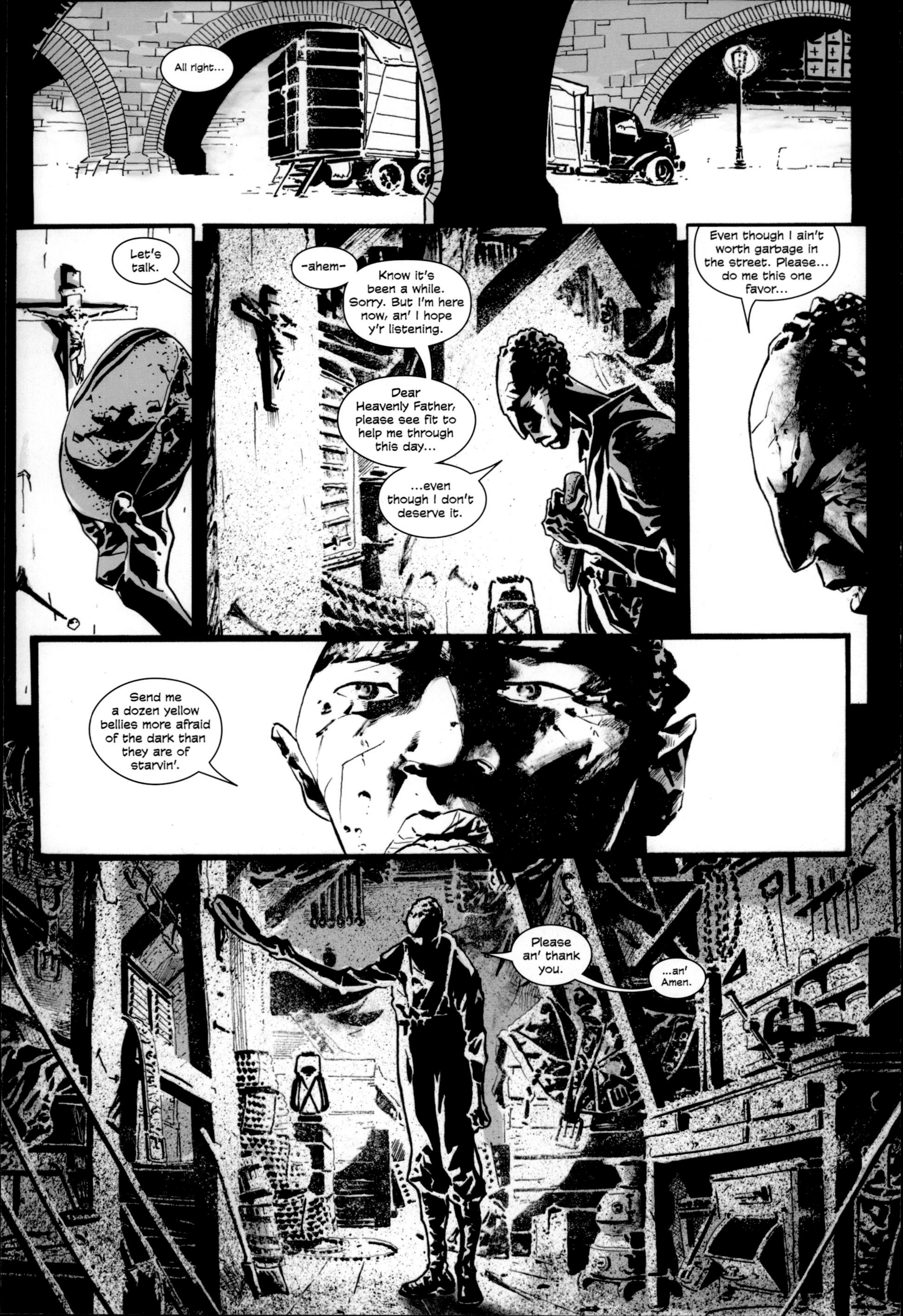
All right...
Let's talk.
-ahem-
Know it's been a while. Sorry. But I'm here now, an' I hope y'r listening.
Dear Heavenly Father, please see fit to help me through this day...
...even though I don't deserve it.
Even though I ain't worth garbage in the street. Please... do me this one favor...
Send me a dozen yellow bellies more afraid of the dark than they are of starvin'.
Please an' thank you.
...an' Amen.

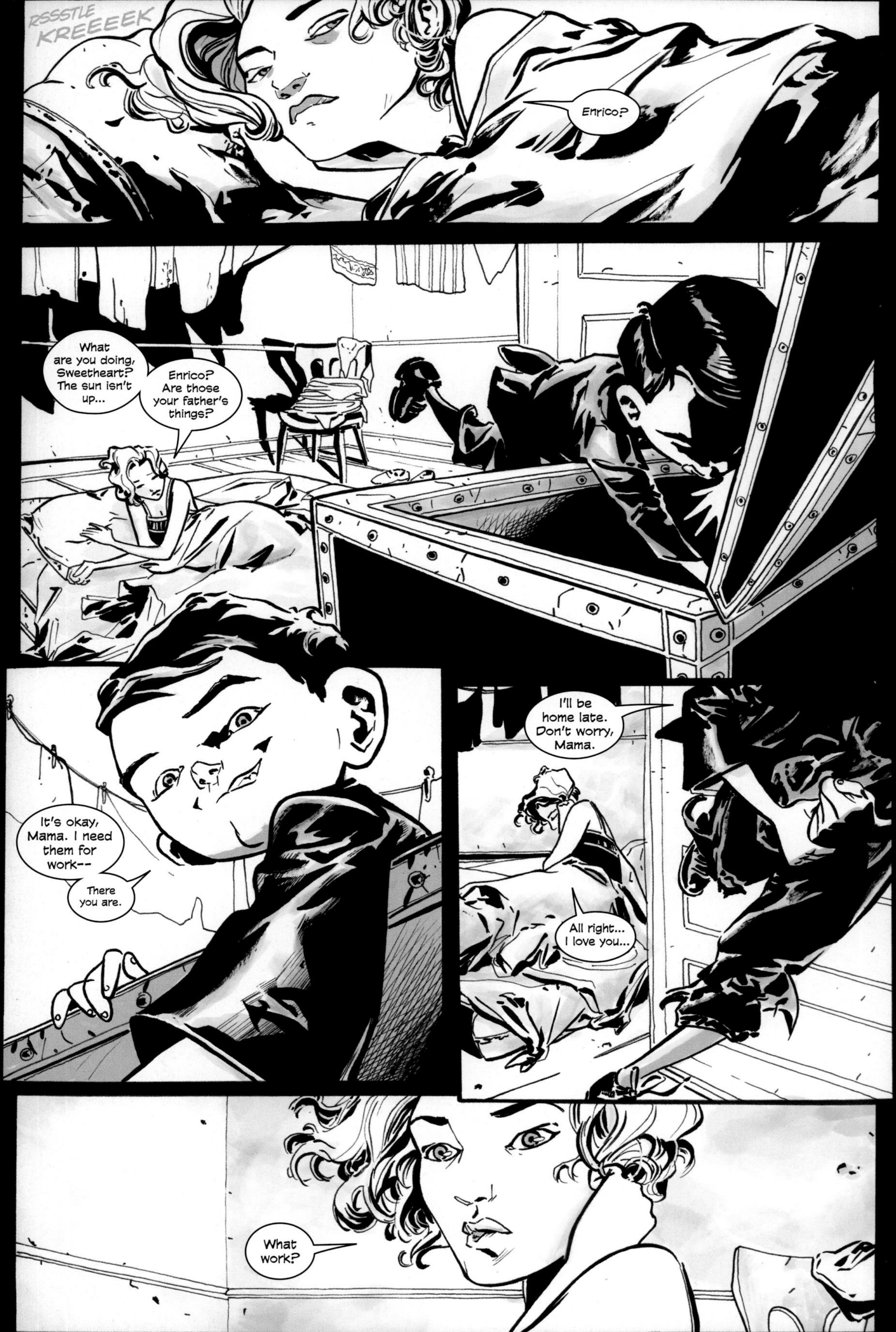
RSSSTLE
KREEEEK
Enrico?
What are you doing, Sweetheart? The sun isn't up...
Enrico? Are those your father's things?
It's okay, Mama. I need them for work--
There you are.
I'll be home late. Don't worry, Mama.
All right... I love you...
What work?

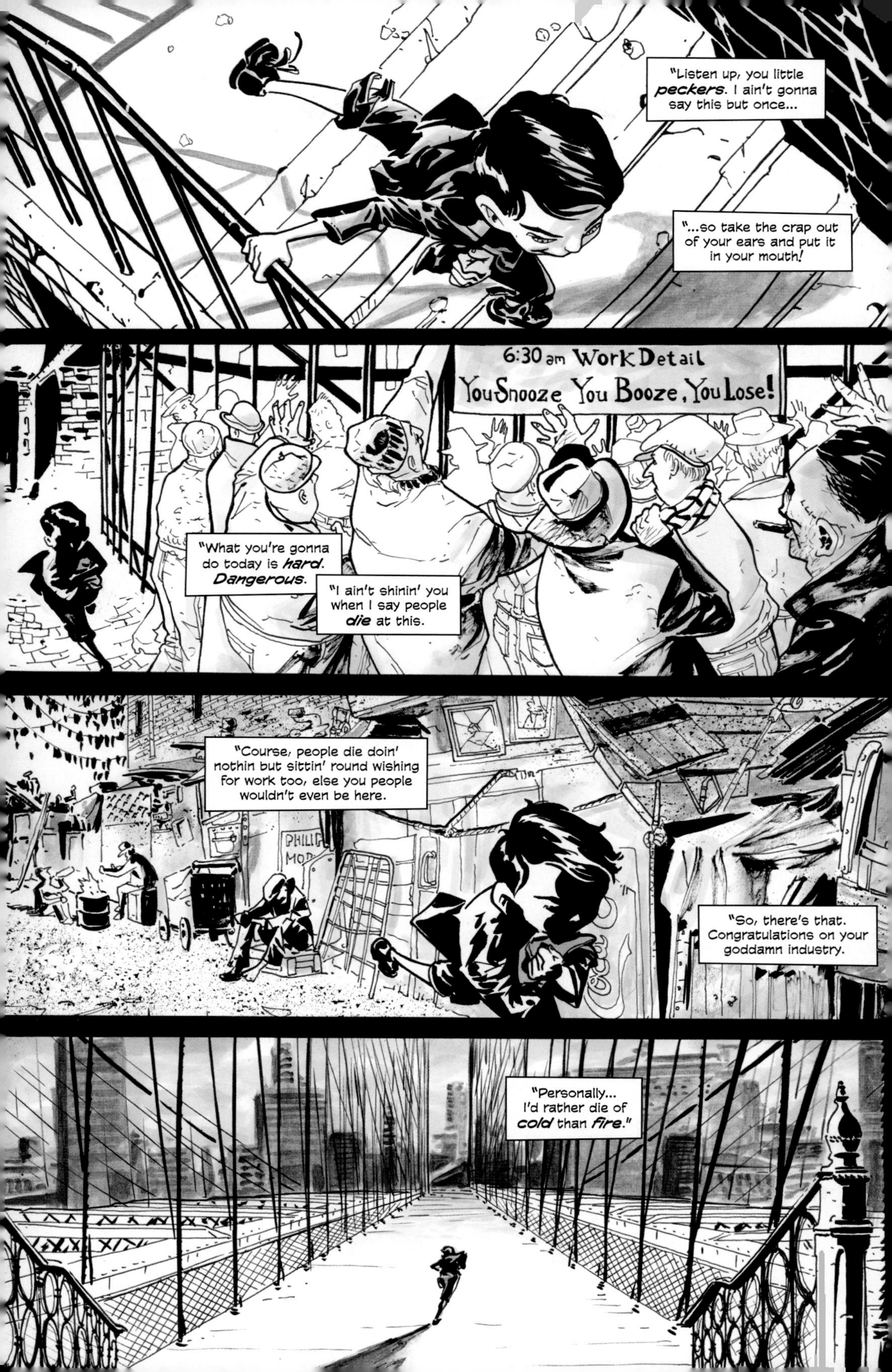
"Listen up, you little **peckers**. I ain't gonna say this but once...
"...so take the crap out of your ears and put it in your mouth!
6:30 am Work Detail
You Snooze You Booze, You Lose!
"What you're gonna do today is **hard**. **Dangerous**.
"I ain't shinin' you when I say people **die** at this.
"Course, people die doin' nothin but sittin' round wishing for work too, else you people wouldn't even be here.
"So, there's that. Congratulations on your goddamn industry.
"Personally... I'd rather die of **cold** than **fire**."

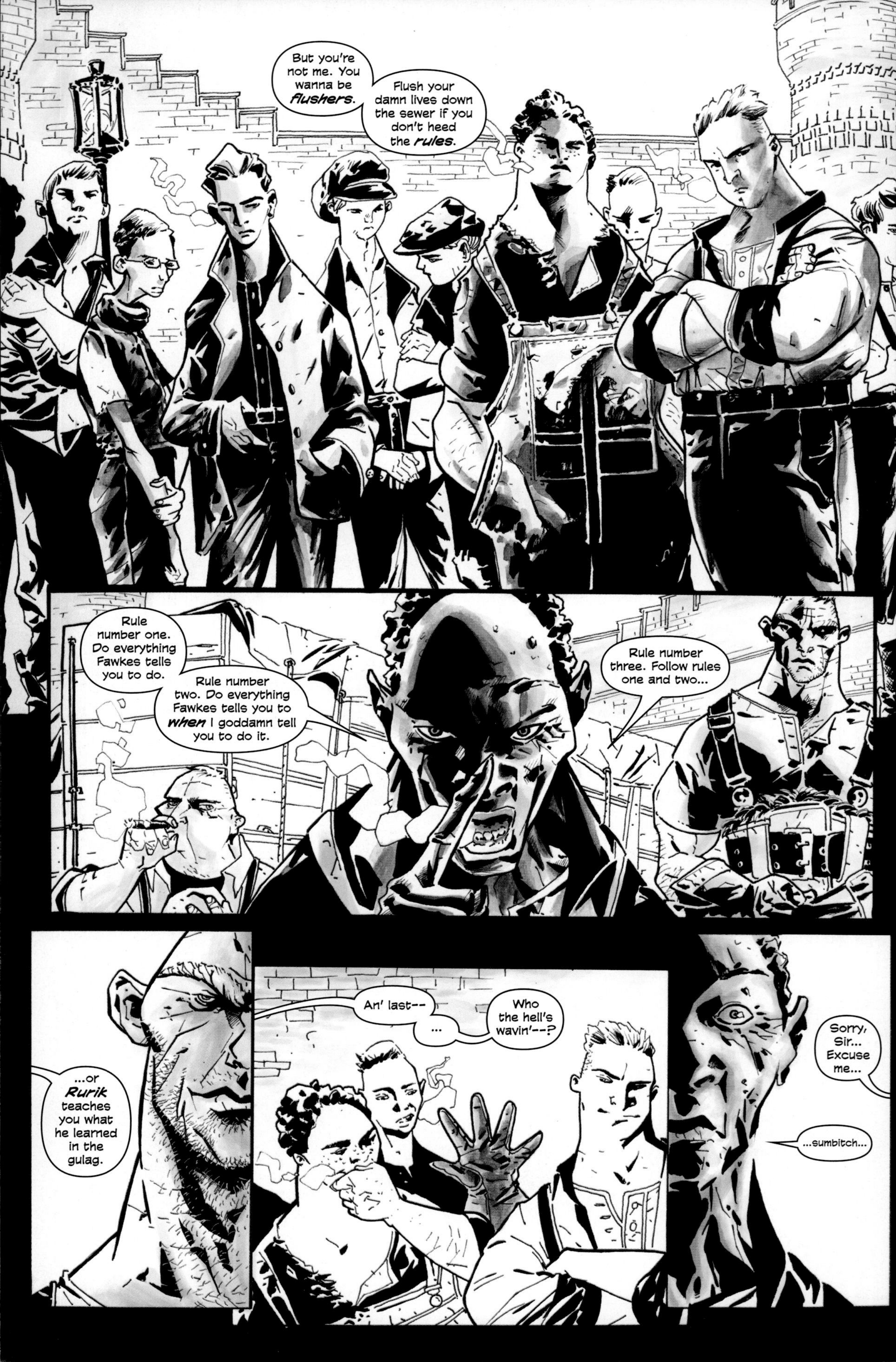

But you're not me. You wanna be flushers.
Flush your damn lives down the sewer if you don't heed the rules.
Rule number one. Do everything Fawkes tells you to do.
Rule number two. Do everything Fawkes tells you to when I goddamn tell you to do it.
Rule number three. Follow rules one and two...
...or Rurik teaches you what he learned in the gulag.
An' last--
...
Who the hell's wavin'--?
Sorry, Sir... Excuse me...
...sumbitch...

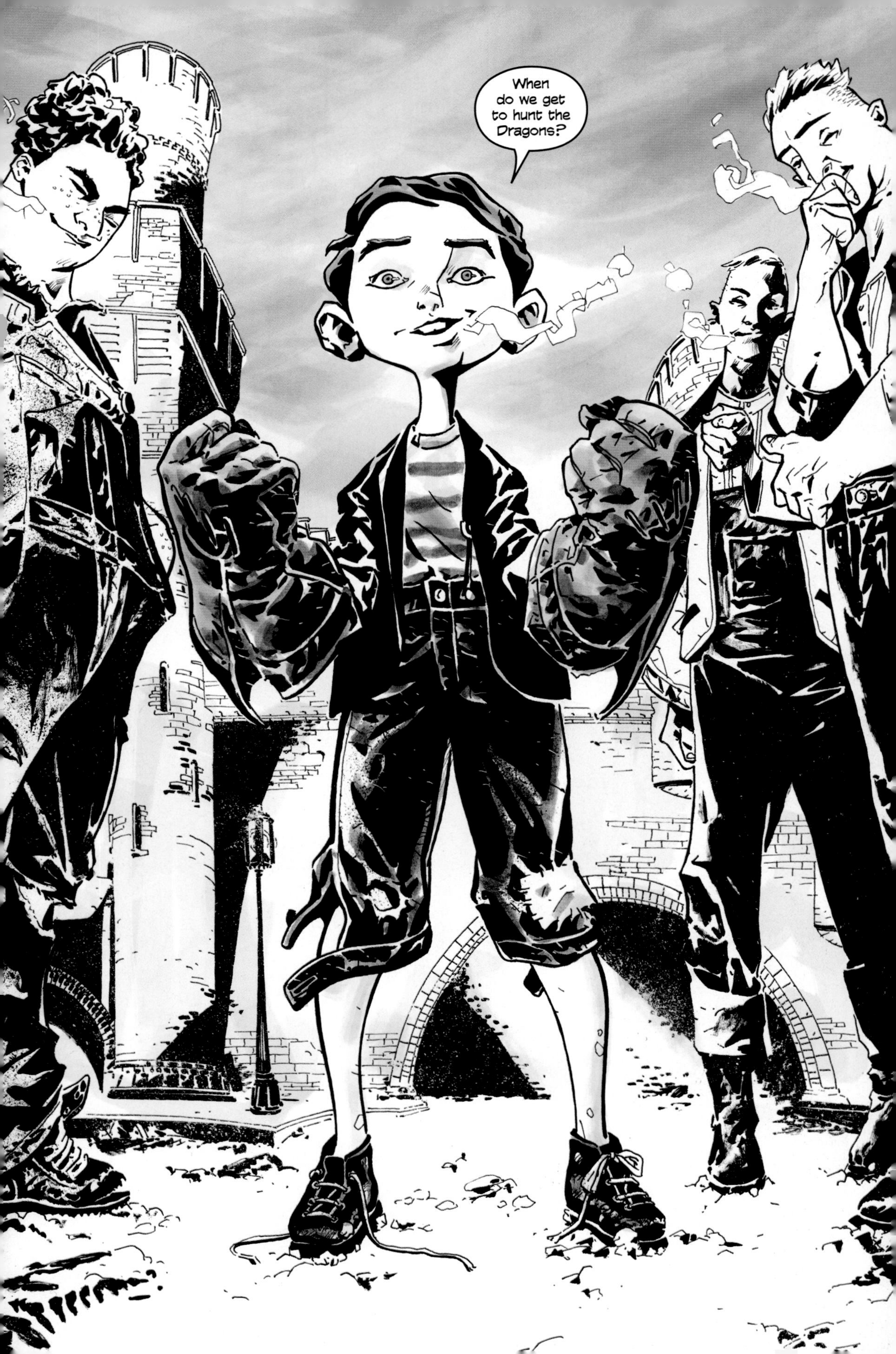
When do we get to hunt the Dragons?

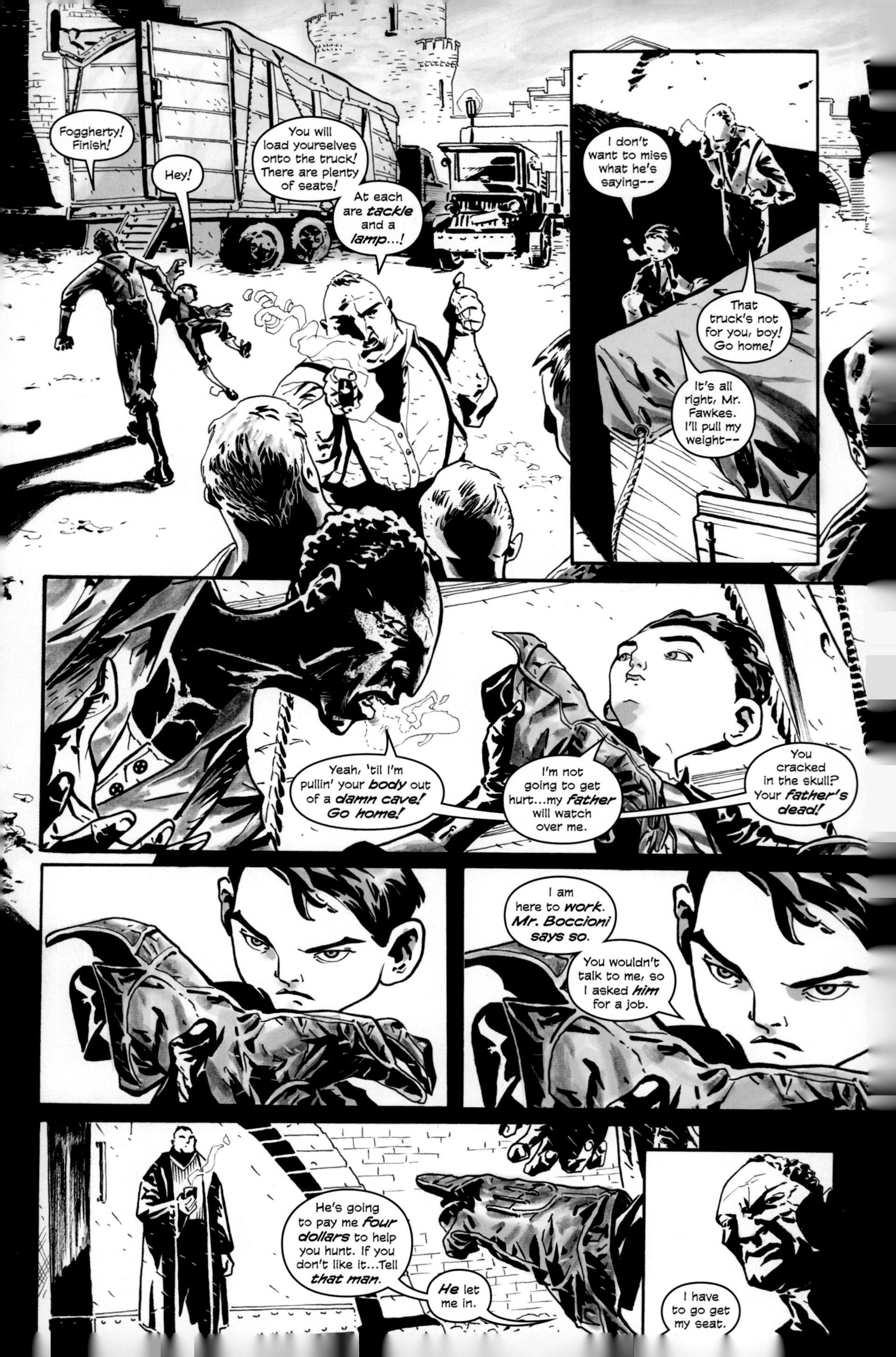
Foggherty! Finish!
Hey!
You will load yourselves onto the truck! There are plenty of seats!
At each are tackle and a lamp...!
I don't want to miss what he's saying--
That truck's not for you, boy! Go home!
It's all right, Mr. Fawkes. I'll pull my weight--
Yeah, 'til I'm pullin' your body out of a damn cave! Go home!
I'm not going to get hurt...my father will watch over me.
You cracked in the skull? Your father's dead!
I am here to work. Mr. Boccioni says so.
You wouldn't talk to me, so I asked him for a job.
He's going to pay me four dollars to help you hunt. If you don't like it...Tell that man.
He let me in.
I have to go get my seat.

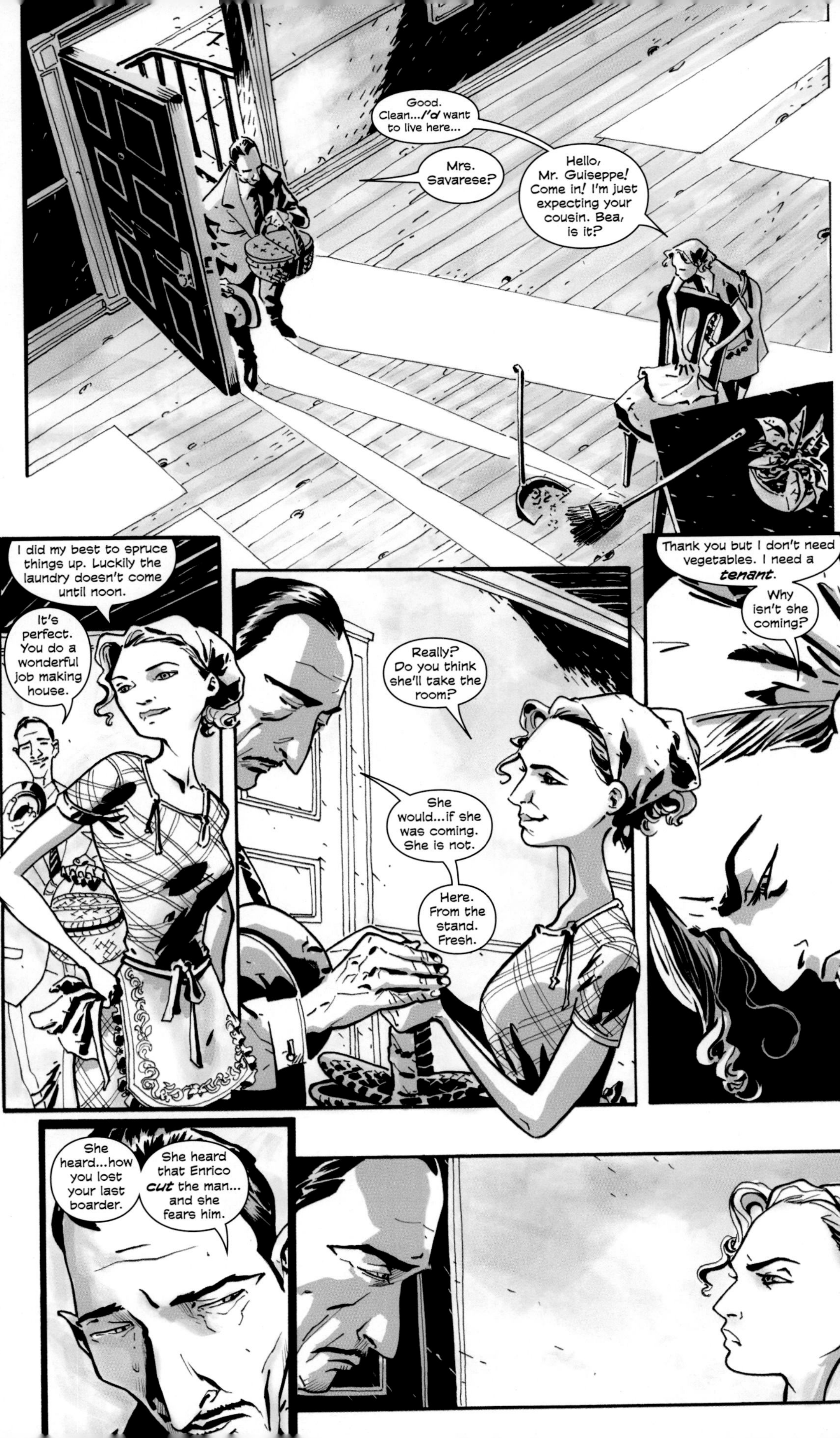
Good. Clean...I'd want to live here...
Mrs. Savarese?
Hello, Mr. Guiseppe! Come in! I'm just expecting your cousin. Bea, is it?
I did my best to spruce things up. Luckily the laundry doesn't come until noon.
It's perfect. You do a wonderful job making house.
Really? Do you think she'll take the room?
She would...if she was coming. She is not.
Here. From the stand. Fresh.
Thank you but I don't need vegetables. I need a tenant.
Why isn't she coming?
She heard...how you lost your last boarder.
She heard that Enrico cut the man... and she fears him.

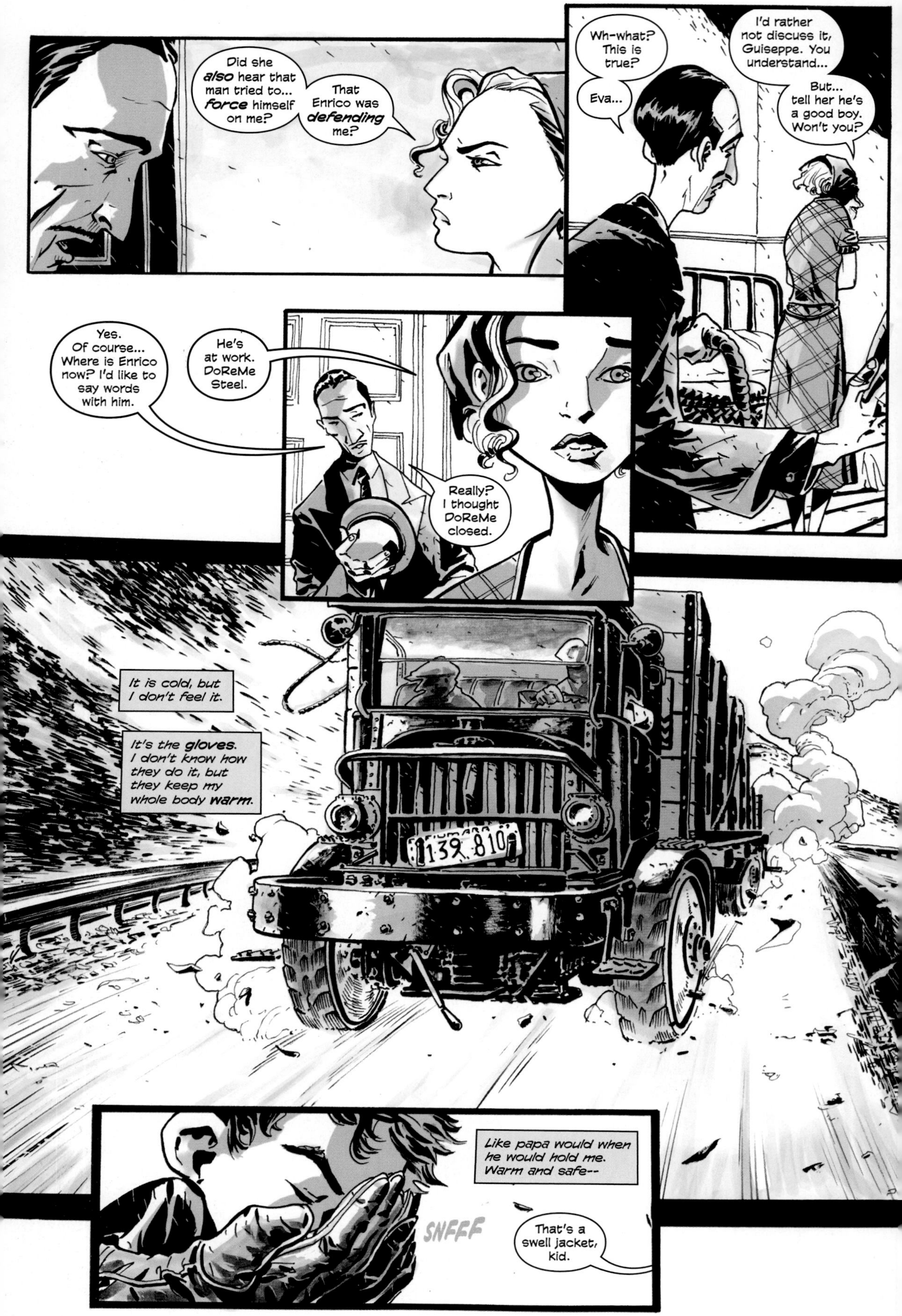
Did she also hear that man tried to... force himself on me?
That Enrico was defending me?
Wh-what? This is true?
Eva...
I'd rather not discuss it, Guiseppe. You understand...
But... tell her he's a good boy. Won't you?
Yes. Of course... Where is Enrico now? I'd like to say words with him.
He's at work. DoReMe Steel.
Really? I thought DoReMe closed.
It is cold, but I don't feel it.
It's the gloves. I don't know how they do it, but they keep my whole body warm.
FIUMARA
139 810
Like papa would when he would hold me. Warm and safe--
SNFFF
That's a swell jacket, kid.

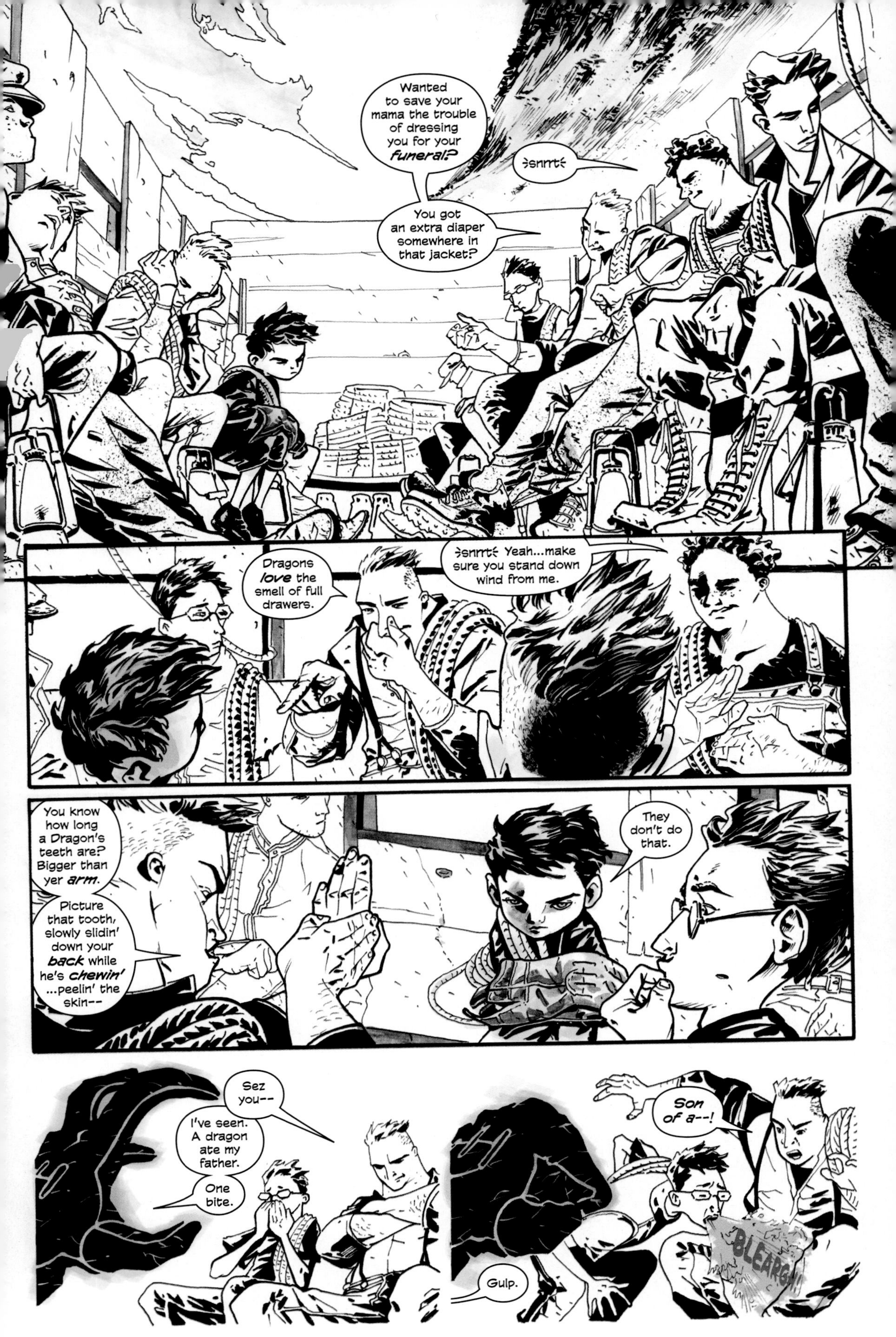
Wanted to save your mama the trouble of dressing you for your funeral?
You got an extra diaper somewhere in that jacket?
snrrt
Dragons love the smell of full drawers.
snrrt Yeah...make sure you stand down wind from me.
You know how long a Dragon's teeth are? Bigger than yer arm.
Picture that tooth, slowly slidin' down your back while he's chewin' ...peelin' the skin--
They don't do that.
Sez you--
I've seen. A dragon ate my father.
One bite.
Son of a--!
Gulp.
BLEARGH

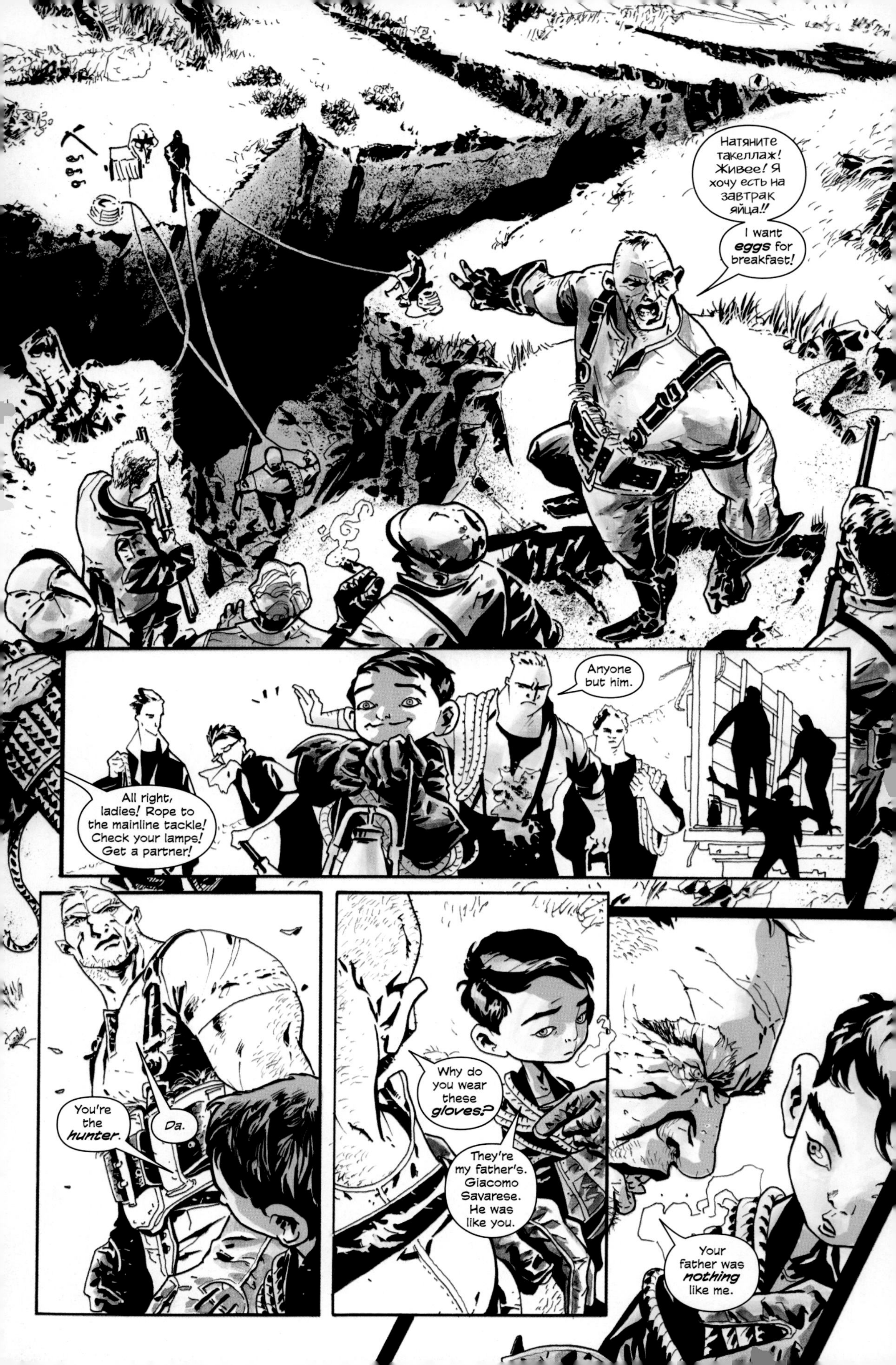
Натяните такеллаж! Живее! Я хочу есть на завтрак яйца!!
I want *eggs* for breakfast!
Anyone but him.
All right, ladies! Rope to the mainline tackle! Check your lamps! Get a partner!
You're the *hunter*.
Da.
Why do you wear these *gloves?*
They're my father's. Giacomo Savarese. He was like you.
Your father was *nothing* like me.

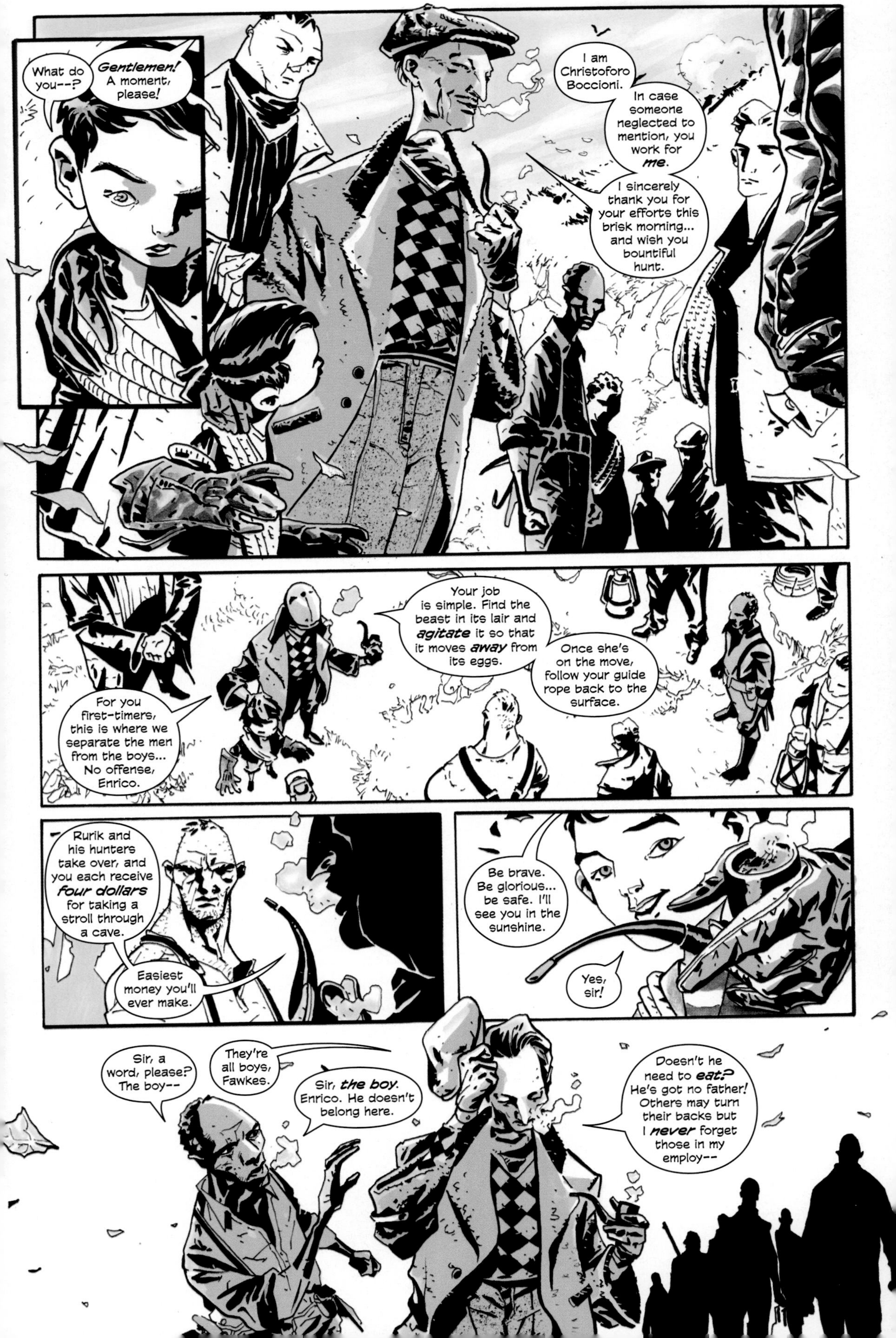

What do you--?
Gentlemen! A moment, please!
I am Christoforo Boccioni.
In case someone neglected to mention, you work for me.
I sincerely thank you for your efforts this brisk morning... and wish you bountiful hunt.
Your job is simple. Find the beast in its lair and agitate it so that it moves away from its eggs.
Once she's on the move, follow your guide rope back to the surface.
For you first-timers, this is where we separate the men from the boys... No offense, Enrico.
Rurik and his hunters take over, and you each receive four dollars for taking a stroll through a cave.
Easiest money you'll ever make.
Be brave. Be glorious... be safe. I'll see you in the sunshine.
Yes, sir!
Sir, a word, please? The boy--
They're all boys, Fawkes.
Sir, the boy. Enrico. He doesn't belong here.
Doesn't he need to eat? He's got no father! Others may turn their backs but I never forget those in my employ--

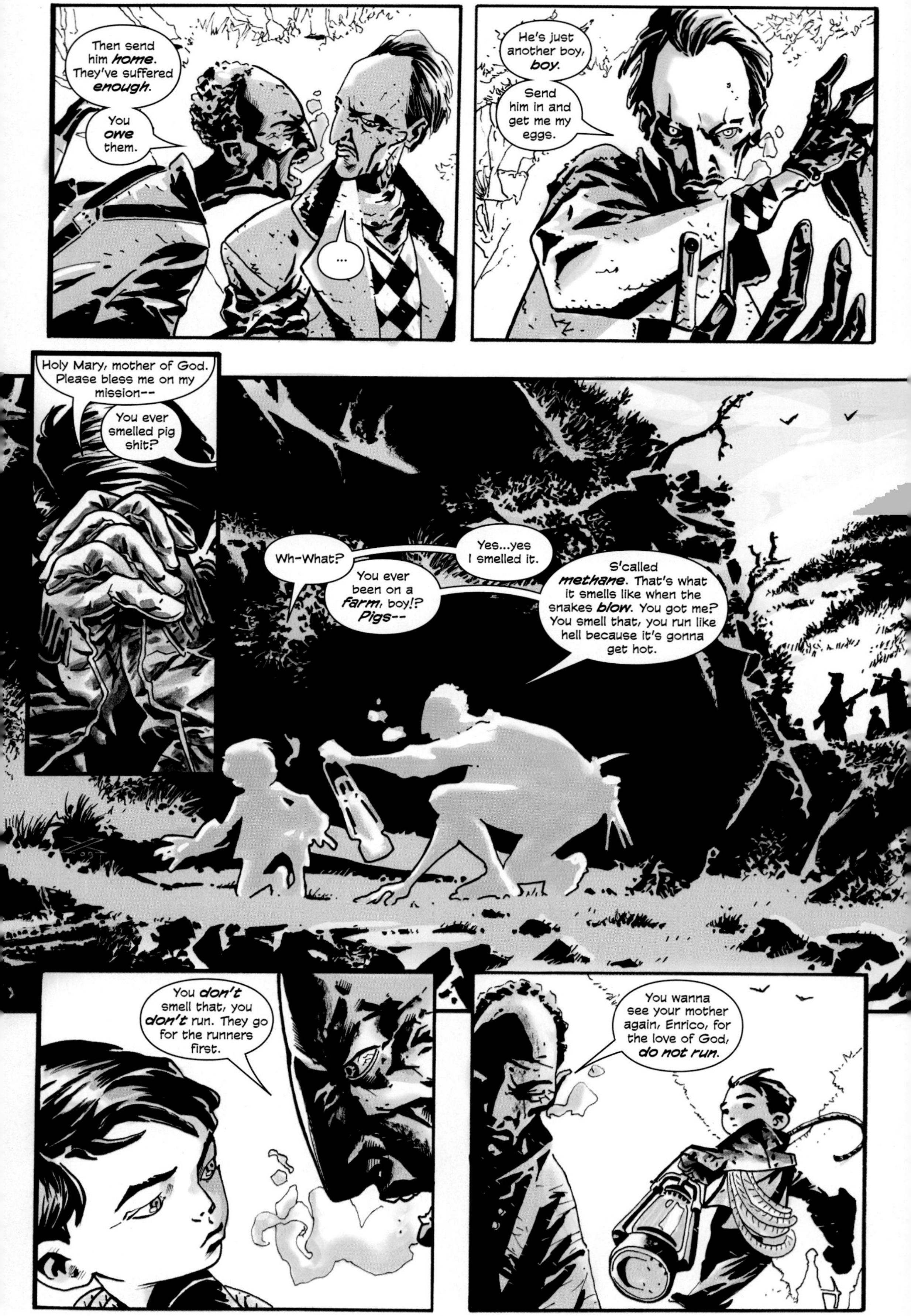
Then send him *home*. They've suffered *enough*.
You *owe* them.
...
He's just another boy, *boy*.
Send him in and get me my eggs.
Holy Mary, mother of God. Please bless me on my mission--
You ever smelled pig shit?
Wh-What?
Yes...yes I smelled it.
You ever been on a *farm*, boy!? *Pigs*--
S'called *methane*. That's what it smells like when the snakes *blow*. You got me? You smell that, you run like hell because it's gonna get hot.
You *don't* smell that, you *don't* run. They go for the runners first.
You wanna see your mother again, Enrico, for the love of God, *do not run*.

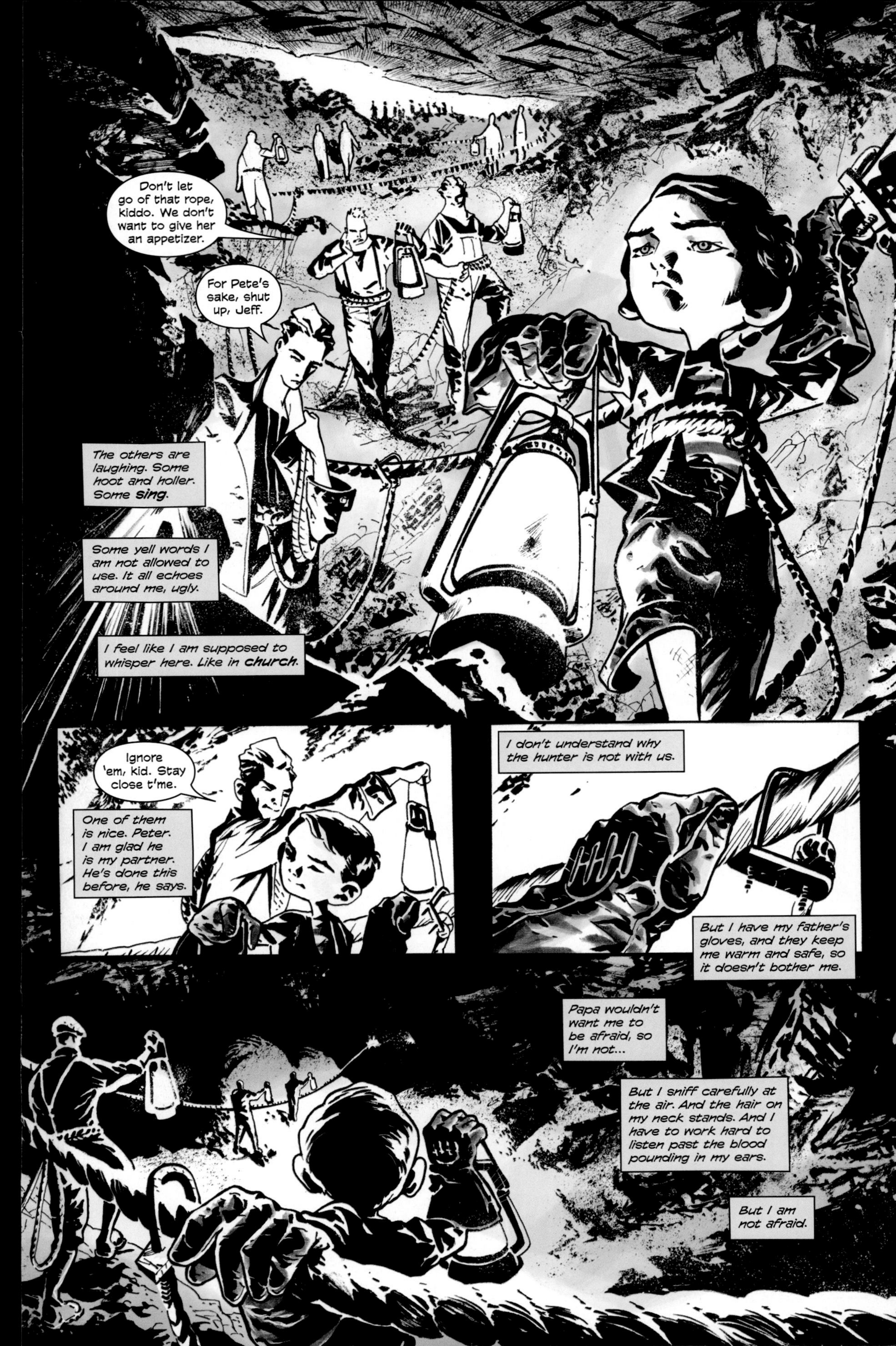
Don't let go of that rope, kiddo. We don't want to give her an appetizer.
For Pete's sake, shut up, Jeff.
The others are laughing. Some hoot and holler. Some **sing**.
Some yell words I am not allowed to use. It all echoes around me, ugly.
I feel like I am supposed to whisper here. Like in **church**.
Ignore 'em, kid. Stay close t'me.
One of them is nice. Peter. I am glad he is my partner. He's done this before, he says.
I don't understand why the hunter is not with us.
But I have my father's gloves, and they keep me warm and safe, so it doesn't bother me.
Papa wouldn't want me to be afraid, so I'm not...
But I sniff carefully at the air. And the hair on my neck stands. And I have to work hard to listen past the blood pounding in my ears.
But I am not afraid.

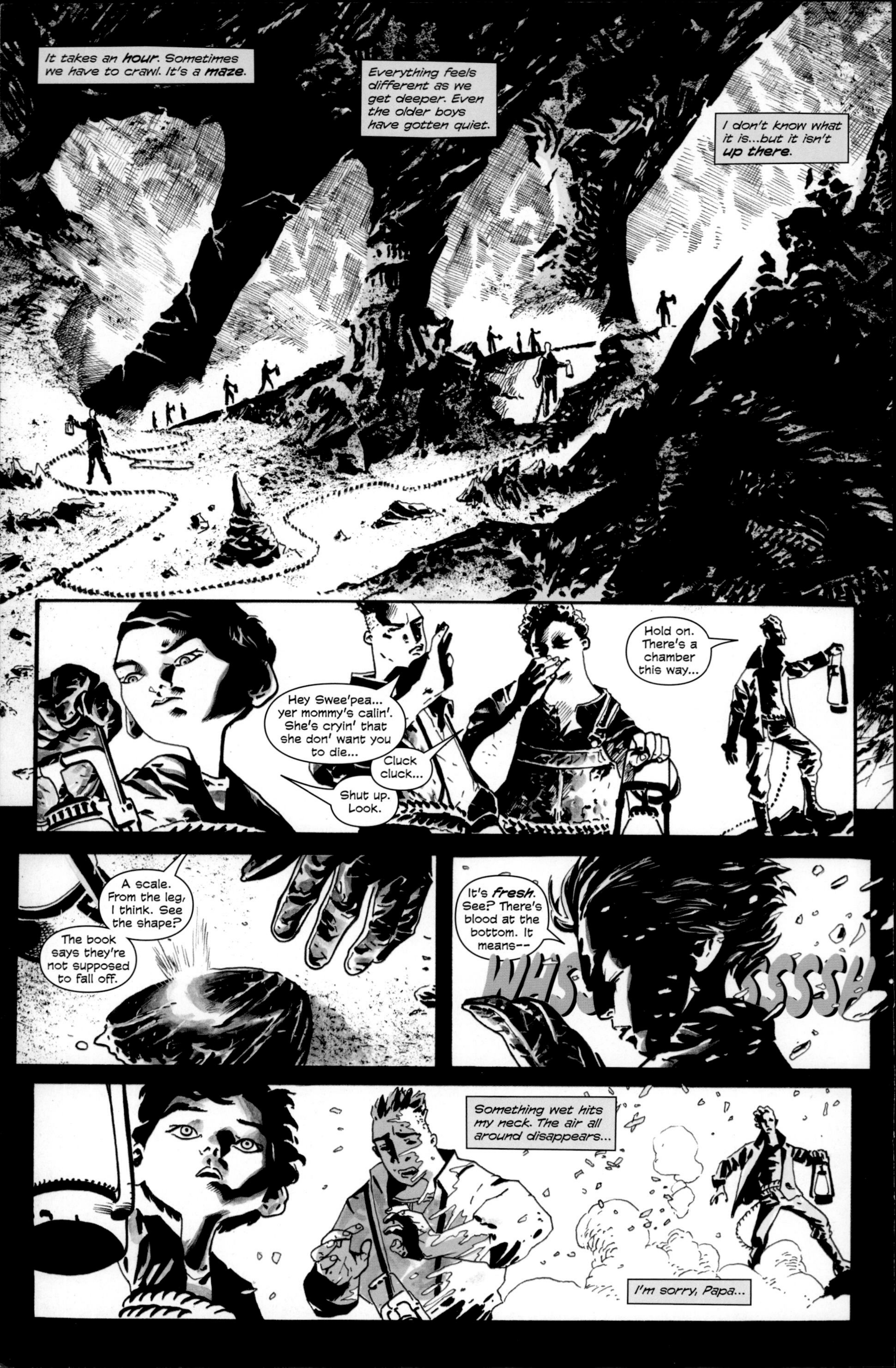
It takes an **hour**. Sometimes we have to crawl. It's a **maze**.
Everything feels different as we get deeper. Even the older boys have gotten quiet.
I don't know what it is...but it isn't **up there**.
Hold on. There's a chamber this way...
Hey Swee'pea... yer mommy's calin'. She's cryin' that she don' want you to die...
Cluck cluck...
Shut up. Look.
A scale. From the leg, I think. See the shape?
The book says they're not supposed to fall off.
It's *fresh*. See? There's blood at the bottom. It means--
Something wet hits my neck. The air all around disappears...
I'm sorry, Papa...

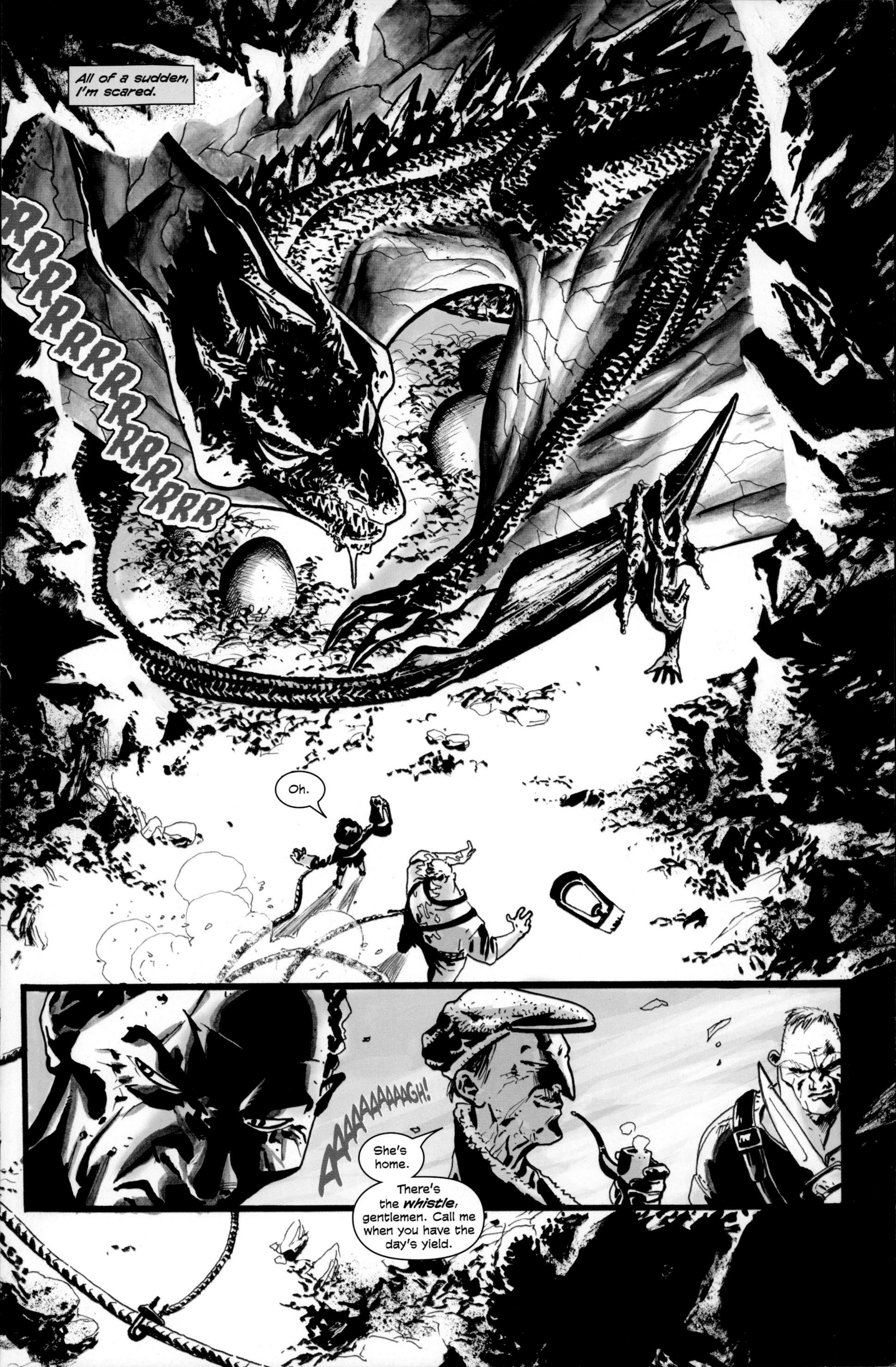

All of a sudden, I'm scared.
RRRRRRRRRRRRRRRRRR
Oh.
AAAAAAAAAAAGH!
She's home.
There's the *whistle*, gentlemen. Call me when you have the day's yield.

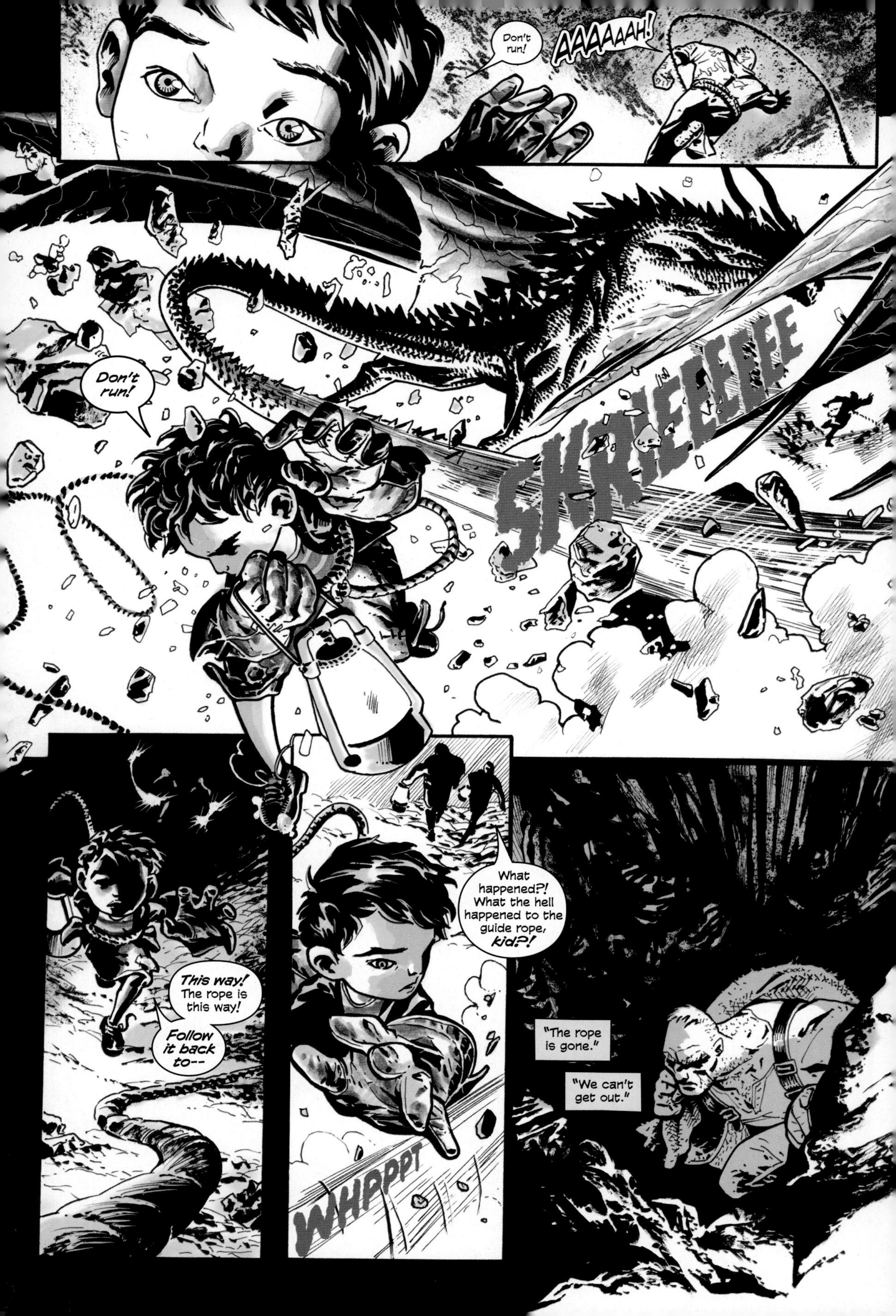

Don't run!
AAAAAAH!
Don't run!
SKRIEEEEEE
This way! The rope is this way!
Follow it back to--
What happened?! What the hell happened to the guide rope, kid?!
WHPPPT
"The rope is gone."
"We can't get out."

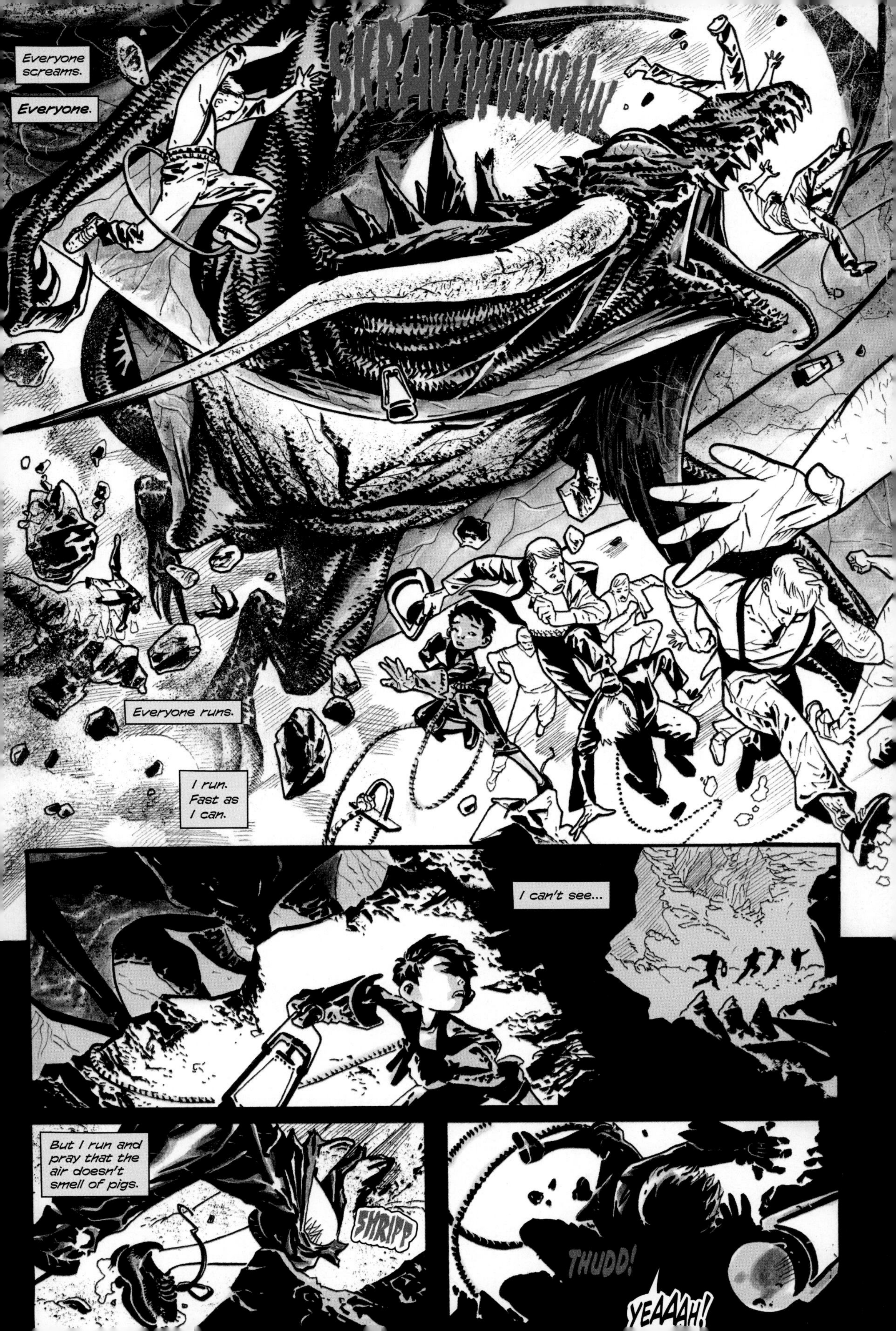
Everyone screams.
Everyone.
SKRAWWWWWW
Everyone runs.
I run. Fast as I can.
I can't see...
But I run and pray that the air doesn't smell of pigs.
SHRIPP
THUDD!
YEAAAH!

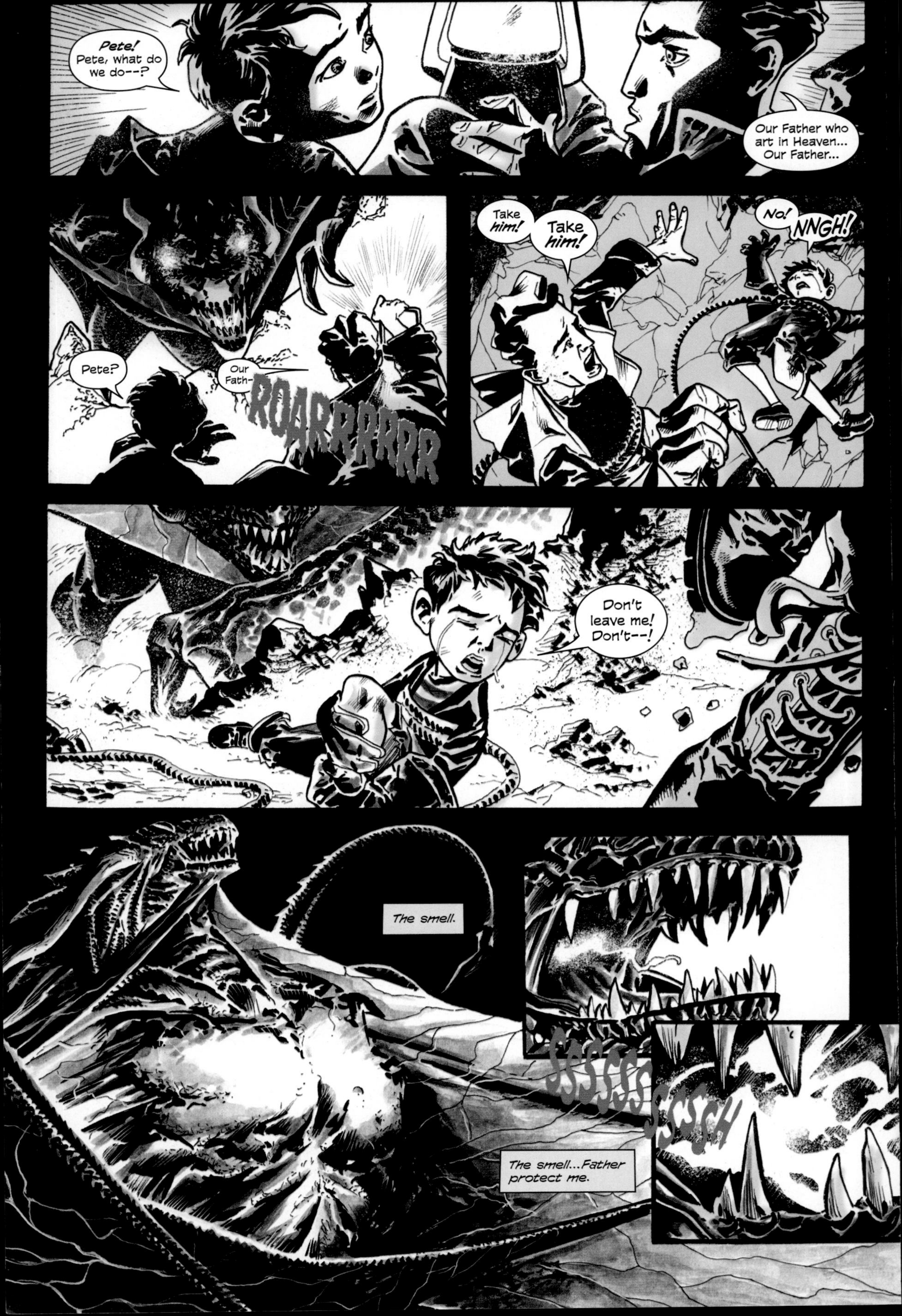
Pete! Pete, what do we do--?
Our Father who art in Heaven... Our Father...
Pete?
Our Fath-
ROARRRRRRR
Take him!
Take him!
No!
NNGH!
Don't leave me! Don't--!
The smell.
SSSSSSSSSSH
The smell...Father protect me.

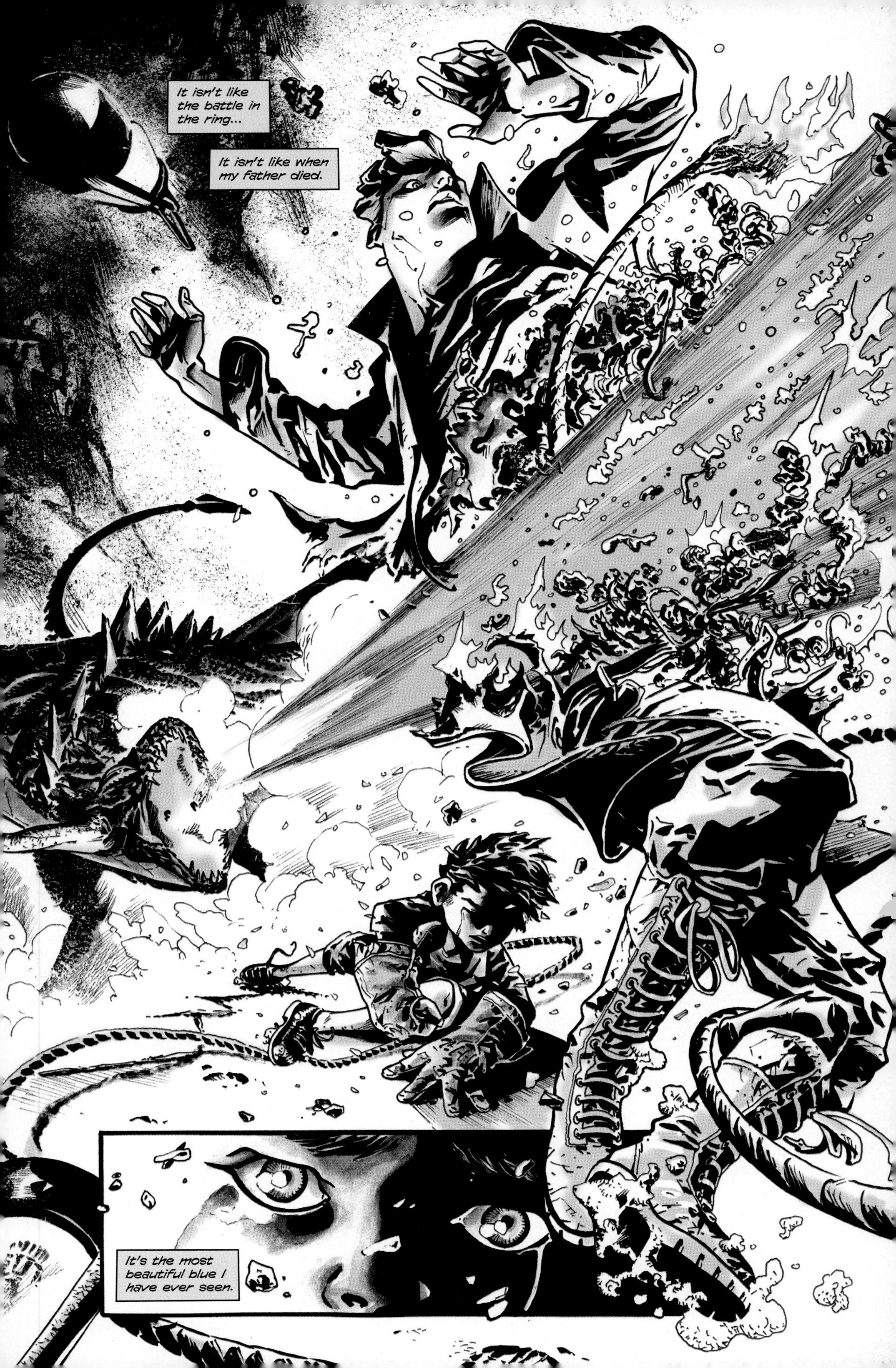
It isn't like the battle in the ring...
It isn't like when my father died.
It's the most beautiful blue I have ever seen.

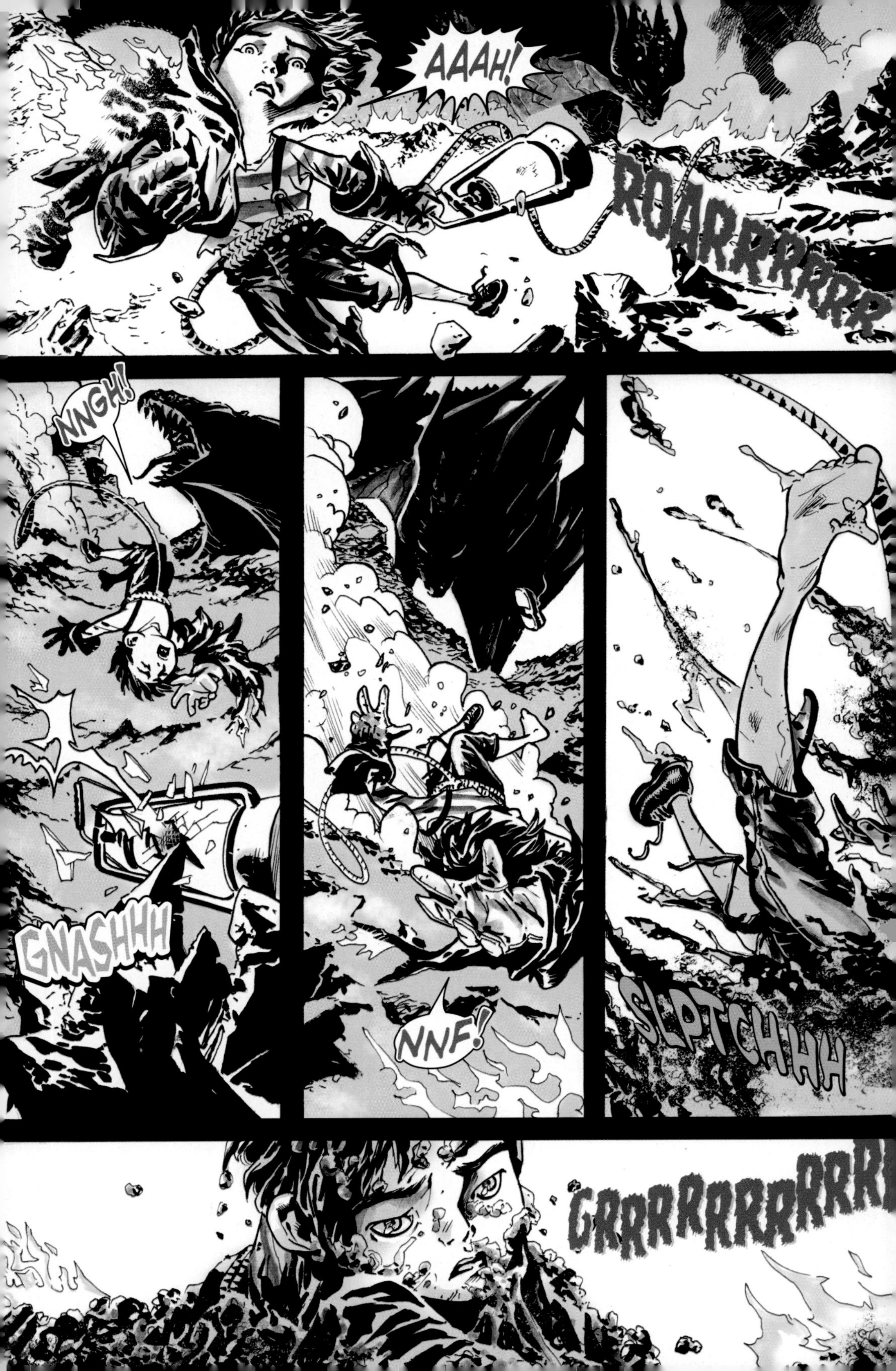
AAAH!
ROARRRRRRR
NNGH!
GNASHHH
NNF!
SLPTCHHH
GRRRRRRRRRR

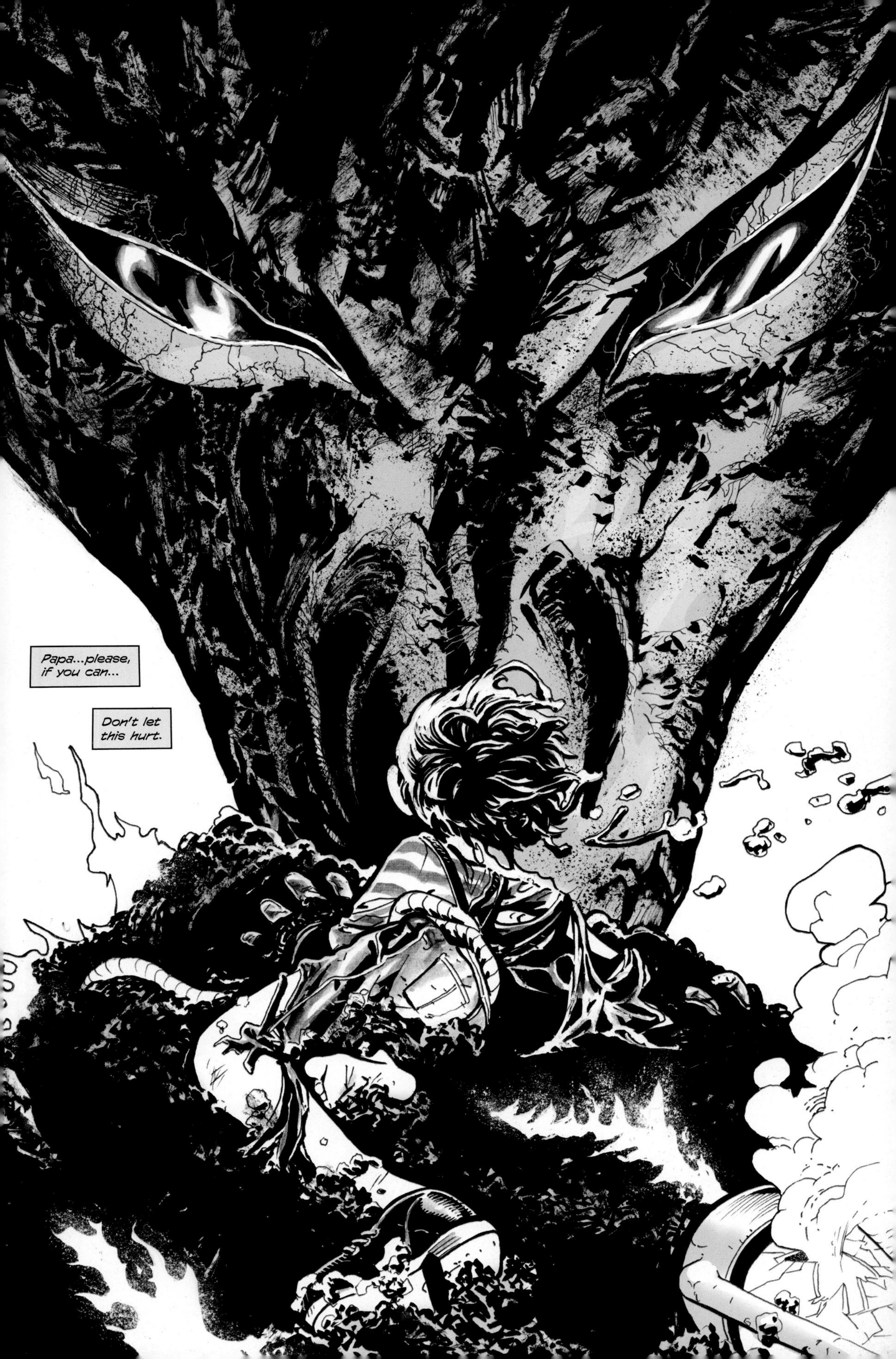
Papa...please, if you can...
Don't let this hurt.

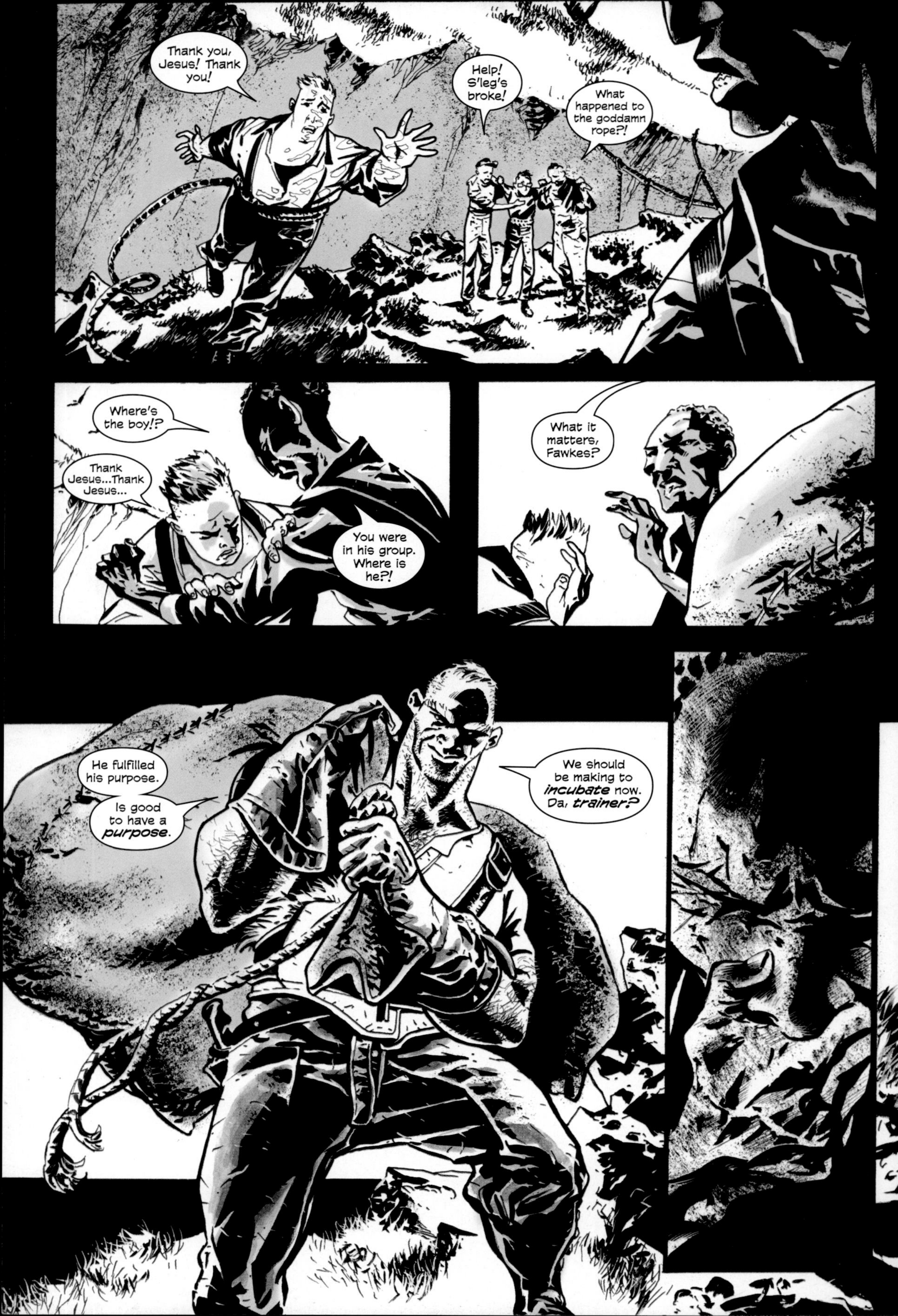
Thank you, Jesus! Thank you!
Help! S'leg's broke!
What happened to the goddamn rope?!
Where's the boy!?
Thank Jesus...Thank Jesus...
You were in his group. Where is he?!
What it matters, Fawkes?
He fulfilled his purpose.
Is good to have a *purpose*.
We should be making to *incubate* now. Da, *trainer?*

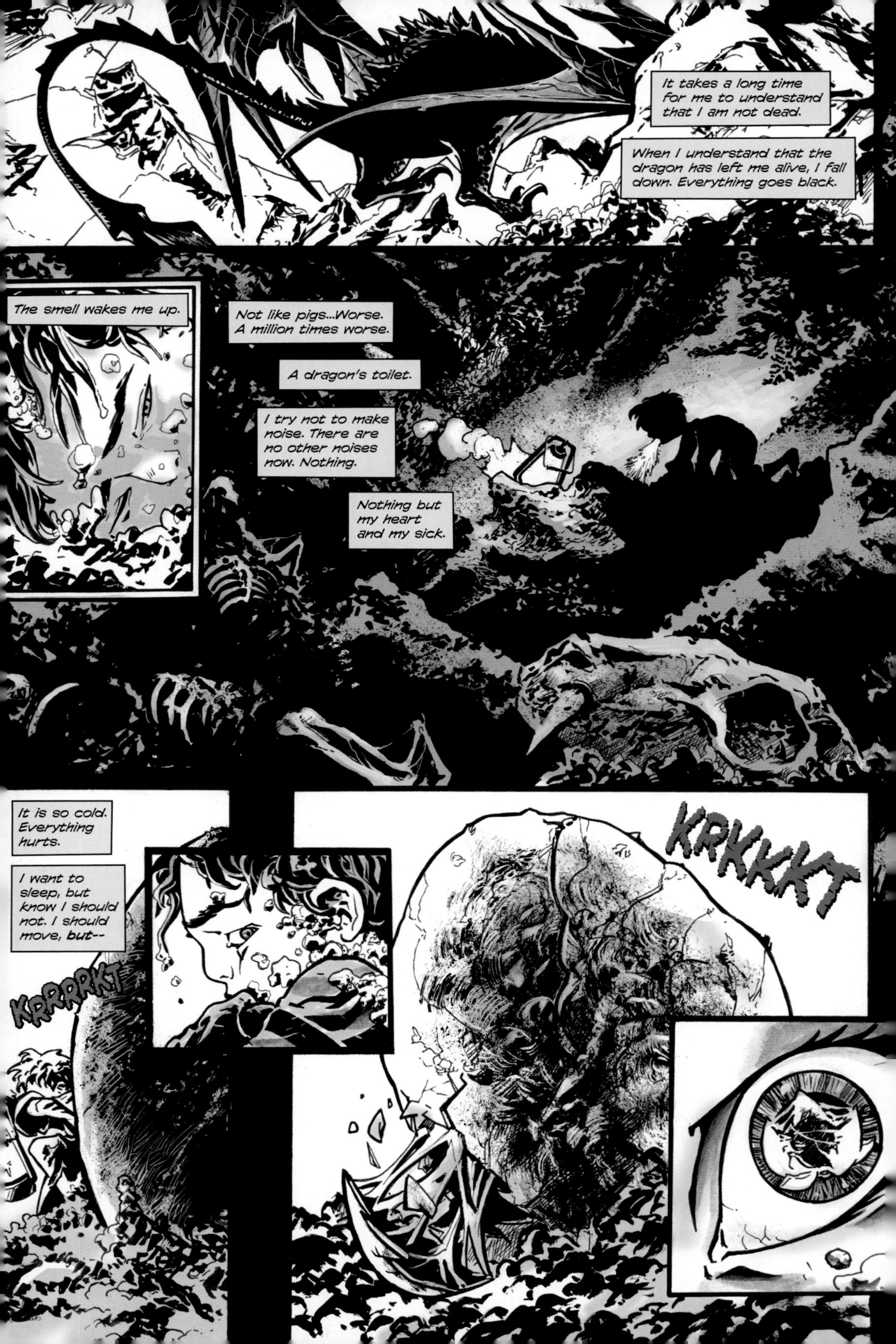
It takes a long time for me to understand that I am not dead.
When I understand that the dragon has left me alive, I fall down. Everything goes black.
The smell wakes me up.
Not like pigs...Worse. A million times worse.
A dragon's toilet.
I try not to make noise. There are no other noises now. Nothing.
Nothing but my heart and my sick.
It is so cold. Everything hurts.
I want to sleep, but know I should not. I should move, **but--**
KRRRRKT
KRKKKT

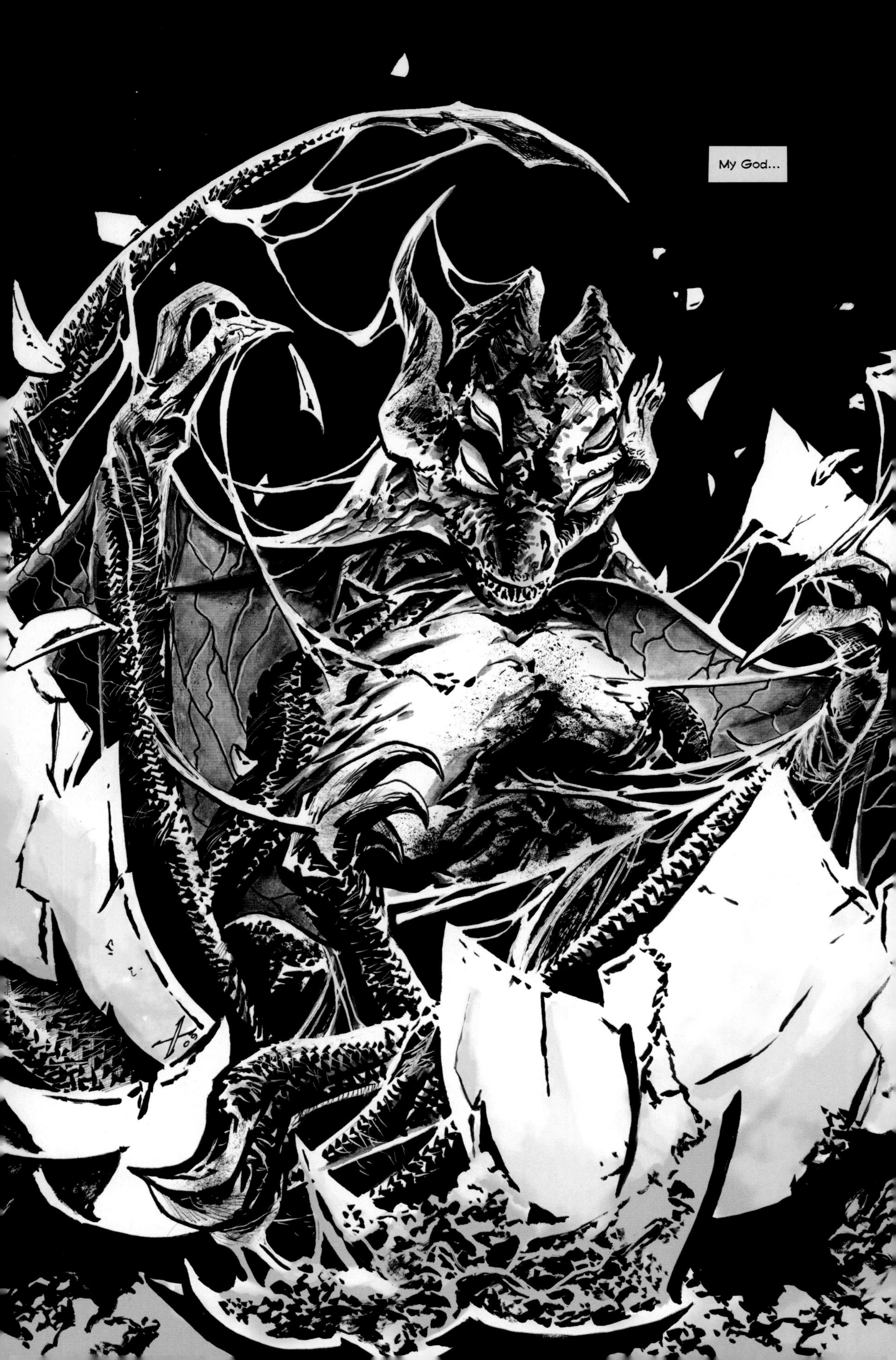
My God...

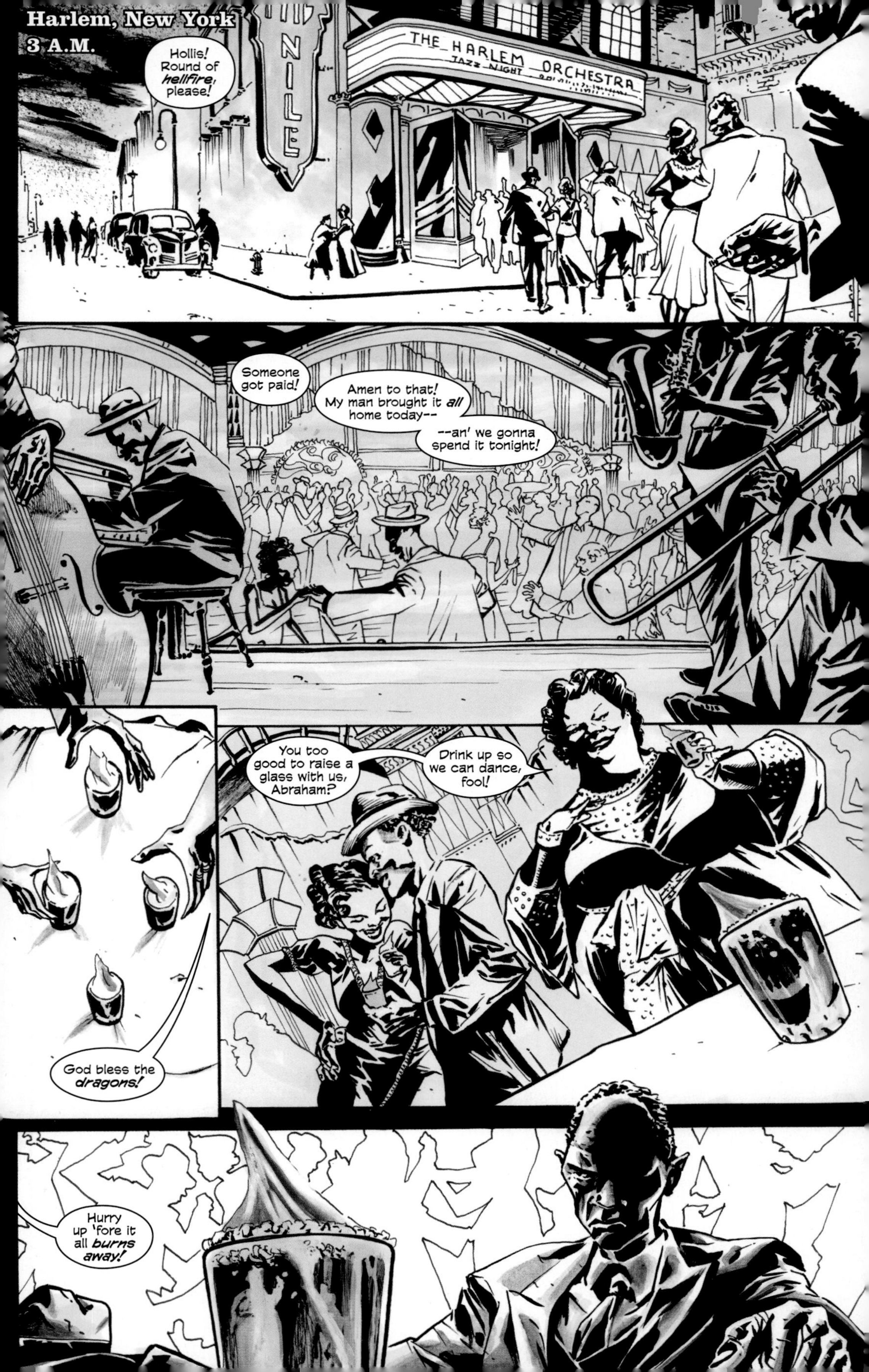
Harlem, New York
3 A.M.
NILE
THE HARLEM ORCHESTRA
JAZZ NIGHT
Hollis! Round of *hellfire*, please!
Someone got paid!
Amen to that! My man brought it *all* home today--
--an' we gonna spend it tonight!
God bless the *dragons!*
You too good to raise a glass with us, Abraham?
Drink up so we can dance, fool!
Hurry up 'fore it all *burns away!*

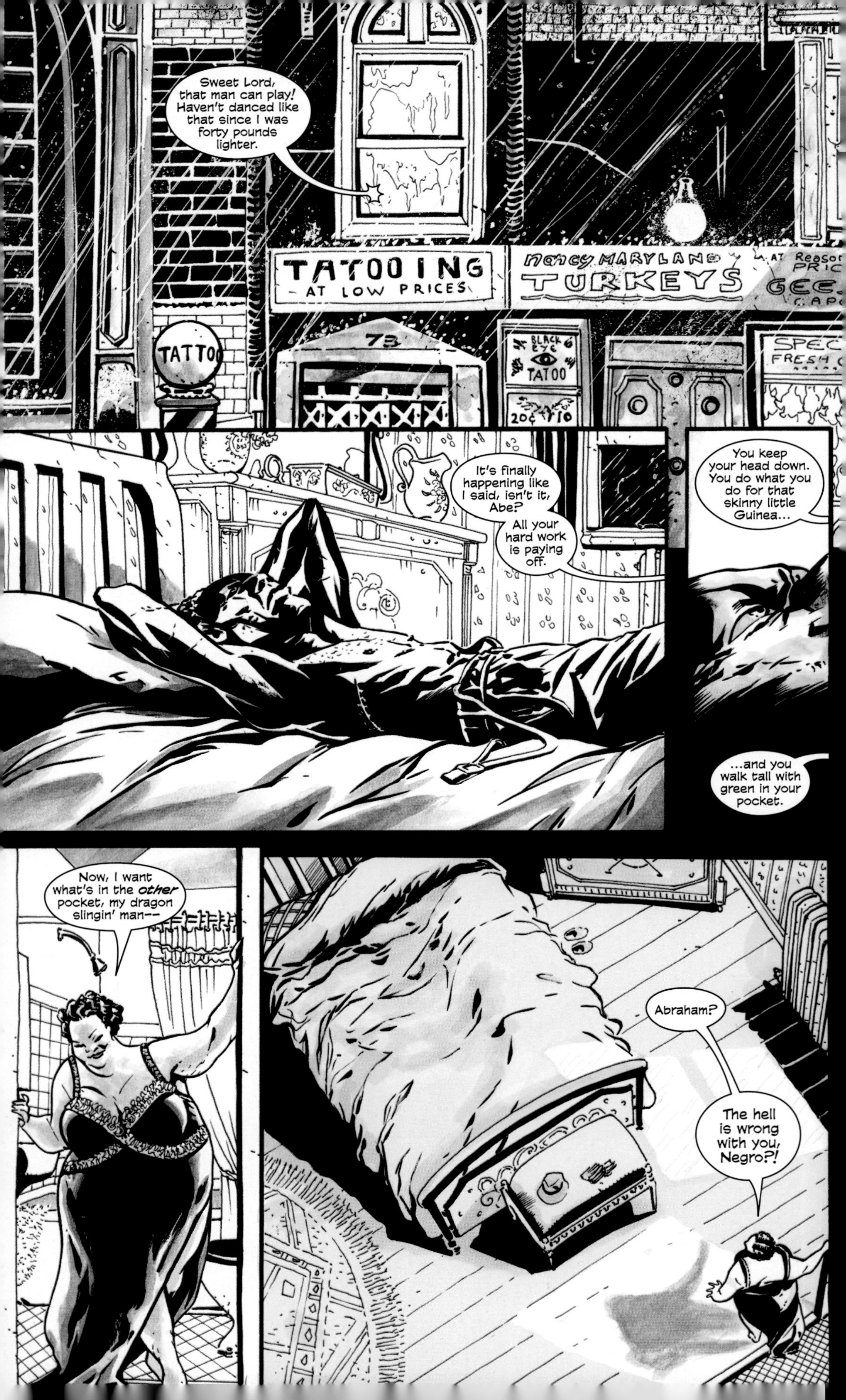
Sweet Lord, that man can play! Haven't danced like that since I was forty pounds lighter.
TATOOING
AT LOW PRICES
nancy MARYLAND
TURKEYS
TATTOO
BLACK EYE
TATOO
It's finally happening like I said, isn't it, Abe?
All your hard work is paying off.
You keep your head down. You do what you do for that skinny little Guinea...
...and you walk tall with green in your pocket.
Now, I want what's in the *other* pocket, my dragon slingin' man--
Abraham?
The hell is wrong with you, Negro?!

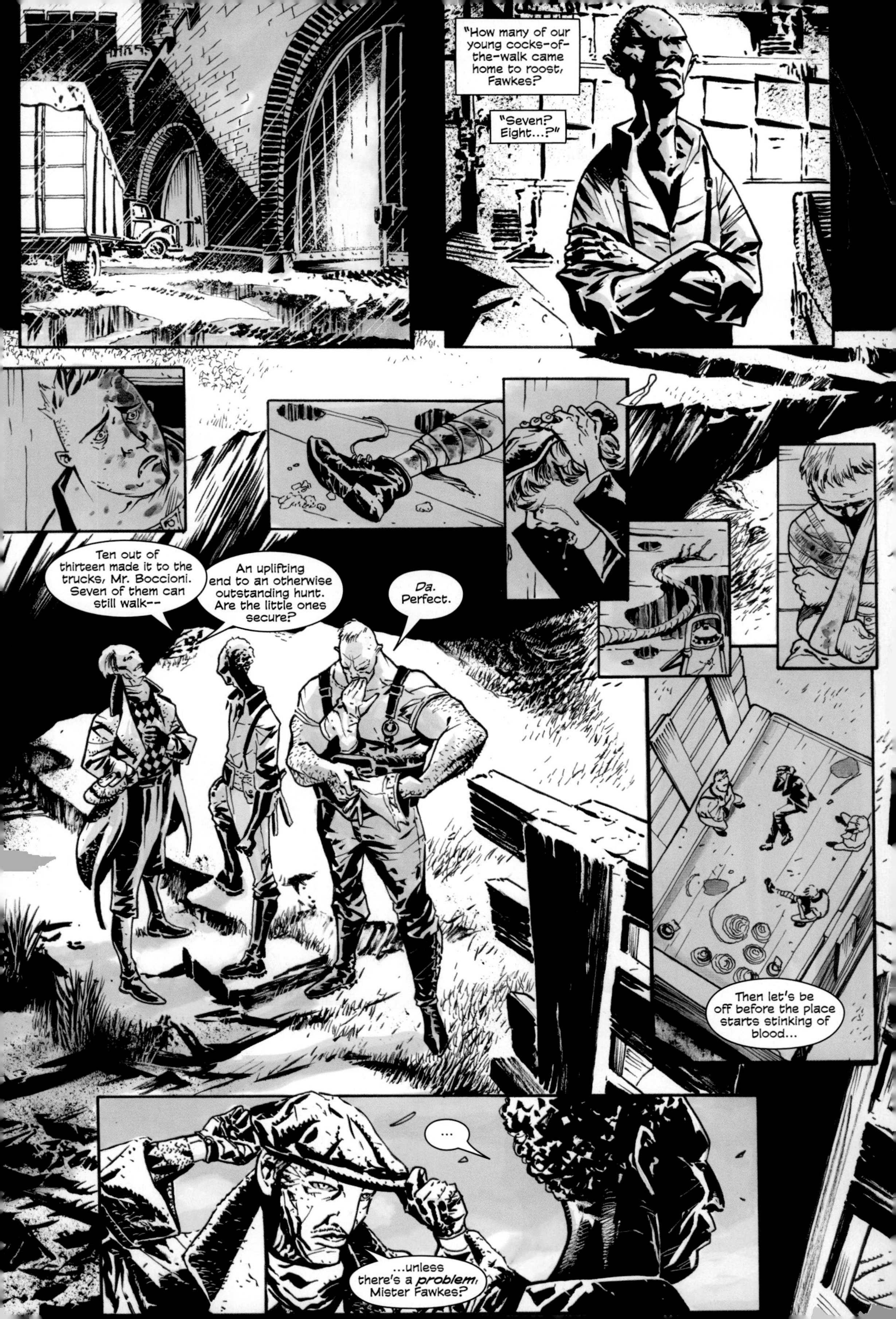
"How many of our young cocks-of-the-walk came home to roost, Fawkes?
"Seven? Eight...?"
Ten out of thirteen made it to the trucks, Mr. Boccioni. Seven of them can still walk--
An uplifting end to an otherwise outstanding hunt. Are the little ones secure?
Da. Perfect.
Then let's be off before the place starts stinking of blood...
...
...unless there's a *problem*, Mister Fawkes?

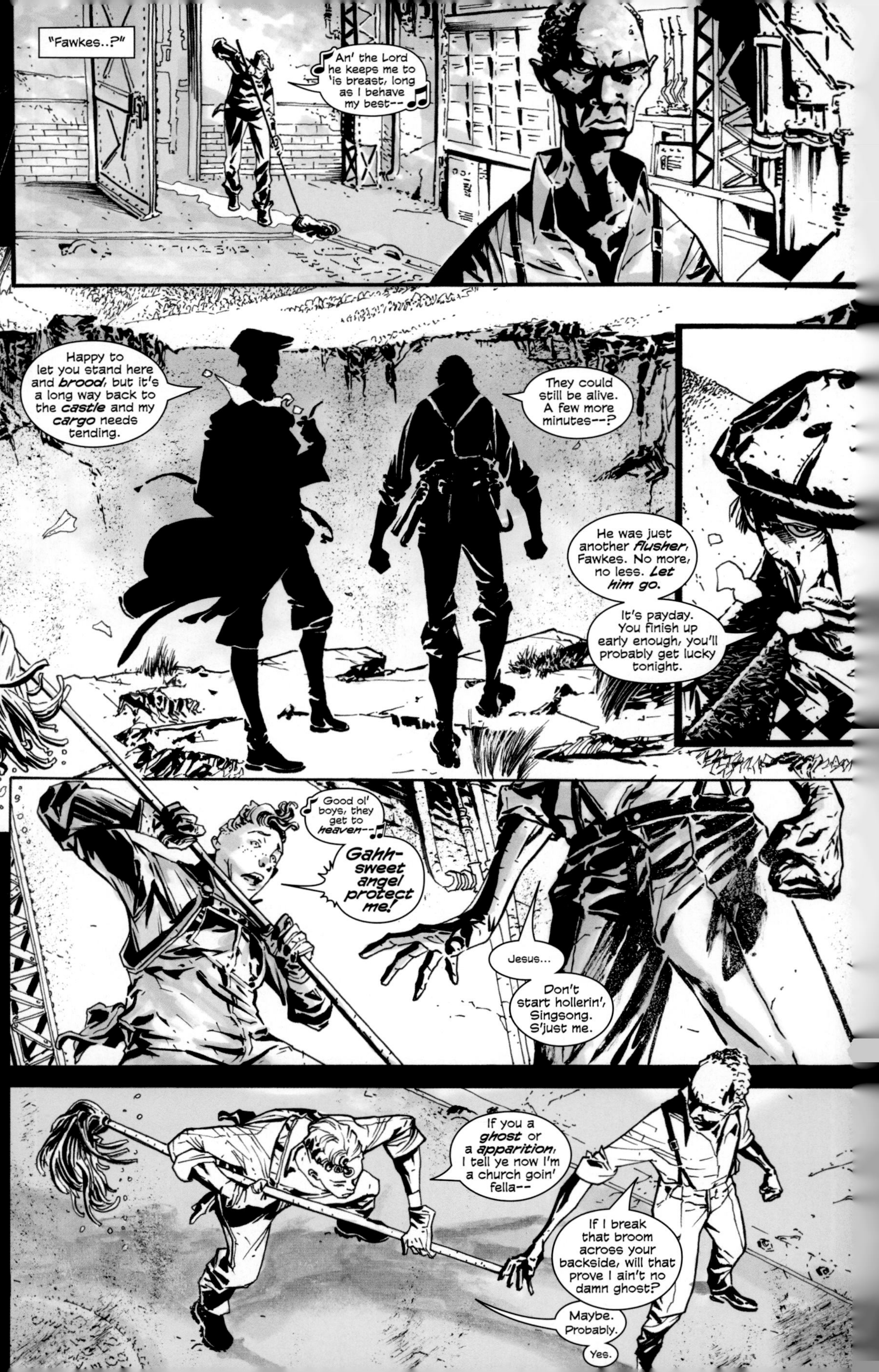
"Fawkes..?"
An' the Lord he keeps me to 'is breast, long as I behave my best--
Happy to let you stand here and *brood*, but it's a long way back to the *castle* and my *cargo* needs tending.
They could still be alive. A few more minutes--?
He was just another *flusher*, Fawkes. No more, no less. *Let him go.*
It's payday. You finish up early enough, you'll probably get lucky tonight.
Good ol' boys, they get to *heaven*--
Gahh-sweet angel protect me!
Jesus...
Don't start hollerin', Singsong. S'just me.
If you a *ghost* or a *apparition*, I tell ye now I'm a church goin' fella--
If I break that broom across your backside, will that prove I ain't no damn ghost?
Maybe.
Probably.
Yes.

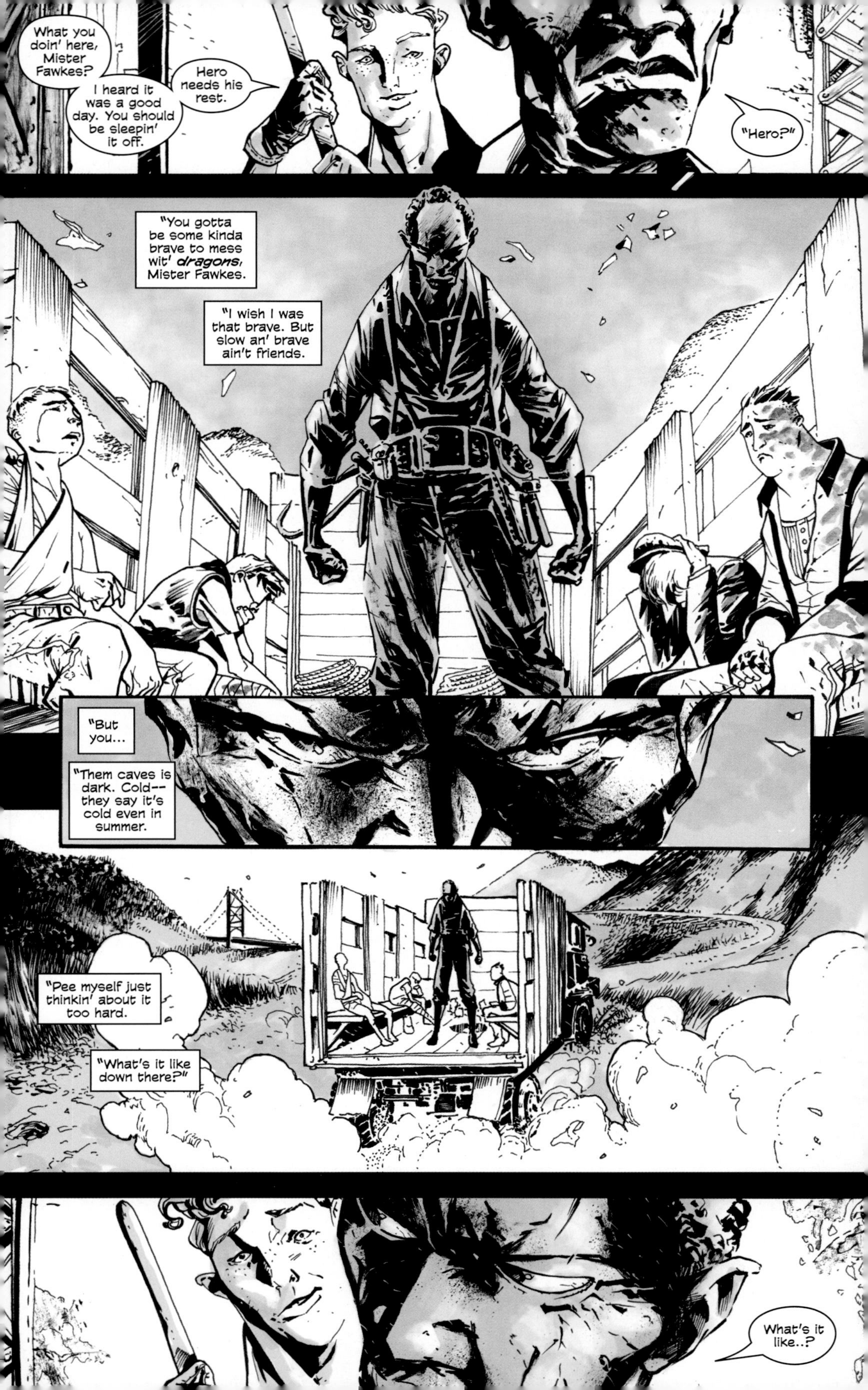
What you doin' here, Mister Fawkes?
I heard it was a good day. You should be sleepin' it off.
Hero needs his rest.
"Hero?"
"You gotta be some kinda brave to mess wit' *dragons*, Mister Fawkes.
"I wish I was that brave. But slow an' brave ain't friends.
"But you...
"Them caves is dark. Cold-- they say it's cold even in summer.
"Pee myself just thinkin' about it too hard.
"What's it like down there?"
What's it like..?

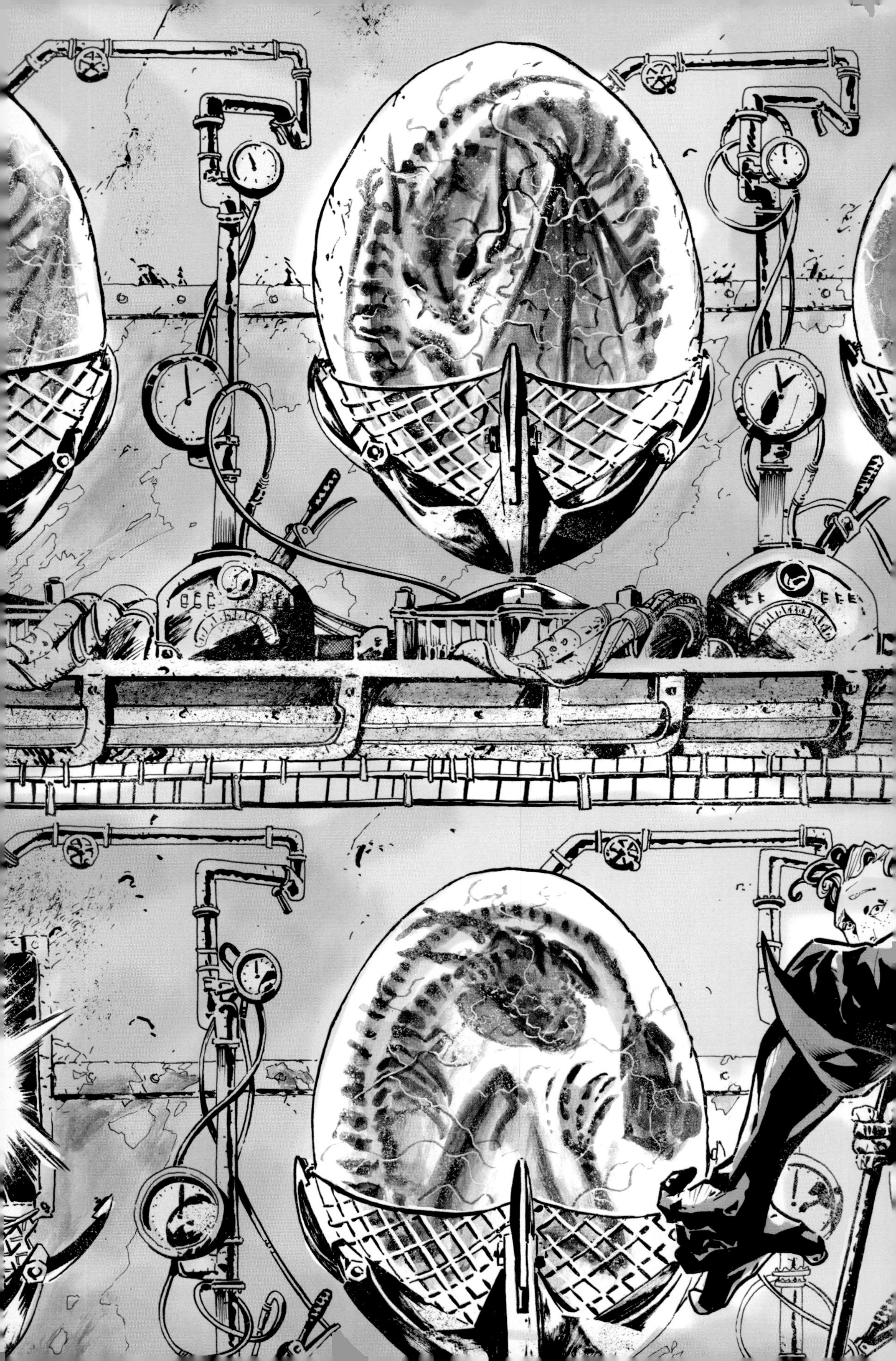

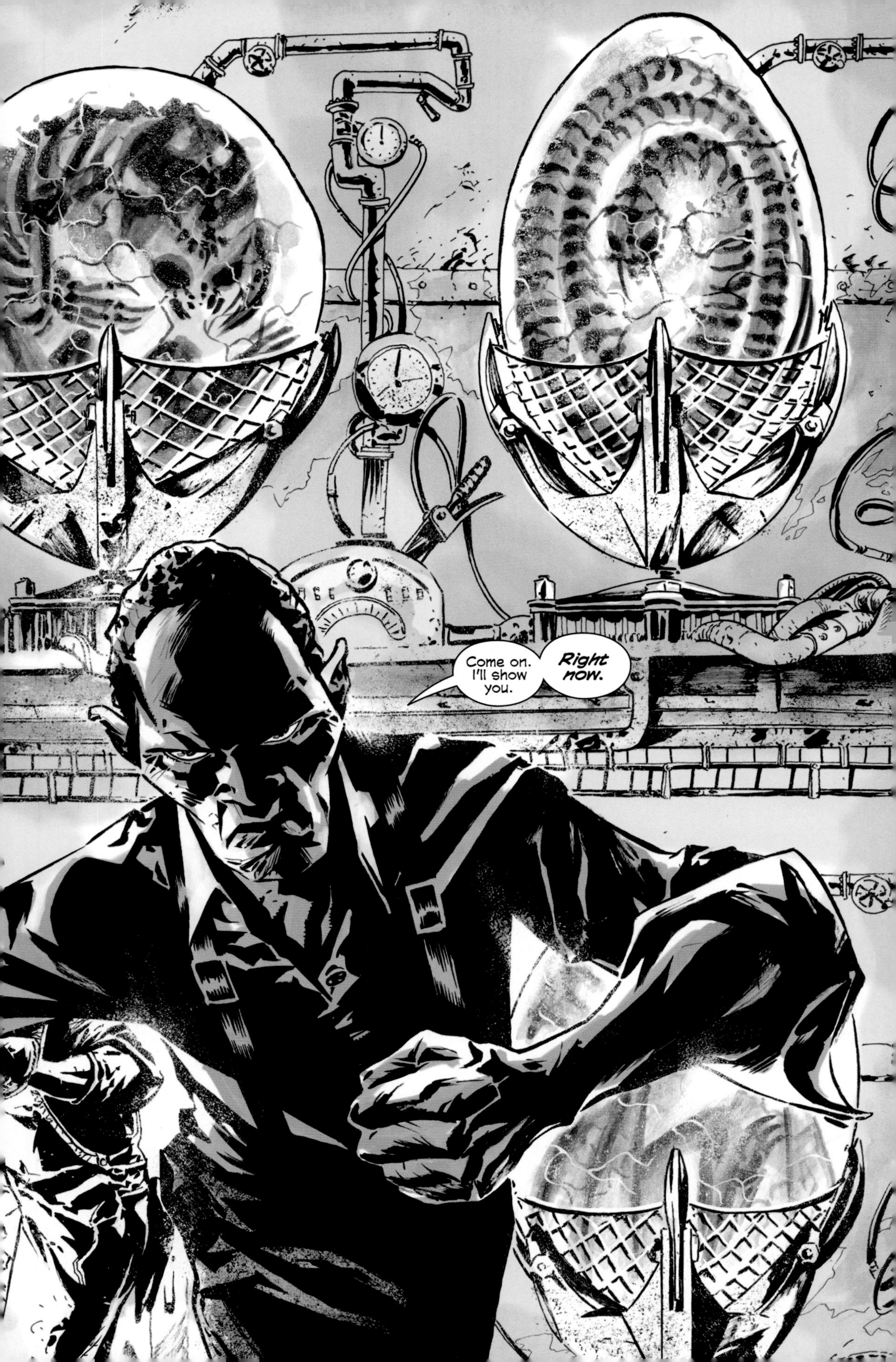
Come on. I'll show you.
Right now.

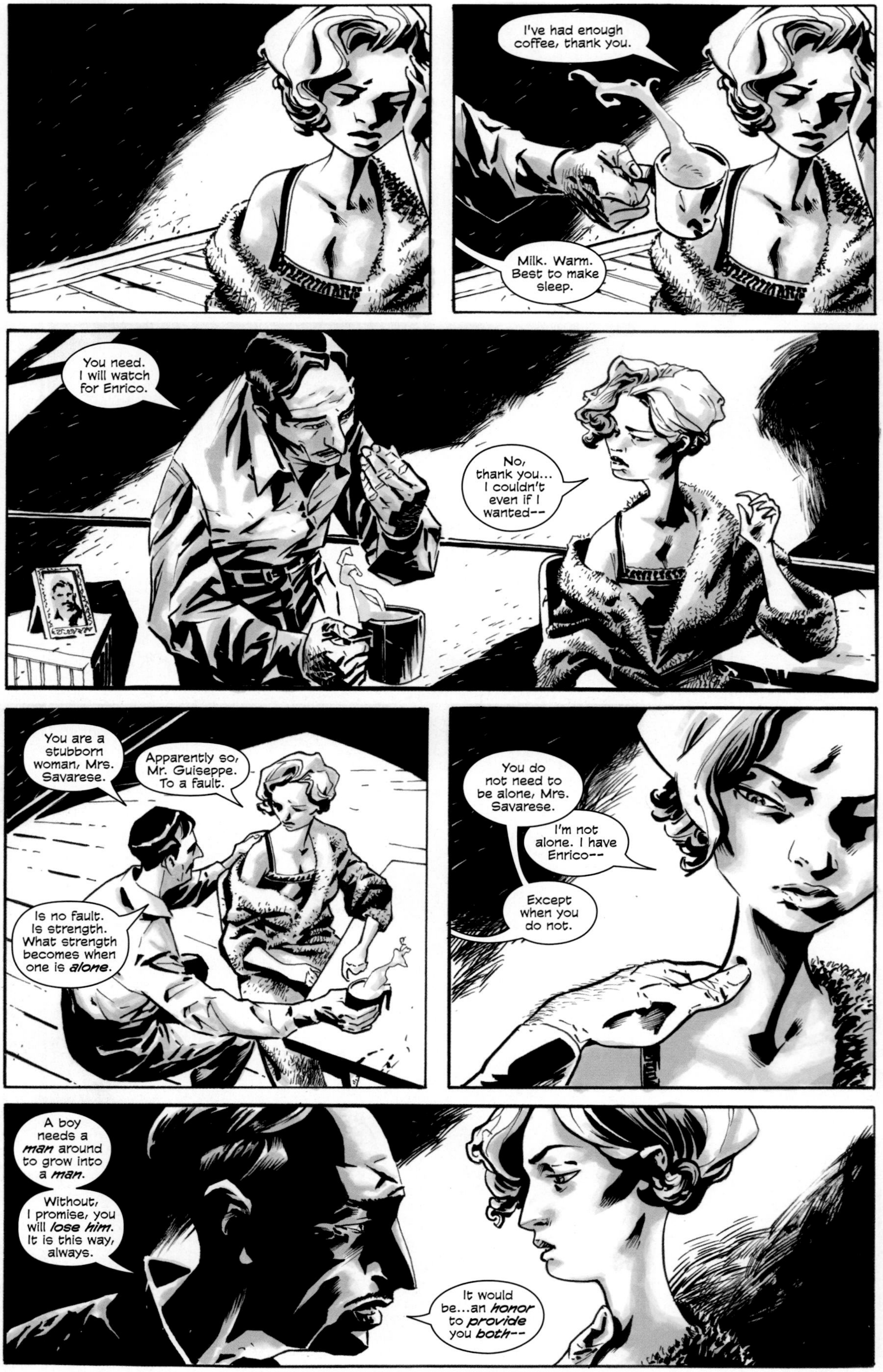
I've had enough coffee, thank you.
Milk. Warm. Best to make sleep.
You need. I will watch for Enrico.
No, thank you... I couldn't even if I wanted--
You are a stubborn woman, Mrs. Savarese.
Apparently so, Mr. Guiseppe. To a fault.
Is no fault. Is strength. What strength becomes when one is *alone*.
You do not need to be alone, Mrs. Savarese.
I'm not alone. I have Enrico--
Except when you do not.
A boy needs a *man* around to grow into a *man*.
Without, I promise, you will *lose him*. It is this way, always.
It would be...an *honor* to *provide* you both--

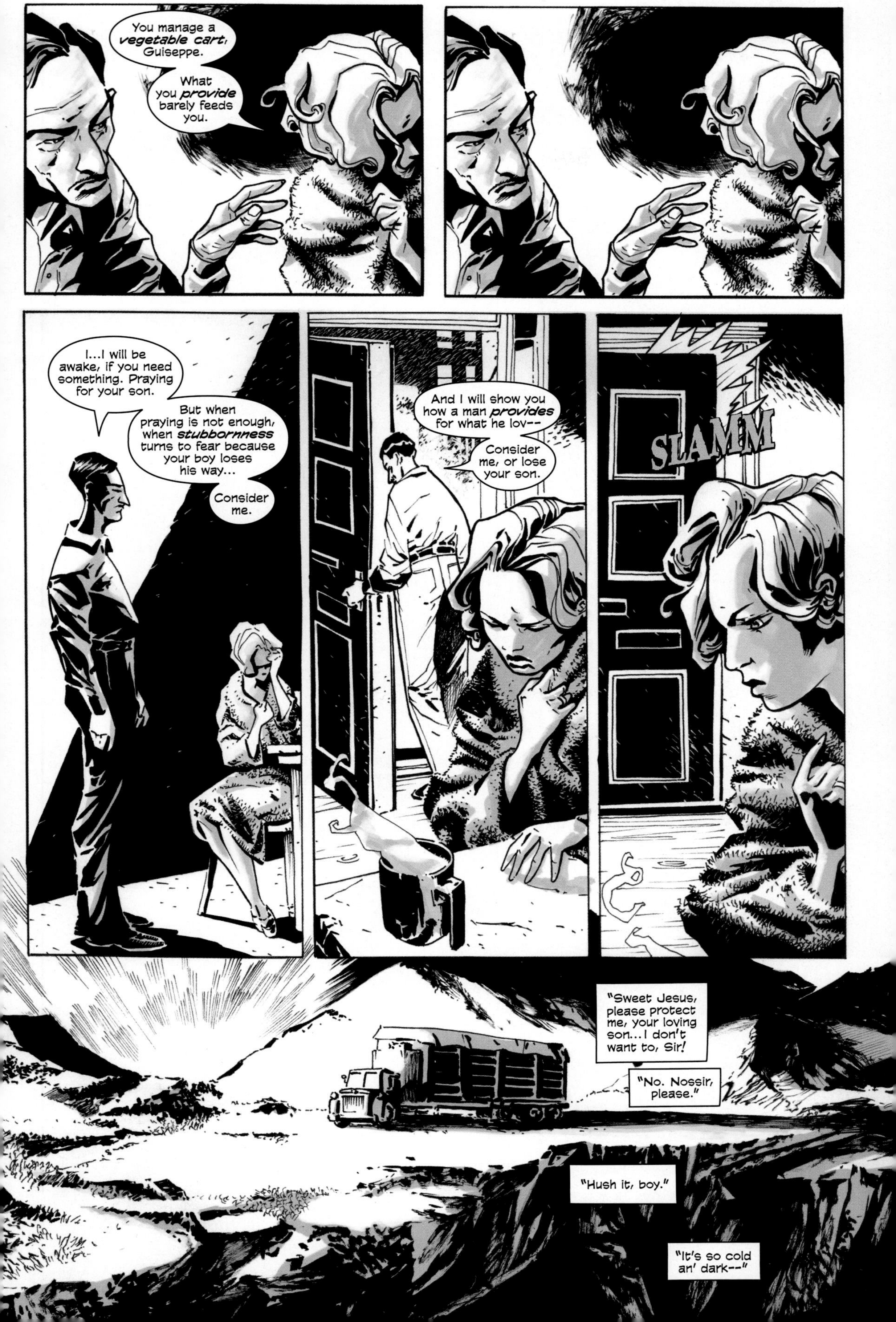
You manage a *vegetable cart*, Guiseppe.
What you *provide* barely feeds you.
I...I will be awake, if you need something. Praying for your son.
But when praying is not enough, when *stubbornness* turns to fear because your boy loses his way...
Consider me.
And I will show you how a man *provides* for what he lov--
Consider me, or lose your son.
SLAMM
"Sweet Jesus, please protect me, your loving son...I don't want to, Sir!
"No. Nossir, please."
"Hush it, boy."
"It's so cold an' dark--"

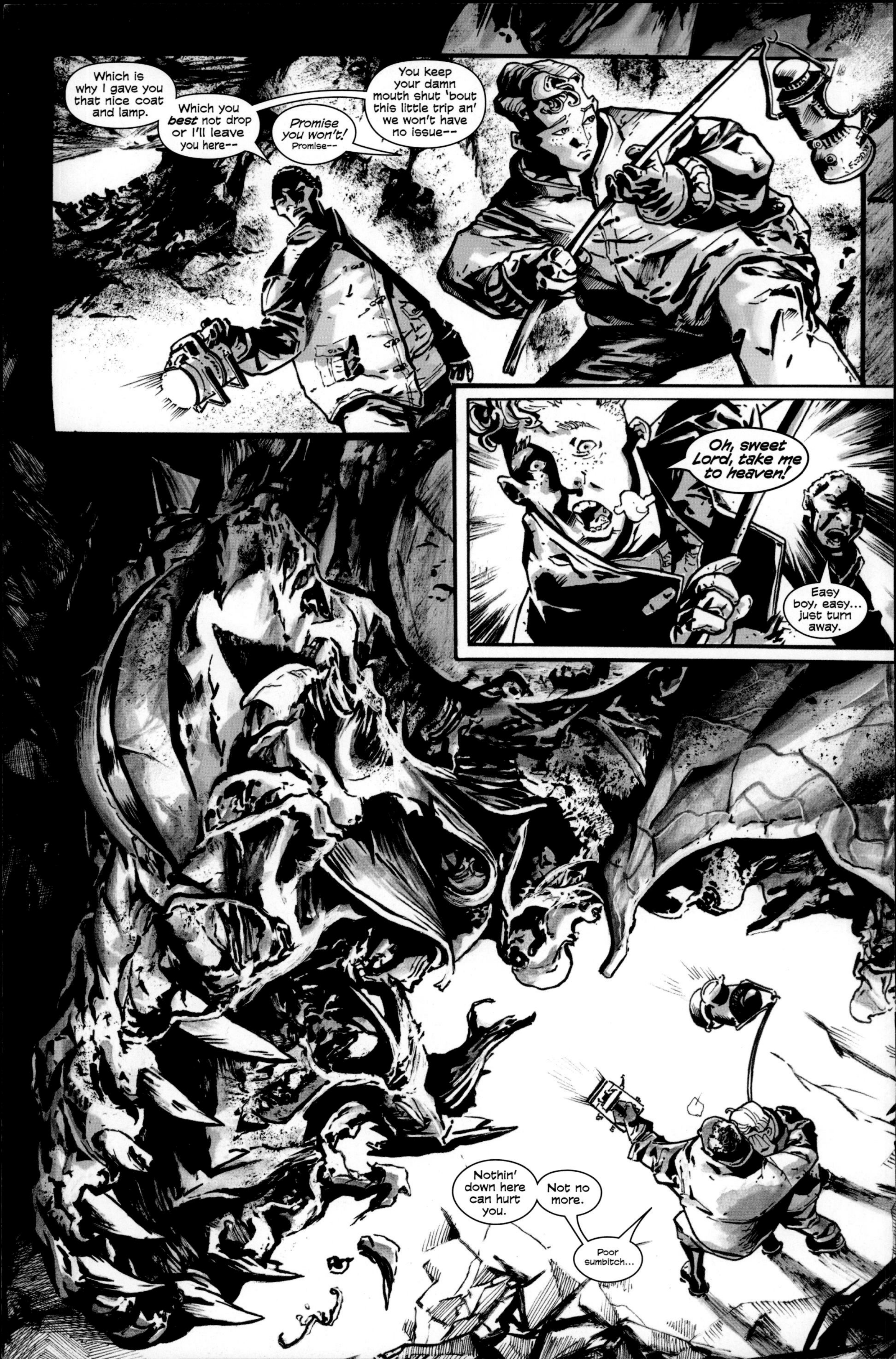
Which is why I gave you that nice coat and lamp.
Which you *best* not drop or I'll leave you here--
Promise you won't! Promise--
You keep your damn mouth shut 'bout this little trip an' we won't have no issue--
Oh, sweet Lord, take me to heaven!
Easy boy, easy... just turn away.
Nothin' down here can hurt you.
Not no more.
Poor sumbitch...

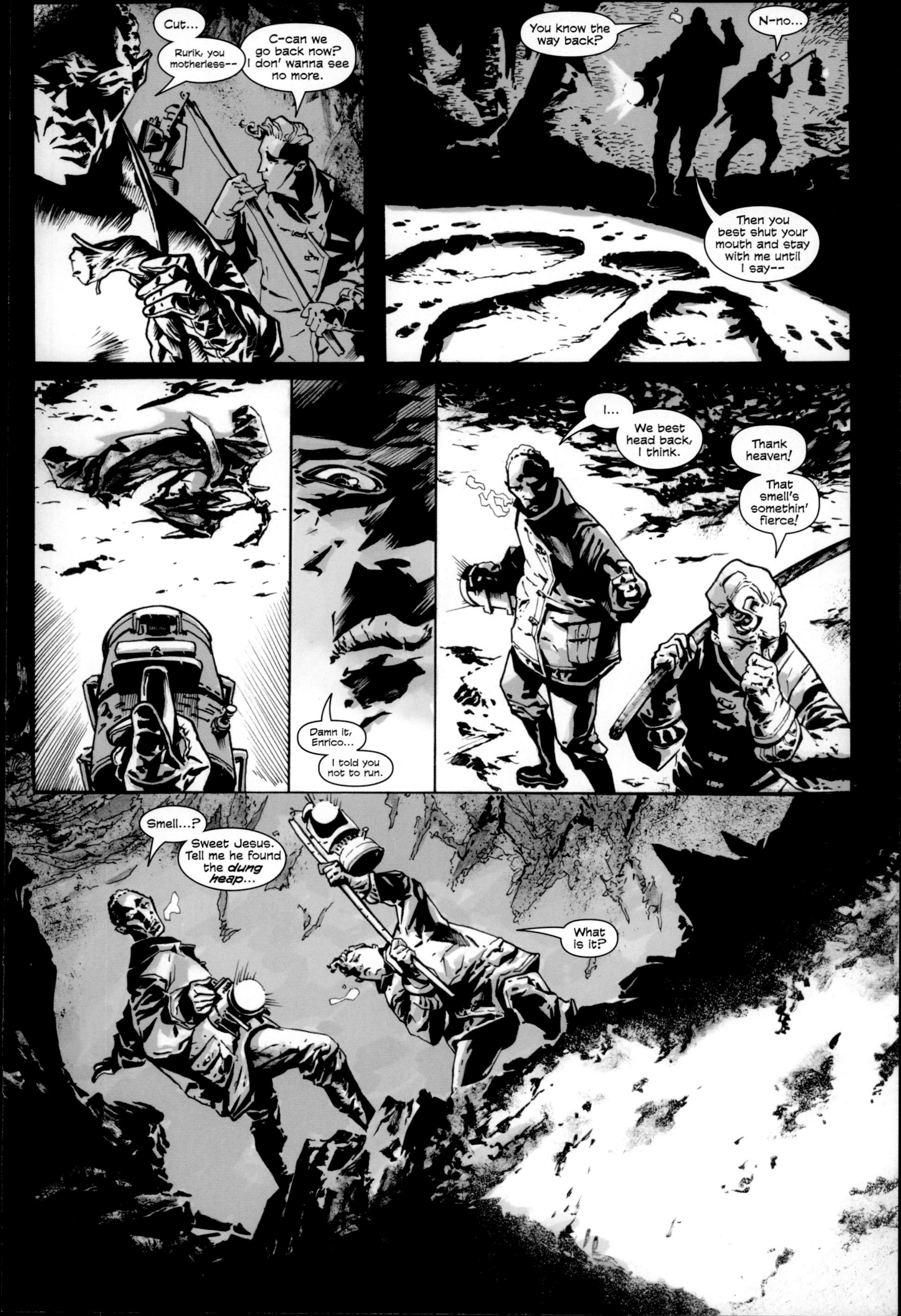
Cut...
Rurik, you motherless--
C-can we go back now? I don' wanna see no more.
You know the way back?
N-no...
Then you best shut your mouth and stay with me until I say--
Damn it, Enrico...
I told you not to run.
I...
We best head back, I think.
Thank heaven!
That smell's somethin' fierce!
Smell...?
Sweet Jesus. Tell me he found the *dung heap*...
What is it?

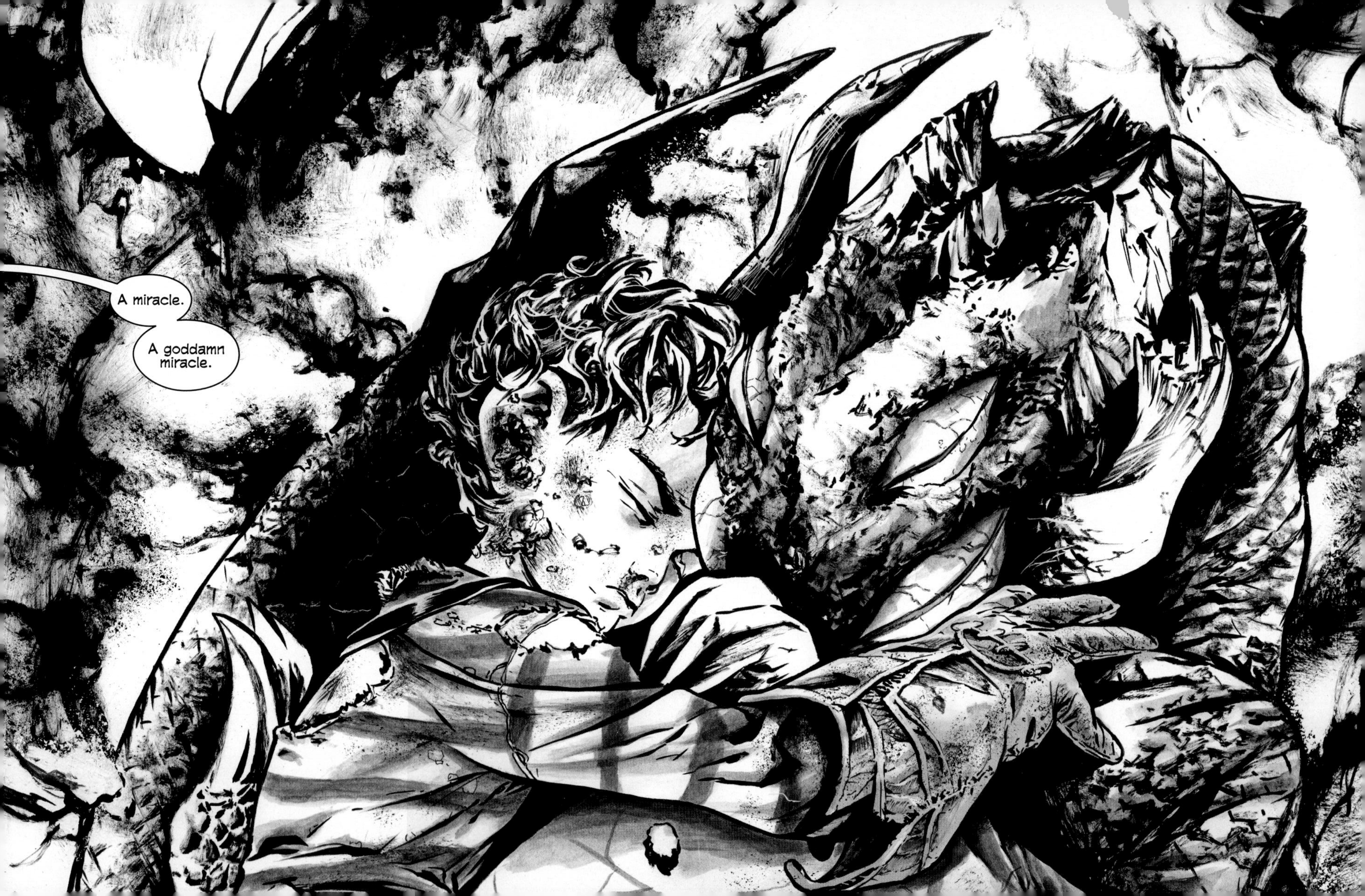
A miracle.
A goddamn miracle.

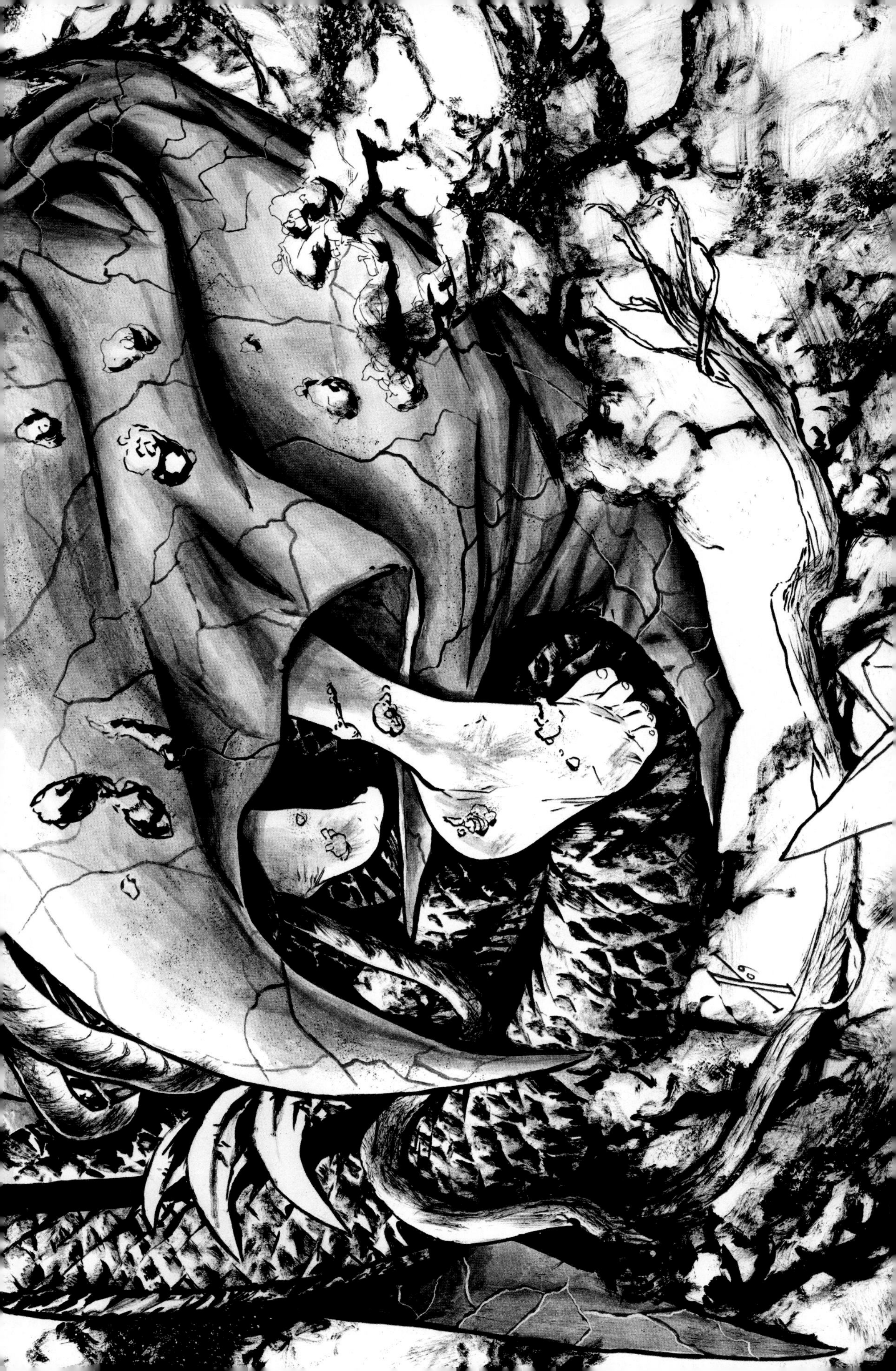

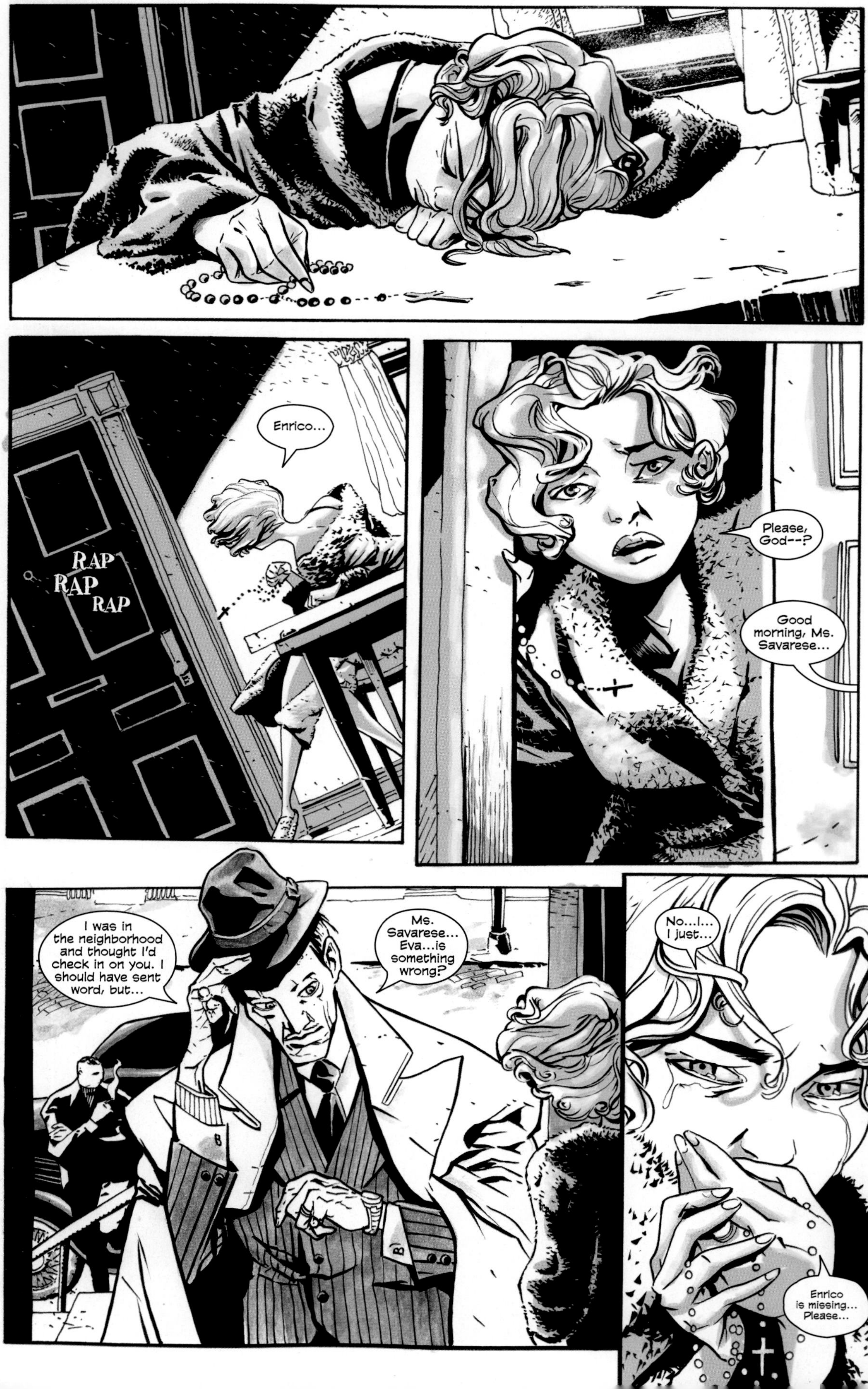

Enrico...
RAP RAP RAP
Please, God--?
Good morning, Ms. Savarese...
I was in the neighborhood and thought I'd check in on you. I should have sent word, but...
Ms. Savarese... Eva...is something wrong?
No...I... I just...
Enrico is missing... Please...

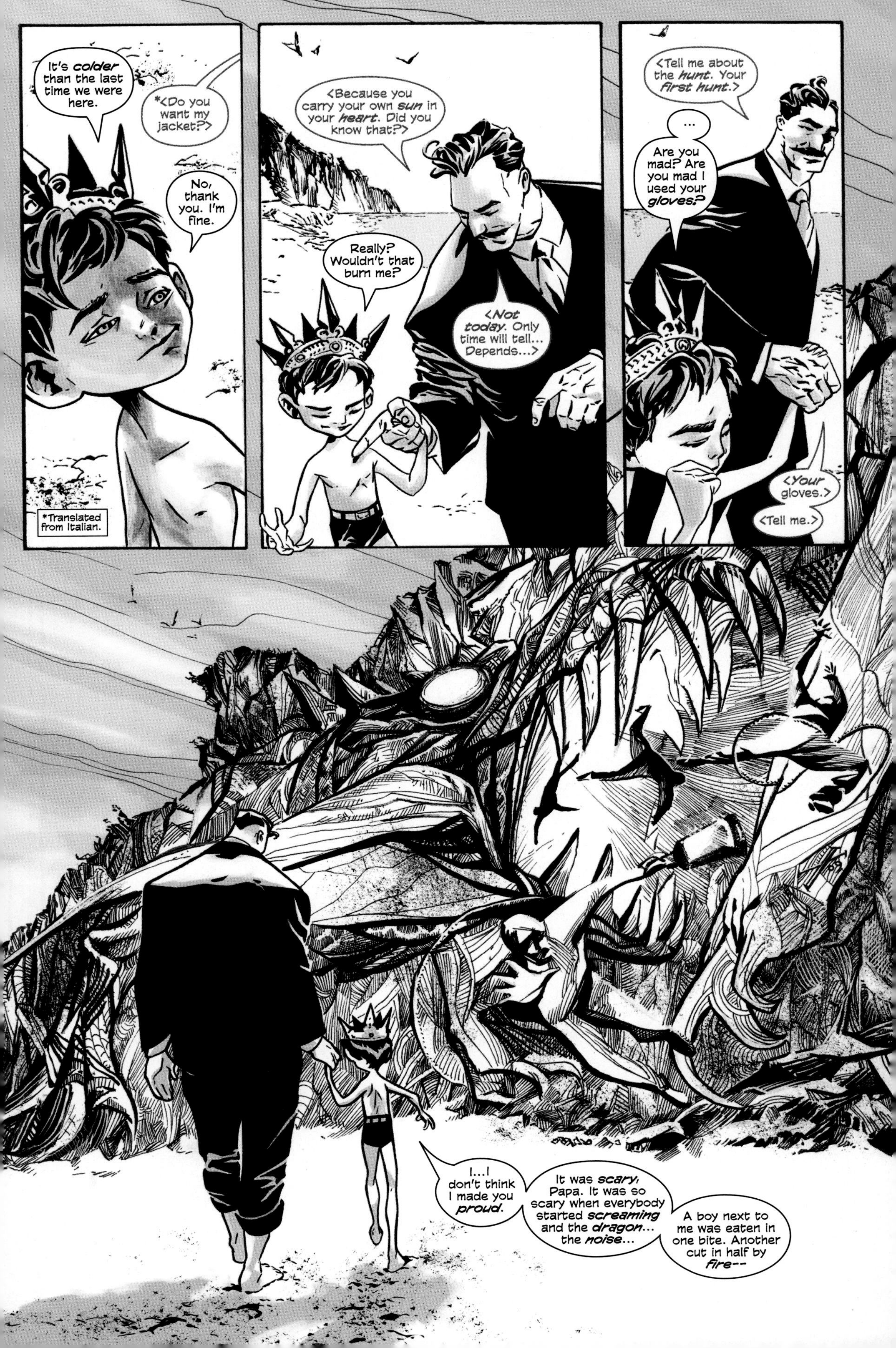

It's *colder* than the last time we were here.
*<Do you want my jacket?>
No, thank you. I'm fine.
*Translated from Italian.
<Because you carry your own *sun* in your *heart*. Did you know that?>
Really? Wouldn't that burn me?
<*Not today*. Only time will tell... Depends...>
<Tell me about the *hunt*. Your *first hunt*.>
...
Are you mad? Are you mad I used your *gloves?*
<*Your* gloves.>
<Tell me.>
I...I don't think I made you *proud*.
It was *scary*, Papa. It was so scary when everybody started *screaming* and the *dragon*... the *noise*...
A boy next to me was eaten in one bite. Another cut in half by *fire*--

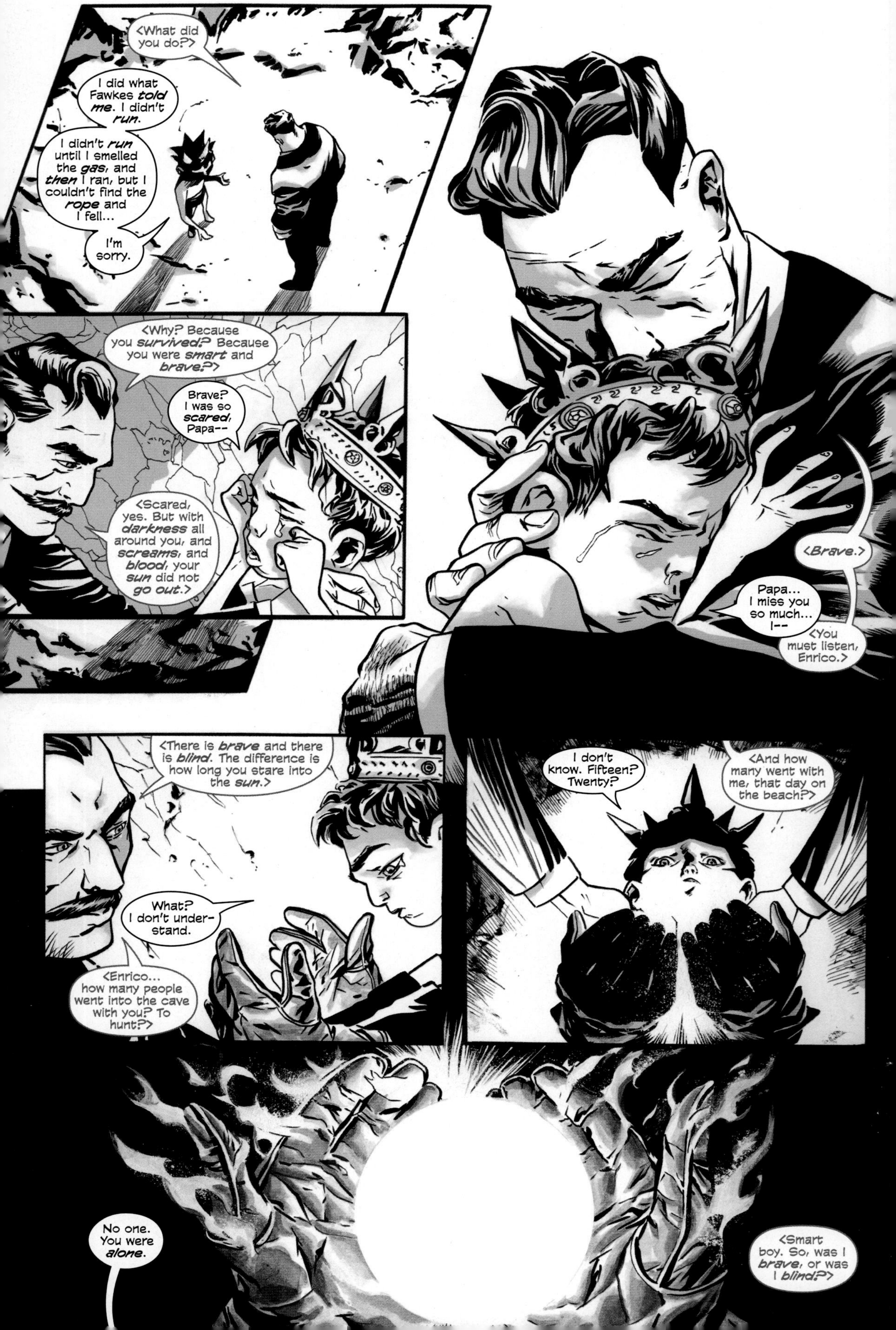

<What did you do?>
I did what Fawkes *told me*. I didn't *run*.
I didn't *run* until I smelled the *gas*, and *then* I ran, but I couldn't find the *rope* and I fell...
I'm sorry.
<Why? Because you *survived?* Because you were *smart* and *brave?*>
Brave? I was so *scared*, Papa--
<Scared, yes. But with *darkness* all around you, and *screams*, and *blood*, your *sun* did not *go out*.>
<*Brave*.>
Papa... I miss you so much... I--
<You must listen, Enrico.>
<There is *brave* and there is *blind*. The difference is how long you stare into the *sun*.>
What? I don't under-stand.
<Enrico... how many people went into the cave with you? To hunt?>
I don't know. Fifteen? Twenty?
<And how many went with me, that day on the beach?>
No one. You were *alone*.
<Smart boy. So, was I *brave*, or was I *blind?*>

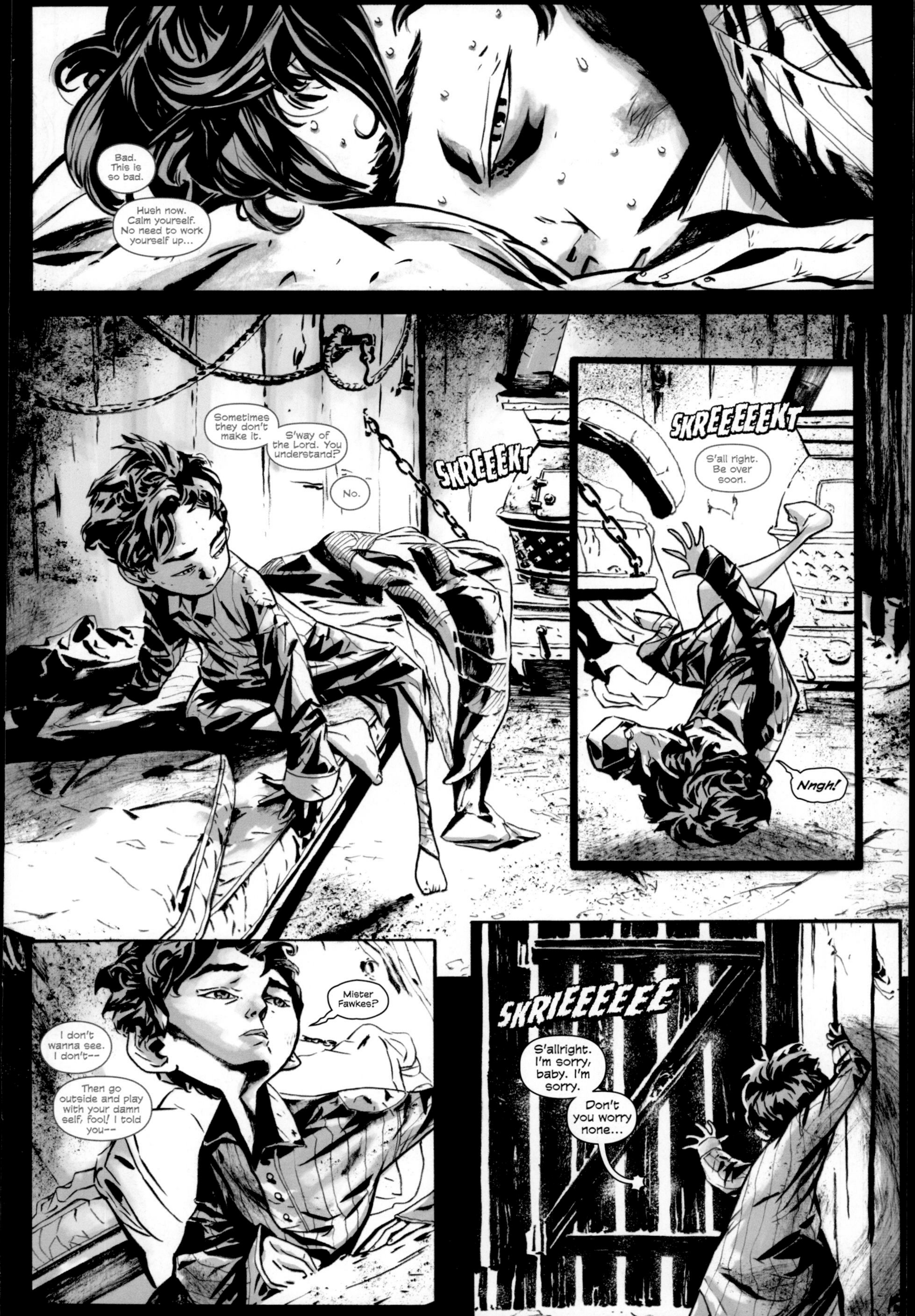
Bad. This is so bad.
Hush now. Calm yourself. No need to work yourself up...
Sometimes they don't make it.
S'way of the Lord. You understand?
No.
SKREEEKT
SKREEEEEEKT
S'all right. Be over soon.
Nngh!
Mister Fawkes?
I don't wanna see. I don't--
Then go outside and play with your damn self, fool! I told you--
SKRIEEEEEEE
S'allright. I'm sorry, baby. I'm sorry.
Don't you worry none...

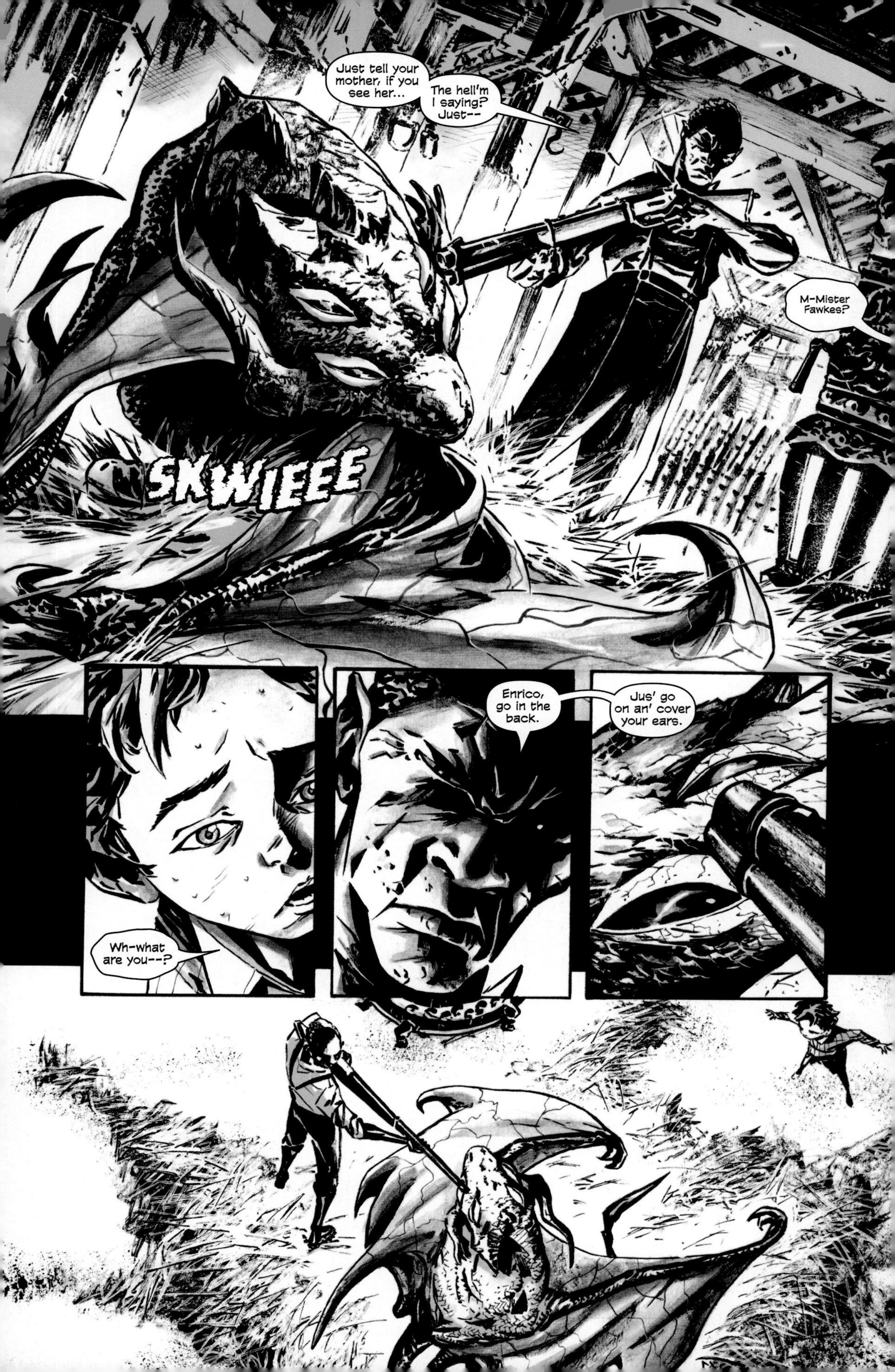
Just tell your mother, if you see her...
The hell'm I saying? Just--
M-Mister Fawkes?
SKWIEEE
Wh-what are you--?
Enrico, go in the back.
Jus' go on an' cover your ears.

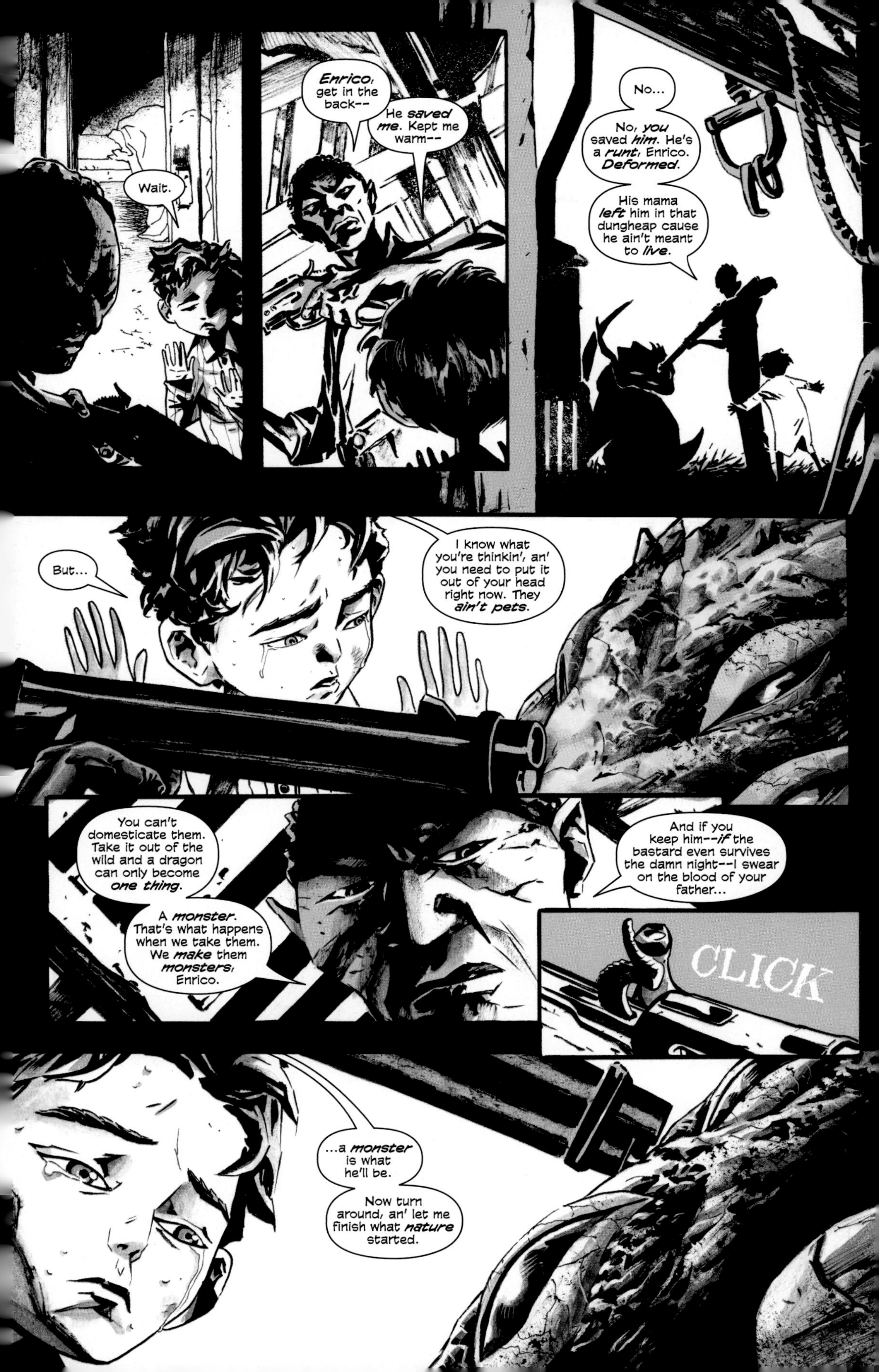
Wait.
Enrico, get in the back--
He saved me. Kept me warm--
No...
No, you saved him. He's a runt, Enrico. Deformed.
His mama left him in that dungheap cause he ain't meant to live.
But...
I know what you're thinkin', an' you need to put it out of your head right now. They ain't pets.
You can't domesticate them. Take it out of the wild and a dragon can only become one thing.
A monster. That's what happens when we take them. We make them monsters, Enrico.
And if you keep him--if the bastard even survives the damn night--I swear on the blood of your father...
CLICK
...a monster is what he'll be.
Now turn around, an' let me finish what nature started.

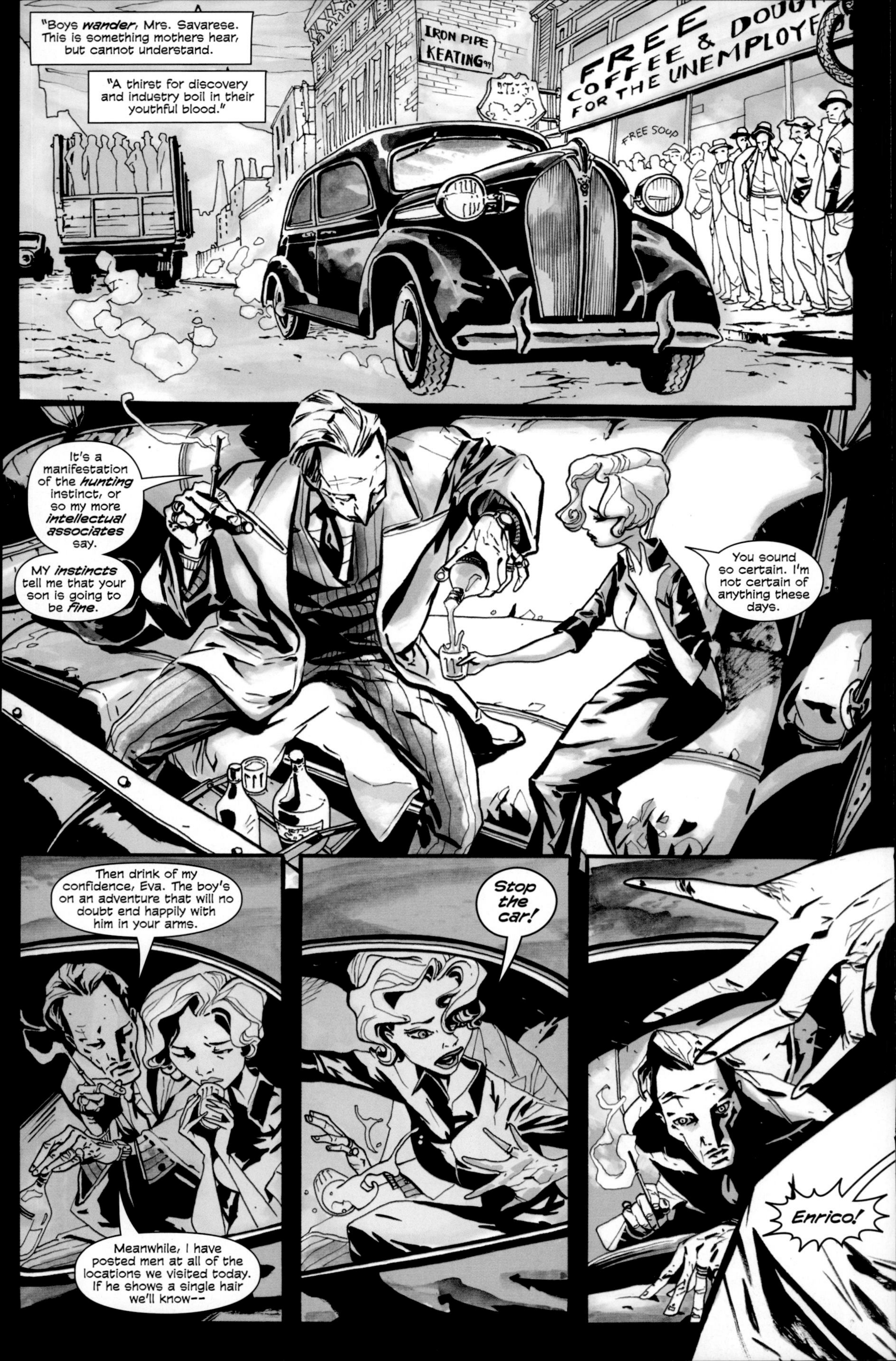
"Boys *wander*, Mrs. Savarese. This is something mothers hear, but cannot understand.
"A thirst for discovery and industry boil in their youthful blood."
IRON PIPE
KEATING
FREE COFFEE & DOUGH
FOR THE UNEMPLOYE
FREE SOUP
It's a manifestation of the *hunting* instinct, or so my more *intellectual associates* say.
MY *instincts* tell me that your son is going to be *fine*.
You sound so certain. I'm not certain of anything these days.
Then drink of my confidence, Eva. The boy's on an adventure that will no doubt end happily with him in your arms.
Meanwhile, I have posted men at all of the locations we visited today. If he shows a single hair we'll know--
Stop the car!
Enrico!

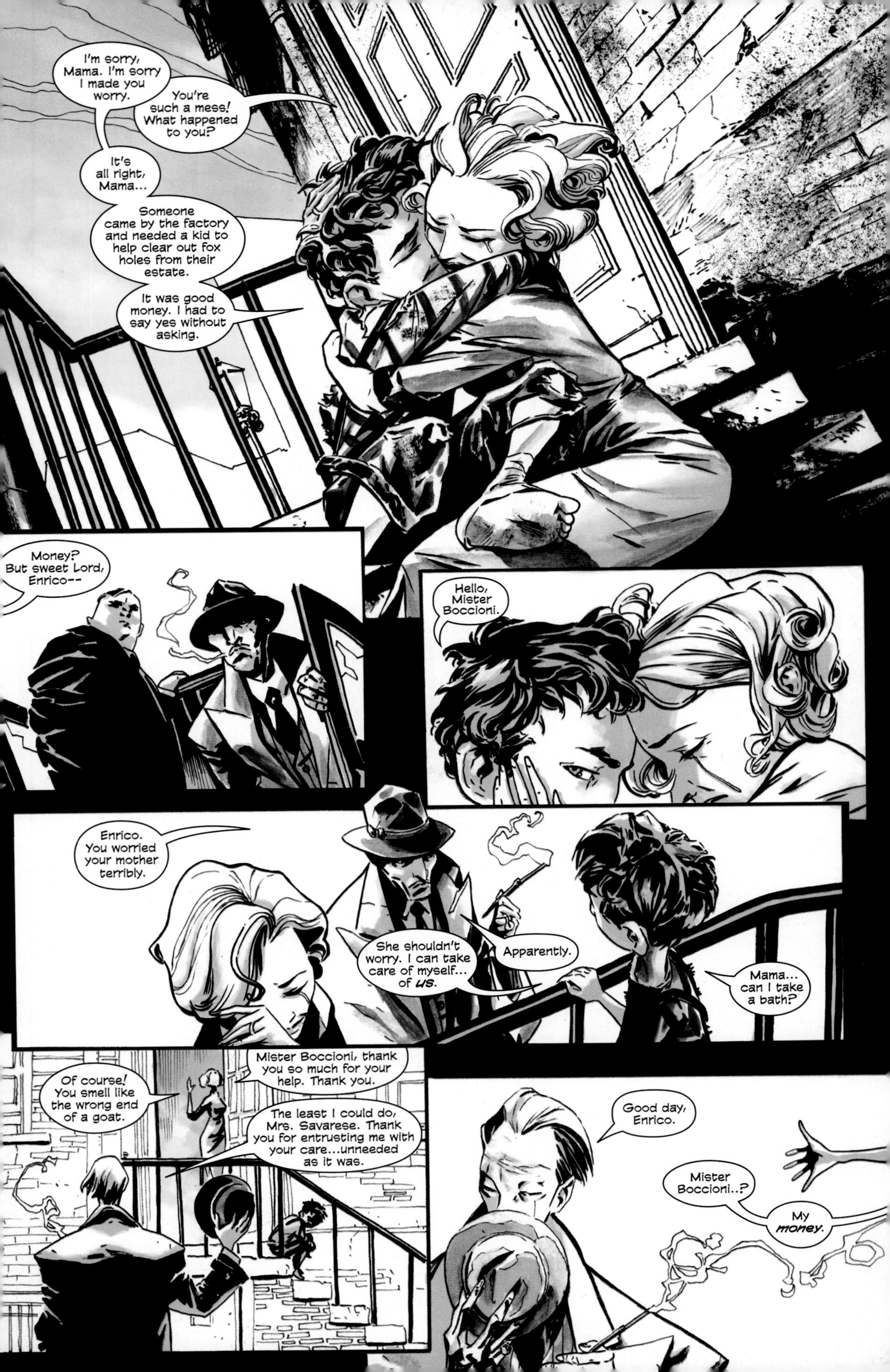
I'm sorry, Mama. I'm sorry I made you worry.
You're such a mess! What happened to you?
It's all right, Mama...
Someone came by the factory and needed a kid to help clear out fox holes from their estate.
It was good money. I had to say yes without asking.
Money? But sweet Lord, Enrico--
Hello, Mister Boccioni.
Enrico. You worried your mother terribly.
She shouldn't worry. I can take care of myself... of *us*.
Apparently.
Mama... can I take a bath?
Of course! You smell like the wrong end of a goat.
Mister Boccioni, thank you so much for your help. Thank you.
The least I could do, Mrs. Savarese. Thank you for entrusting me with your care...unneeded as it was.
Good day, Enrico.
Mister Boccioni..?
My *money*.

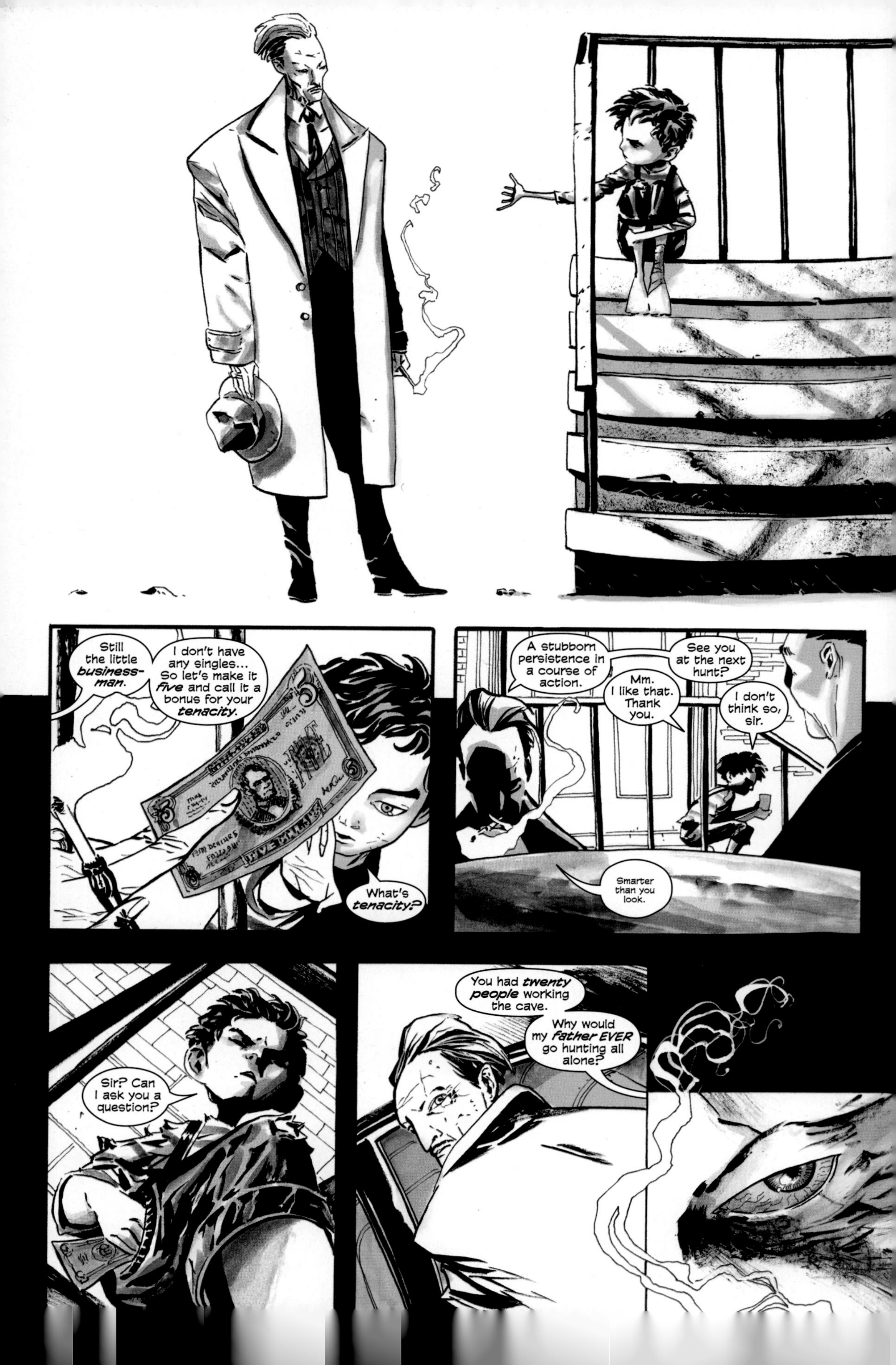
Still the little *business-man.*
I don't have any singles... So let's make it *five* and call it a bonus for your *tenacity.*
What's *tenacity?*
A stubborn persistence in a course of action.
Mm. I like that. Thank you.
See you at the next hunt?
I don't think so, sir.
Smarter than you look.
Sir? Can I ask you a question?
You had *twenty people* working the cave.
Why would my *father EVER* go hunting all alone?

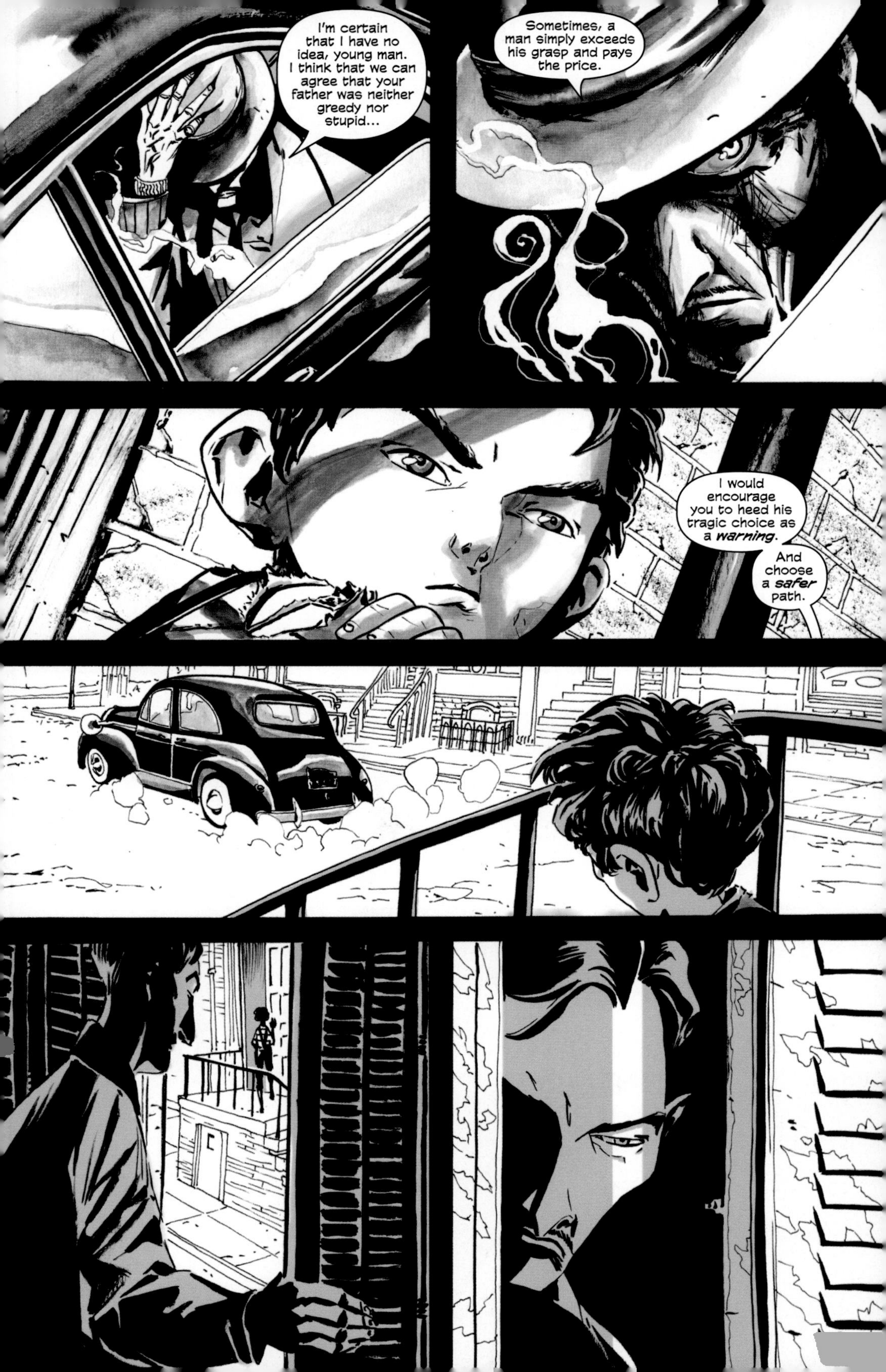
I'm certain that I have no idea, young man. I think that we can agree that your father was neither greedy nor stupid...
Sometimes, a man simply exceeds his grasp and pays the price.
I would encourage you to heed his tragic choice as a *warning*.
And choose a *safer* path.

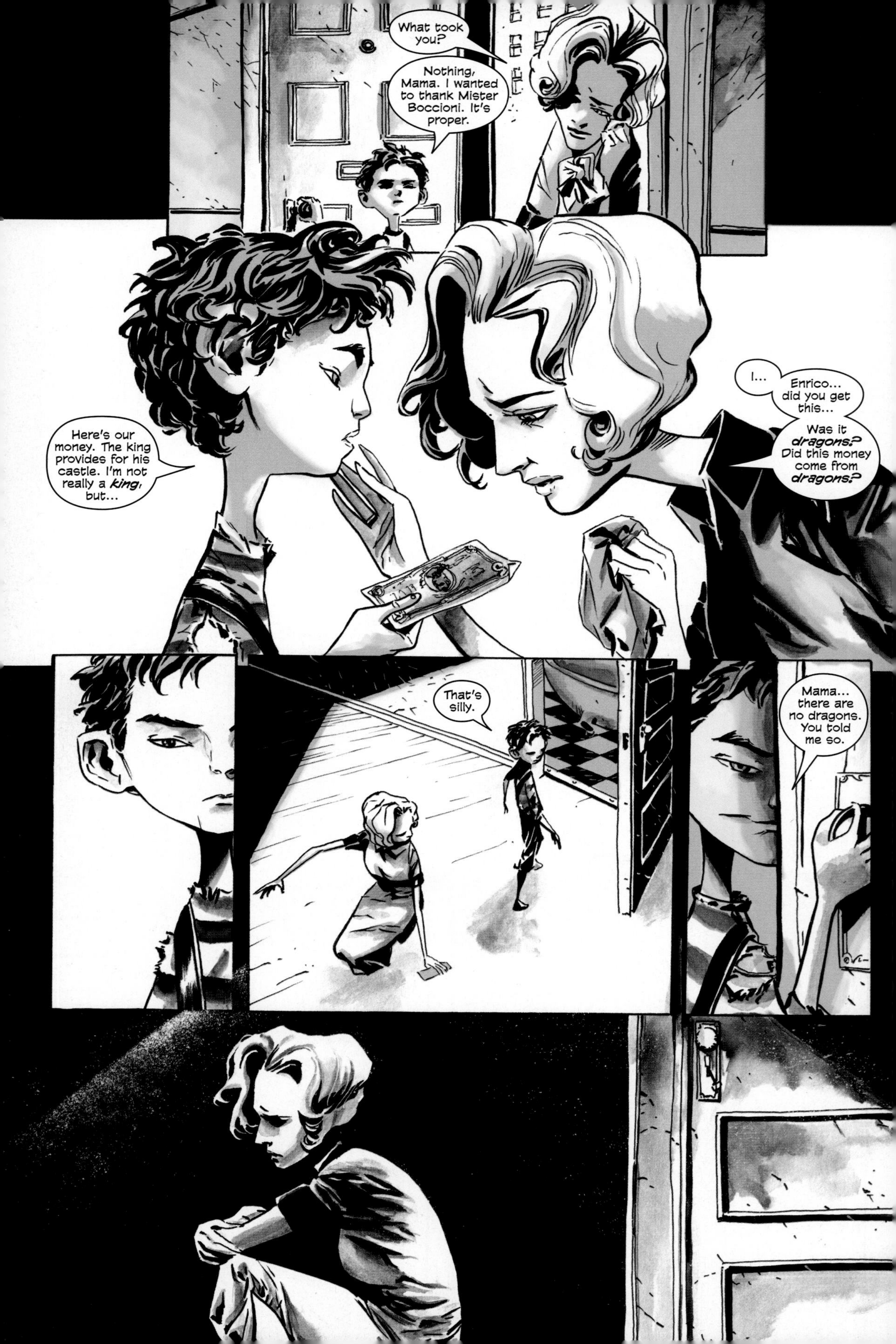
What took you?
Nothing, Mama. I wanted to thank Mister Boccioni. It's proper.
Here's our money. The king provides for his castle. I'm not really a *king*, but...
I...
Enrico... did you get this...
Was it ***dragons?*** Did this money come from ***dragons?***
That's silly.
Mama... there are no dragons. You told me so.

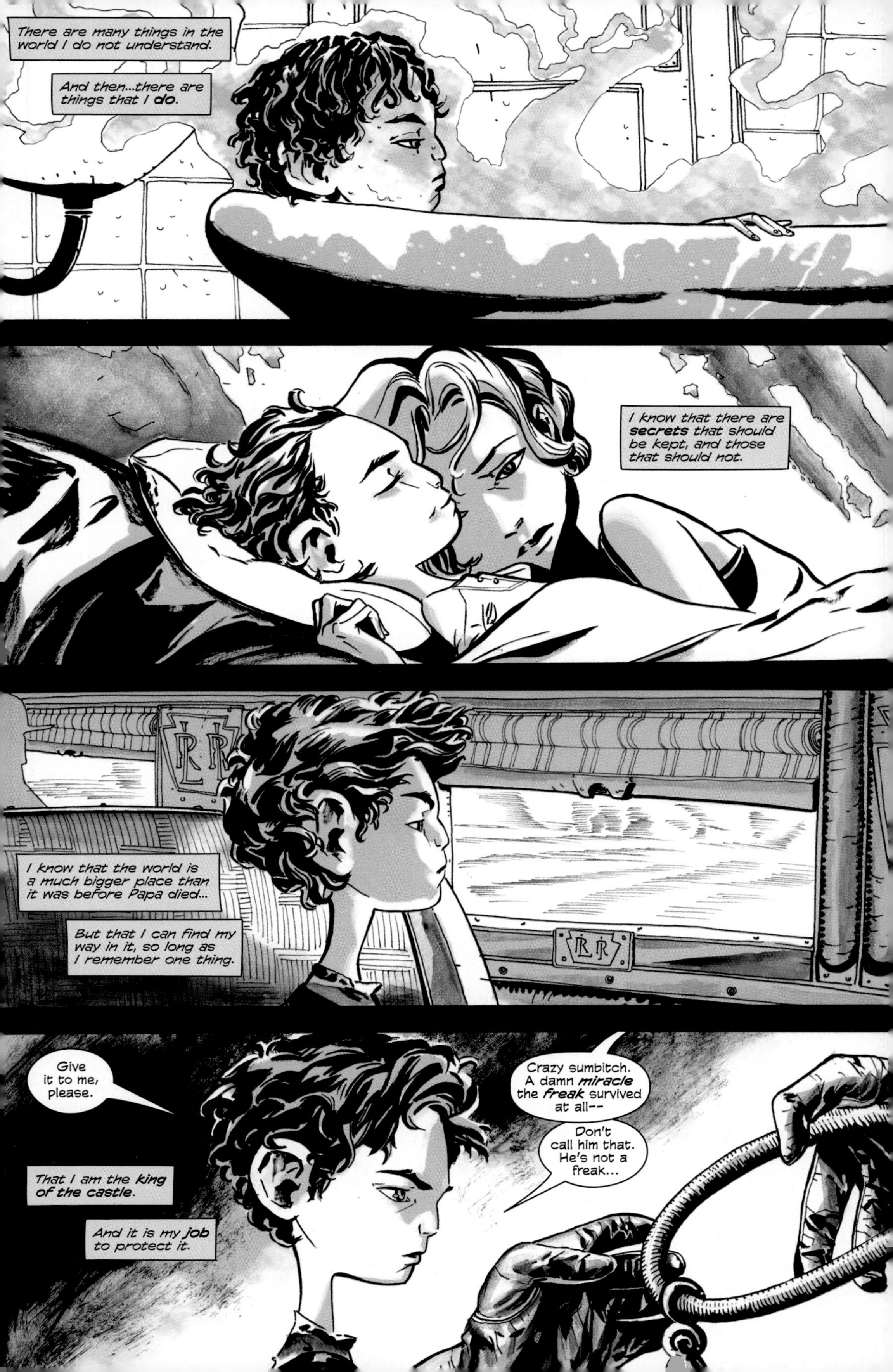

There are many things in the world I do not understand.
And then...there are things that I **do**.
I know that there are **secrets** that should be kept, and those that should not.
I know that the world is a much bigger place than it was before Papa died...
But that I can find my way in it, so long as I remember one thing.
Give it to me, please.
Crazy sumbitch. A damn ***miracle*** the ***freak*** survived at all--
Don't call him that. He's not a freak...
That I am the **king of the castle**.
And it is my **job** to protect it.

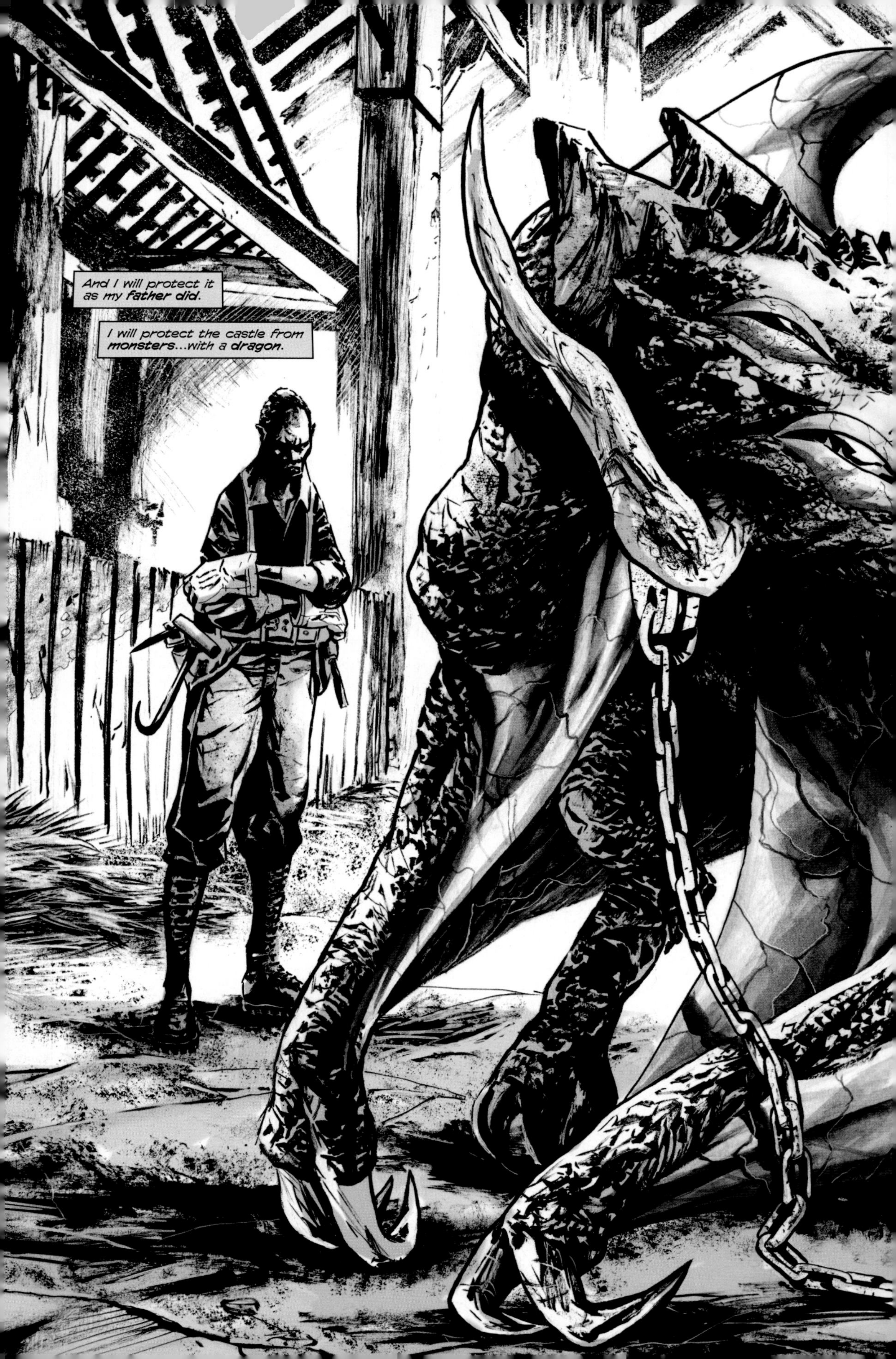
And I will protect it as my **father did**.
I will protect the castle from **monsters**...with a **dragon**.

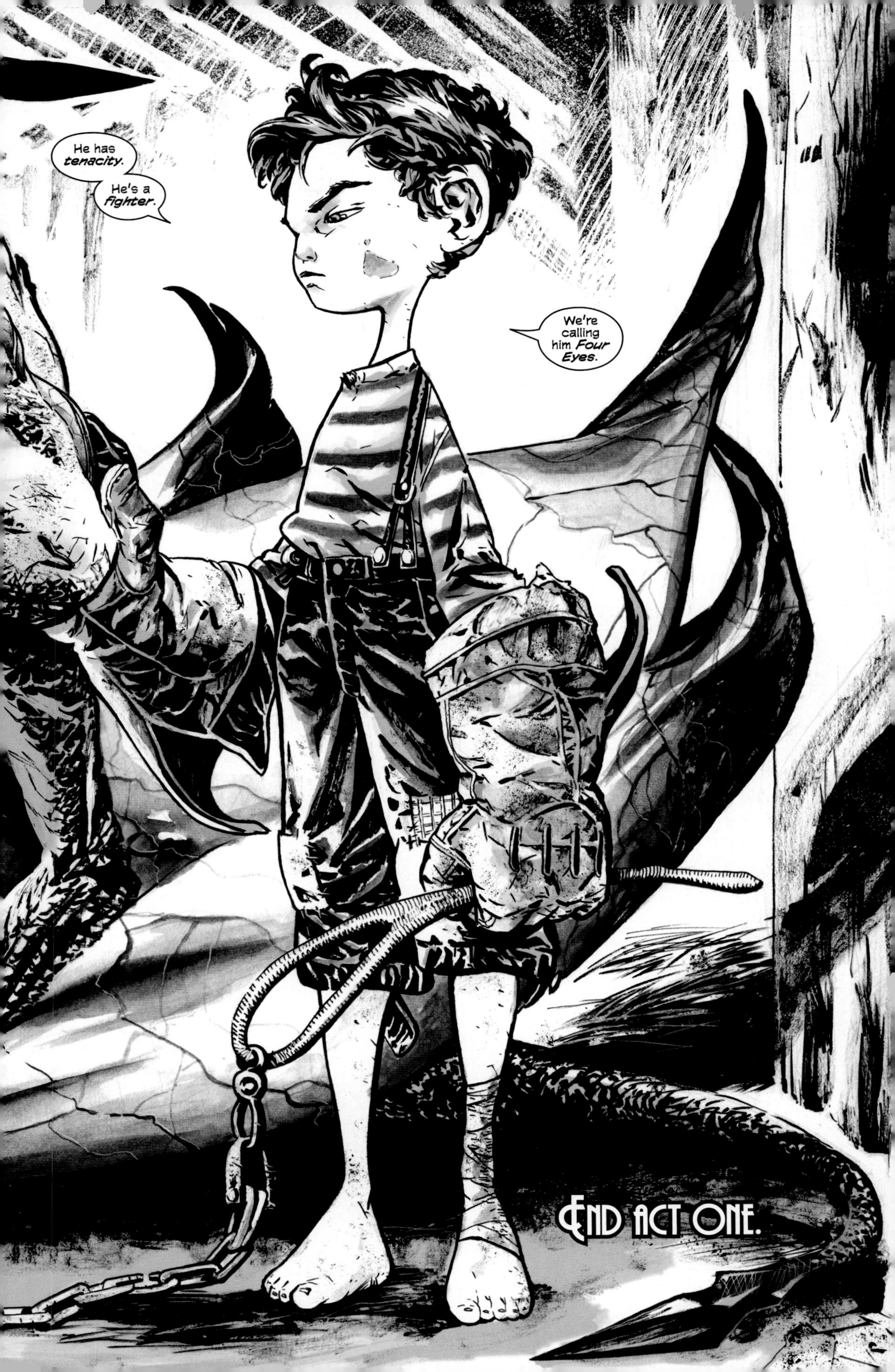
He has *tenacity*.
He's a *fighter*.
We're calling him *Four Eyes*.
END ACT ONE.

Big Burners Busted!

Borough of Richmond, New York

This Saturday, local and state authorities conducted a daring joint raid on a dragon fighting operation set in an abandoned stone quarry on Staten Island. Fifty Peace Officers took part in the maneuver, resulting in the arrest of over thirty poachers, trainers, and fight organizers. Nearly twenty-five thousand dollars in "house money" set to back illegal wagers was confiscated. The raid was a cooperative effort by Sergeant Russell Fitzgerald of the Richmond Police Department, and Sergeant Anthony Tabone of the New York State Troopers.

According to eyewitness accounts, the initial assault on the quarry went off without any bloodshed. However, the night turned deadly when one of the dragon handlers removed the protective blind from a primed bluefin and turned it loose on the officers. Bluefins are "primed" when they ingest the minimum amount of coal needed to exhale flames in combat. Five officers were burned to death before the beast could be destroyed.

This barbaric "sport" of dragon fighting has been on the rise in New York since the turn of the century when seemingly sterile dragon populations began breeding again, confounding biologists and dracospecialists alike. Though an underground phenomena, the spectacle has captured the imagination of many Americans seeking relief from the drudgery of these troubled times. Betting on dragon matches is rampant, especially in our poorest neighborhoods.

When questioned by a reporter for the Star about allegations that both state and local police are bribed to "turn a blind eye" to dragon fighting, Sgt. Fitzgerald became noticeably agitated. "We lost five men before the beast went down. Why don't you go ask their widows if they were on the take?" The remainder of the sergeant's comment cannot be printed in this article for concerns of decency.

Dracospecialists insist that Dragons are relatively harmless and have no interest in human beings when left to their own. They often quote a dubious statistic that there have been fewer than eighty unprovoked dragon attacks reported worldwide in the last half century. Dragons of every breed are considered "endangered species" and it is illegal to own, train, or fight them. Once a dragon has been taken from its natural habitat and "trained" for combat in the ring, federal law requires its destruction as it has proven impossible to release the creatures back into the wild without endangering human lives.

Announcing an evening of majestic brutality and incomparable sportsmanship!

An exhibition of the "Sport of Emperors" is to be conducted this September the 24th including four undercard battles and one title match!

Thrill to the gladiatorial mastery of "Darwin's Darlings" as five different species of dragons clash for supremacy before your very eyes!

Bouts Start At 10:00 P.M. Standard Time

TITLE BOUT:
Maximus Class   60-Unlimited ft.
The Old Man (BF) *vs.* True Emperor (Go)

UNDERCARD:
Tiberius Class   10-18 ft.
Gail's Fortune (BF) *vs.* Fang and Claw (BF)

Augustus Class   19-25 ft.
The Little Emperor (BF) *vs.* The Great Wall (Y)

Imperator Class   25-39 ft.
D'amato's Glory (A) *vs.* Mucho Gusto (Gi)

Caesar Class   40-55 ft.
Casey's Bat (BF) *vs.* Yellow Menace (Y)

Admission: 25 cents   (TAX INCLUDED)

Wagers begin at 5 cents

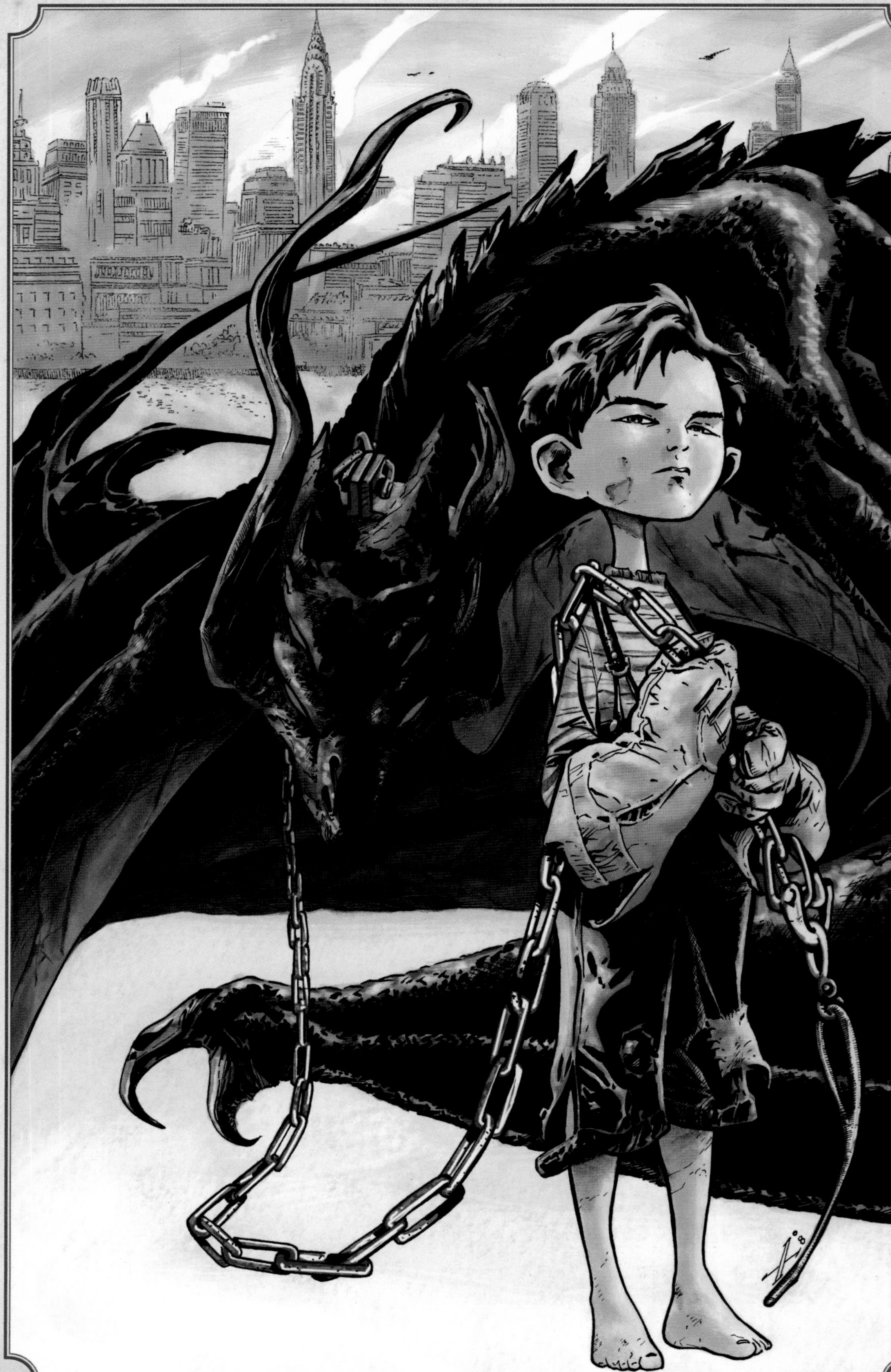

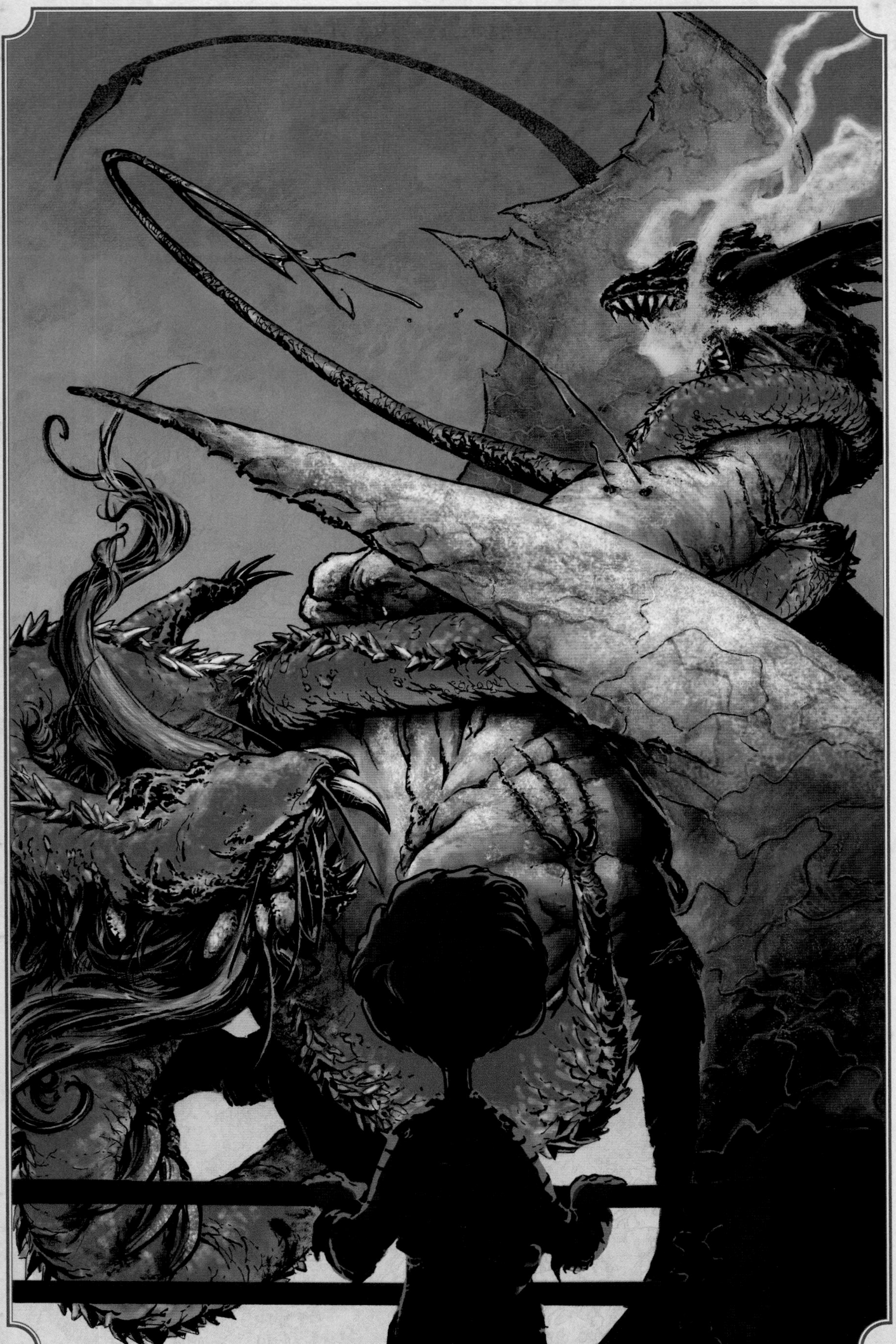

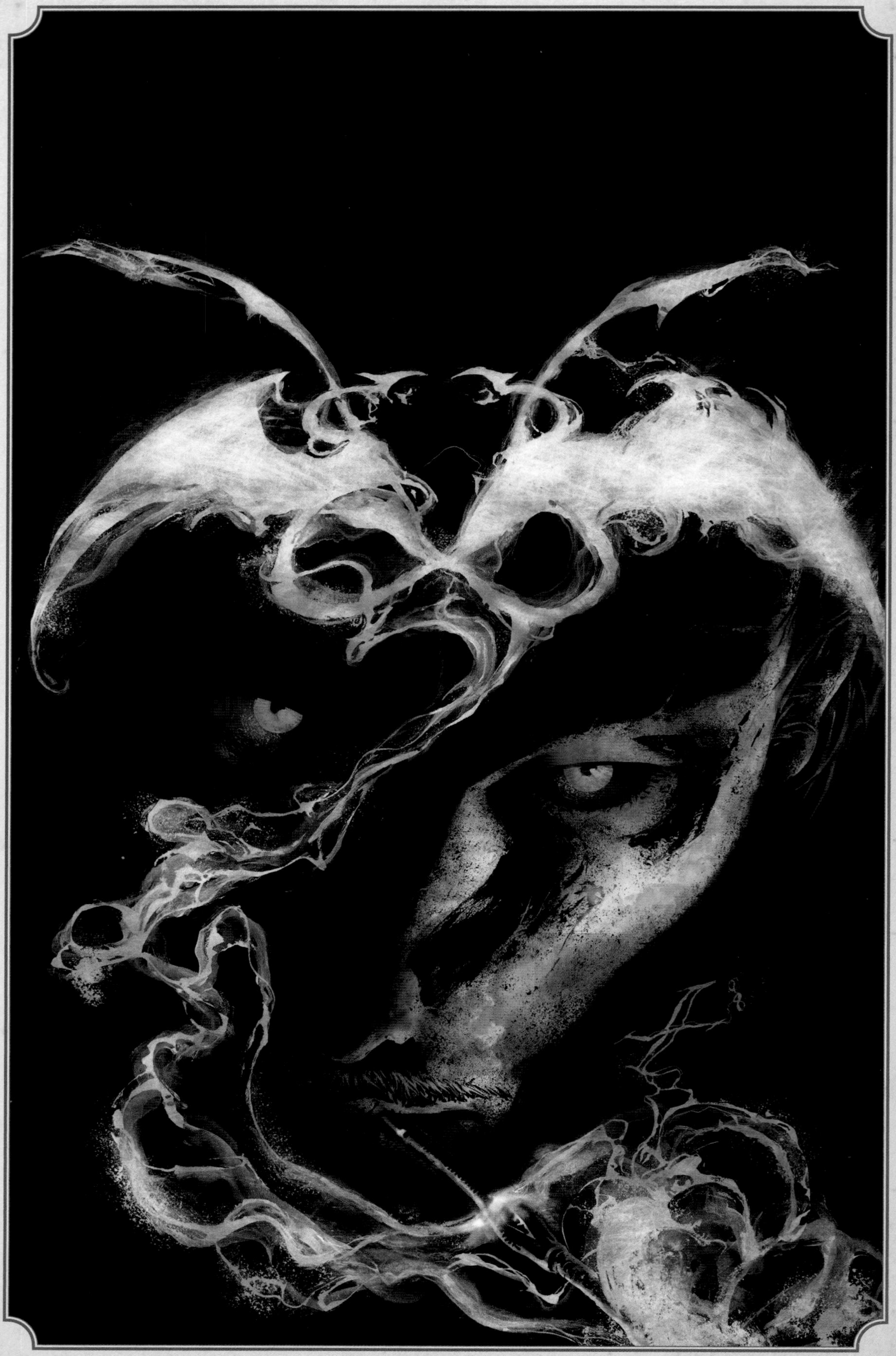

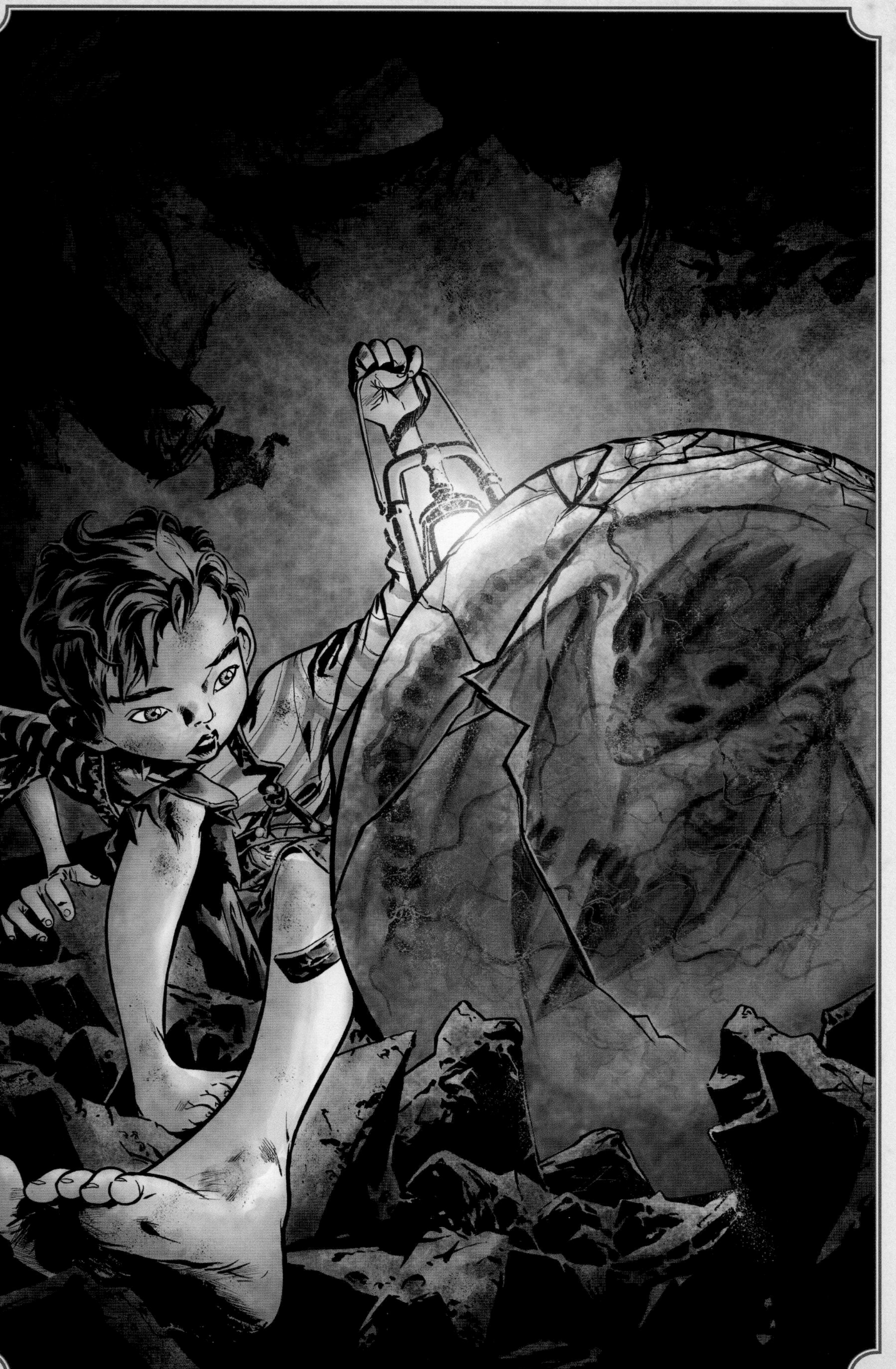

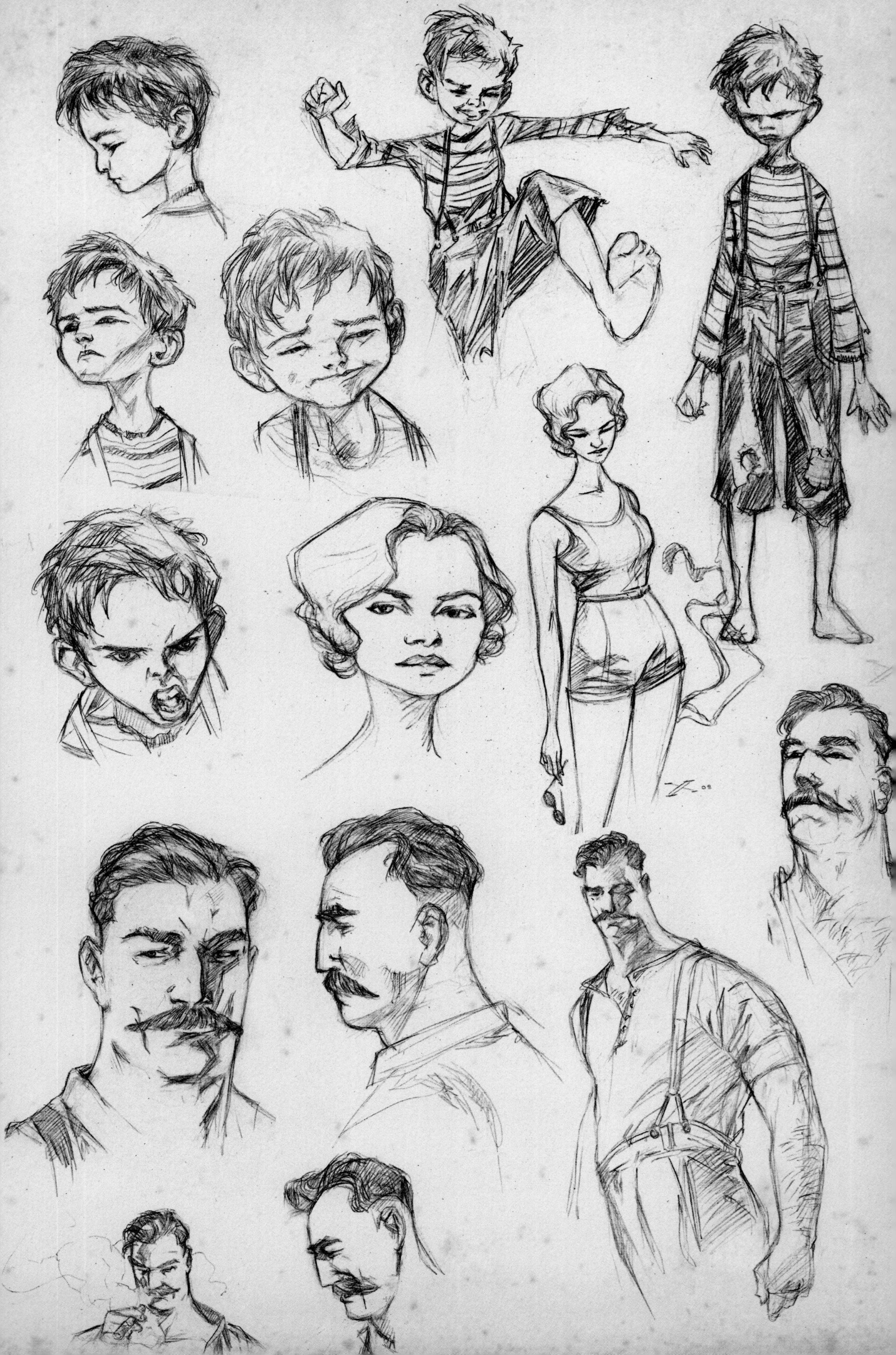

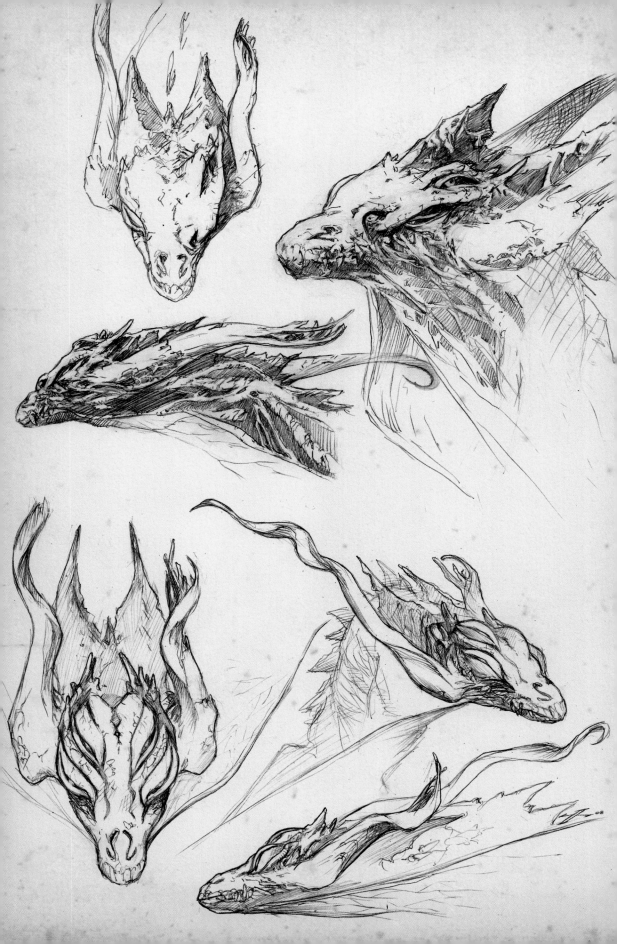

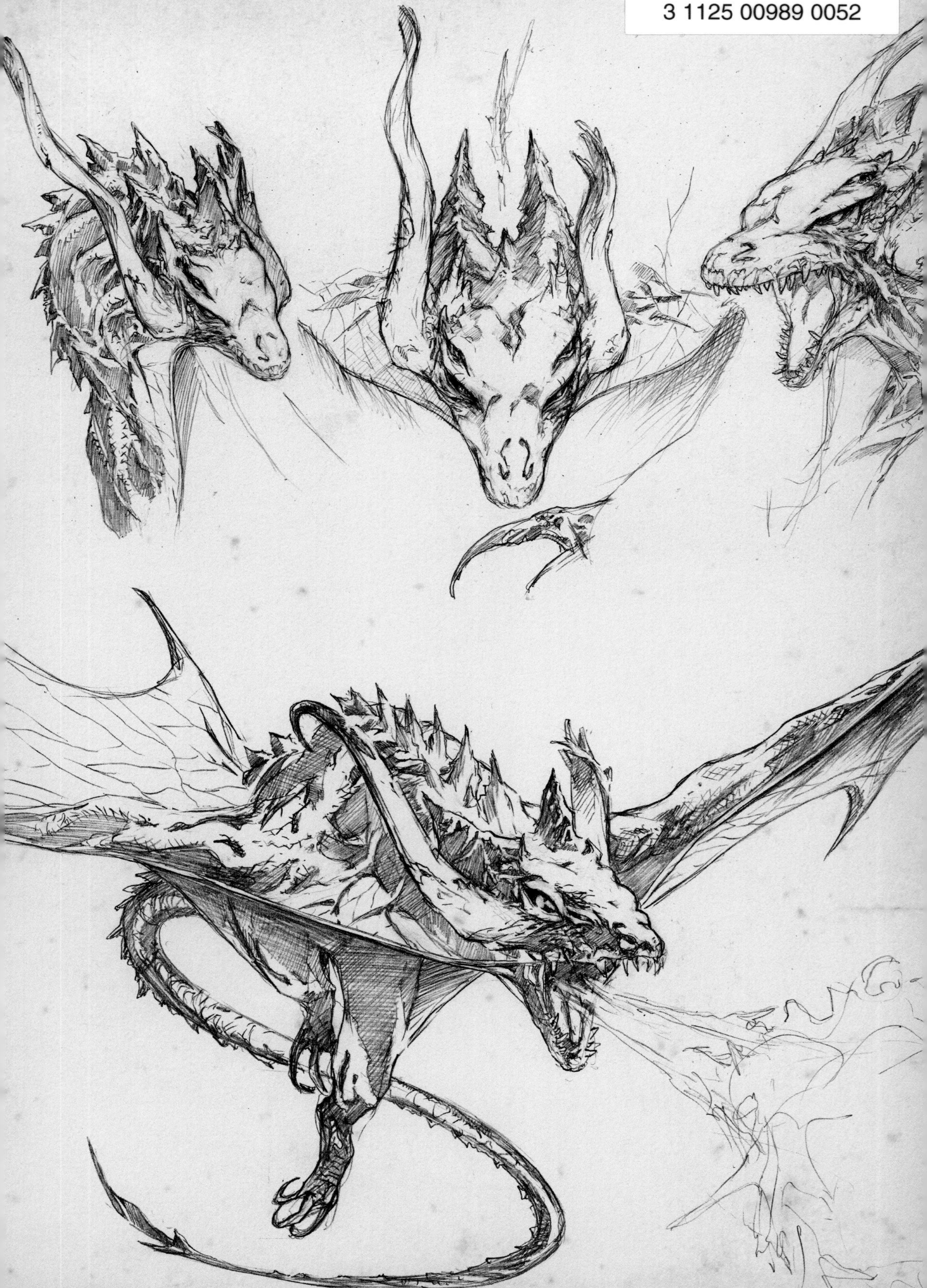